THE GREEK INTERPRETER

Nobody who stayed at the Europa hotel had got their money's worth until they had tried complaining to Mr Lo. Mr Lo was the assistant manager in charge of customer relations: he sat at a separate desk in the corner of the lobby and handled any whingeing guests. He was shrewd and tenacious, a past master of stonewalling. Getting a refund agreed by him was like discovering a Rembrandt in the attic or making love in a moving vehicle: many aspired to it, but few succeeded. His genius was to listen to the most vitriolic outburst without losing his air of concerned beneficence. He smiled incessantly: he *never* answered back. In time the vitriol would burn itself out, the plaintiff retire exhausted, the life of the hotel go sweetly on. The Great Wall of China – Lo's parents had fled from Peking during the cultural revolution – was never breached.

About the author

Max Davidson was born in 1955 and now divides his time between London and Cheltenham. His first novel, *The Wolf*, was published in 1983 and was followed by *Beef Wellington Blue* in 1985, *Hugger Mugger* in 1986 and his most recent success *Suddenly, In Rome* in 1988.

The Greek
Interpreter

Max Davidson

New English Library
Hodder and Stoughton

Copyright © 1990 by Max Davidson

First published in Great Britain in 1990 by Hodder and Stoughton Ltd

NEL edition 1991

The right of Max Davidson to be identified as the author of this work has been asserted by him in accordance with the Copyright, Designs and Patents Act 1988.

British Library C.I.P.

Davidson, Max, *1955–*
  The Greek interpreter.
  I. Title
823'.914[F]

ISBN 0-450-55098-2

Printed and bound in Great Britain for Hodder and Stoughton Paperbacks, a division of Hodder and Stoughton Ltd., Mill Road, Dunton Green, Sevenoaks, Kent TN13 2YA (Editorial Office: 47 Bedford Square, London WC1B 3DP) by Clays Ltd., St Ives plc.

To my darling Anna,
who makes her first
appearance

ONE

I

The three men queuing for a taxi outside Don Muang airport were like different sizes of tailor's dummy: small, medium and large. The small man bristled with impatience and kept looking at his watch. The large man was older, chunkier, more composed: he had the massive, granite-jawed confidence which you see in middle-aged Americans of comfortable means. The medium-sized man was entirely nondescript. He was thinking about a woman called Christine.

It was after ten. The other passengers had already left and the night was warm and heavy with the promise of rain. The men's suits hung limply from their shoulders and their shirts were mottled with sweat. A taxi-driver slouched out from behind a pillar. 'Where to?' he asked the small man, throwing a cigarette-end to the ground.

'Europa hotel,' said an indelibly English voice. 'How much?'

The driver shrugged. 'Hundred *baht*.'

'Too much, too much. Sixty *baht*.'

'Ninety *baht*. Europa long way from here.'

'Sixty *baht* only.' The Englishman wagged a stumpy little finger in admonition; in the heat of battle a mad, waspish energy seemed to shake his entire frame. 'Ninety *baht* no good price.'

'Eighty *baht*. Last price.'

'Sixty *baht* or I get different taxi.'

'Seventy *baht*. Last price.'

'Sixty.'

'Sixty-five.'

'Sixty.'

The driver's head dropped in defeat. 'Sixty *baht*.' He threw the man's cases into the boot and got into the car.

The man turned to the others.

'Can I offer you a lift?'

7

'Thank you,' said the American. 'I'm staying at the Europa myself.'

'Thank you,' said the other man. 'So am I.'

They drove off at speed, with the Englishman in the front seat and the other two clutching on to their cases in the back. The slip-road joined a highway and the driver weaved across the traffic into the fast lane.

'You drive a hard bargain,' the American observed, with a dry irony which the Englishman missed. He picked up the point enthusiastically.

'Oh you have to, you know. Bartering's a way of life in this place. They pretend to get indignant, but they love it – it's the only language they know. If you settle at their price, you'll be ripped off every time. We'd have paid twenty *baht* more if I hadn't stood firm.'

'How much is twenty *baht*?' the American asked blandly – he knew the answer already. Still his irony passed unnoticed. The Englishman twisted round in his seat, so that he was facing him.

'About fifty pence. Eighty-five cents for you. It doesn't sound much, I know, but it's the principle that counts. I heard of someone who paid a hundred and fifty *baht* for a shirt in one of the markets here. He walked round the corner and saw exactly the same shirt – same design, same colour, everything – for a hundred and twenty. It makes you think, doesn't it? I'd have felt miserable wearing that shirt. It would have been' – he gave a prim shudder – 'like handling stolen goods.'

'It's still a cheap shirt,' the American noted.

'That's true.' A suspicion that he was being teased wandered into the man's head – but the thought was too disturbing, too revolutionary in its implications; he hurried on. 'Mind you, the quality of the stuff here isn't too hot. You can get what you think is a fantastic bargain and be disappointed. I heard of a man who bought a transistor radio in the market for a hundred and ninety-five *baht* – that's less than five pounds and the batteries were thrown in. It was one of these tiny ones you can slip into your pocket – you know the sort of thing. He took it back to England, got through customs without paying a penny and then found he couldn't get Radio Four – it was made in Taiwan, you see, and the frequencies were all wrong.

8

I'd have felt really sick if that had been me.' A skyscraper drifted past on the right side of the car, followed by another. The road narrowed from three lanes to two and the traffic intensified. The Englishman looked gloomily out of the window. 'We're lucky it's Sunday. You can sit in this stuff for hours on a weekday.'

'You really know Bangkok,' the American said, in tones of approval. Again the Englishman had the sensation of being teased.

'Actually, it's my first time,' he admitted.

'Then I'm impressed with your research.'

'Well, you know how it is. The odd friend, the odd newspaper article. And, of course, I was in Africa as a boy, so I'm used to the tropics, used to the whole way of life. The Third World' – he arched his eyebrows coyly, risking a joke – 'is my oyster.'

The American nodded solemnly and tried to catch the third man's eye – but he wasn't listening. He was sitting with his eyes half shut and wondering what Christine would be wearing. The American turned back to the Englishman.

'Are you here for the conference too?'

'That's right. I'm acting secretary to the British delegation – sort of glorified bag-carrier. Not much to it but, if our MPs misbehave, I'll get it in the neck from the ambassador. The name's Tight, by the way.' A hand was passed awkwardly to the back of the car like a superfluous piece of luggage. 'Peter Tight.'

'Bill Ledgerwood. I'm the No. 2 on the American delegation.'

Tight pondered. 'That's Congressman Ledgerwood, isn't it? From Delaware?'

'Now I am impressed. Half the folk in Wilmington don't know me from Adam. Don't tell me I'm a household name in London.'

'Well, perhaps not a household name – you know how little most people know about politics. But the better English papers do carry the main news from' – quotation marks flanked the Americanism like sentinels – '"Stateside". Perhaps the story I read was just speculation, but aren't you "running" in '91?'

The Congressman winked, relishing the sudden fame. 'Not – officially. I've got six months to decide and I don't know

9

myself which way I'm going to jump. You need a power-base and you need backing. I think I've got the power-base, but I'm mighty doubtful about the backing. It's not cheap running for President, Peter.'

'No, I imagine not.' Tight blinked. The cost of a taxi suddenly seemed rather small beer. The Congressman stuck out his chest slightly. He seemed to be growing in stature the whole time, like a slowly inflating balloon.

'We're proud to believe, Peter, that any American citizen can make the White House, wherever he starts from. At school we're taught that we're all born equal – children of the free world. We don't have a rigid class system like you British. We get where we get on merit – at least that's the theory. But what we've done is create a system for ourselves that makes a monkey of all that. Small-town boys like me have to become goddam millionaires before anyone in DC takes us seriously. If I don't have enough money behind me by the New Hampshire primary – and I'm not talking peanuts – I'm a dead man. Is that the price of democracy? You tell me, Peter.'

Tight said nothing. A sudden sense of being one of life's bit-part players overwhelmed him, contorting his face into a sad, foolish mask. He wiped a few beads of sweat off his brow with the back of his hand and leant across to the driver.

'Could you put the air-conditioning on? *Air*-conditioning.'

The driver shrugged. 'Thirty *baht*.'

'On top of the fare? Ten *baht* and you're lucky to get it.'

'Twenty *baht*. Last price.'

'No, no, no. Ten *baht*. Who do you think we are?'

'Twenty *baht*.'

'Ten *baht* or we report you to the police. Not legal, charge extra for air-conditioning. Sharp practice. Cheating. Oh, sod this. Just put the bloody thing on, would you?'

'Twenty *baht*.'

'I'm warning you.'

The daydreaming figure on the back seat opened his eyes.

'*Karuna*,' he murmured.

The driver nodded and turned on the air-conditioning.

Tight went crimson. 'Congratulations,' he muttered sourly.

The Congressman chuckled.

'Well, I'll be damned. Like pressing a button. What did you say to him?'

'*Karuna*' – the man tried to avoid sounding smug, but it was quite impossible – 'is the Thai for please.'

The Congressman laughed aloud.

'Is it now? That's useful. So you speak the language?'

'A little. It's part of my job.'

'Your job?'

'I'm a simultaneous interpreter.'

'Is that right? Must be interesting work.'

'It can be.' He smiled wryly and shifted the position of his knees. All thoughts of Christine had to be abandoned as the conversation took root. 'At this sort of conference, I sit in a glass booth with earphones and a microphone and provide English translation of any speeches in French or Italian. Spanish too sometimes.'

'That's a lot of languages to remember.'

'I get by.' The man had the intellectual's terror of sounding big-headed: he retreated into modesty like an animal running for cover. 'It's about the only thing I am good at.'

'Now that I don't believe, Mr –'

'De Battista. Stavros de Battista.'

'So you're an Italian?'

Stavros hesitated. 'Not exactly.' He wanted to explain that he was really a nothing, a nobody. Born in India to the half-Greek wife of a half-German diplomat who had died when he was three; adopted by an Italian journalist who had married his mother in Vienna and left her in Madrid; educated in Paris, Oxford and Heidelberg; domiciled in Switzerland with an Irish wife ... But it was too much to regurgitate in a taxi. 'Greek,' he said, out of respect for his mother. In the driving-mirror he saw Tight's lips curl into a sneer.

The Congressman nodded.

'So where's your home? Athens?'

'No.' Again there was a slight hesitation. Home was a three-bedroomed apartment in Geneva, with two cats and a sauna and a wife who no longer loved him. Home was long silences punctuated by rows and fumbled reconciliations in bed on Sunday morning. But how could you explain these things to a stranger? And wasn't the truth simpler? Home was where Christine was. 'Geneva,' he said.

'Nice place, I'm told.'

'It's all right.'

'Ever get to Washington?'

'Sometimes. Actually, I'm doing a conference there next week – the World Symposium on Small Businesses. Another bloody talking-shop.'

'Is that right?' A note of genuine interest entered the Congressman's voice. He had been making small talk and making it well, with the easy courtesy of his countrymen. Now he moved up a gear: he asked the question as if he cared about the answer. 'Are you flying Sunday?'

'Yes.'

'On the Thai Airways flight via Dallas?'

'I think so. It leaves at seven in the morning.'

The Congressman gave a broad smile. 'Then you're on the same flight as me.' And, with what seemed to Stavros excessive enthusiasm at such a coincidence, he shook him warmly by the hand. 'Now, that *is* funny. It really is.'

Tight sat silently in the front seat and failed to see the joke.

2

The Europa was on the outskirts of the city, marooned on an island where three access roads converged on a highway. Thirty storeys of crude concrete climbed into the night sky: halfway up, a banner welcomed delegates to the 57th Conference of the World League of Parliaments. In the lobby a big-bottomed Australian woman was shouting at a porter; there was an argument going on in German by the fruit-machines. Visitors in search of the real Bangkok would have felt victimised by a bad practical joke, but Stavros smiled like a man walking on to a beach and smelling the sea for the first time. Christine was the sea. In five minutes, he'd be in her.

In their way stood a local man in a white jacket holding up a placard marked 'Senator William Ledgerwood'.

'You've been promoted,' Tight said drily.

The Congressman looked shifty. 'Don't for Christ's sake tell him who I am. I need a shower before I do anything.' He took a roundabout route to reception past a screen of tropical plants.

Stavros got there before him.

'Which room is Miss Golding staying in, please?'

The clerk tapped the question into a computer and peered at the screen. 'Room 722, sir. You're in Room 703, which is on the same floor. Shall I page Miss Golding for you?'

'No, it's all right. There are no messages for me, are there?'

The clerk consulted the computer again. 'There is one message, sir. Could you telephone Mrs de Battista as soon as possible. Is that your wife?'

'My – mother.'

The Congressman was listening to the exchange and slapped him gently on the back. 'If that's your mother, I'm the goddam King of Thailand. Enjoy yourself with Miss Golding, Stavros.'

'Thank you. I will.' With anyone else he would have been furious, but there was a beguiling innocence in the Congressman's attempts at friendship. On one of those absurd impulses which only international conferences generate, he found himself shaking hands with him again. 'See you in the morning.'

'Good night, Stavros.'

A Lufthansa air-crew followed him into the lift. The steward was flirting with one of the stewardesses; he made a joke in German and the buttons on the jacket of his uniform seemed to glisten with self-satisfaction as the girl laughed. They got out at the third floor; one of them said something about going dancing later. A black man with a thick moustache and enormous spectacles took their place in the lift. He was wearing a delegate's badge on the lapel of his jacket. 'P. Achapong, People's Republic of the Congo', Stavros read. He nodded politely; the man nodded back. At the next floor a Frenchwoman got in (she could only have been French) and a tall blond man who might have been Danish. There were more polite nods. The blond man said wasn't it hot, *ya*, and everyone else said, *ya*, it was hot. Stavros felt an unaccountable glow of pleasure: it was good sometimes to move in this world, the world of the international nobody where the barriers were down and everyone was a stranger looking for friends.

He found Room 703 and put his single black case down beside the bed. He always travelled light – possessions were

13

as superfluous to him as nationality. A quick shave, an anxious examination in the mirror and he was out in the corridor again. Room 722 was round the other side of the hotel, opposite something called the Executive Suite.

'Stavvy. Darling.'

She hadn't changed. She never changed. She was the unbroken thread on which his whole life hung. Her very smile inflamed him and they kissed like a couple half their age, pressing tight against each other as they inched past the minibar towards the bed. They didn't hear the first knock on the door, but the second was louder. Stavros swore and went to open it.

'Yes, what is it?'

'Senator Ledgerwood?' He recognised the Thai man who had been waiting in the lobby with a placard. The placard was still sticking out of his pocket and his hand was trembling. He was a shrunken, rather pitiable figure, with fear in his eyes – the sort of man you gave money to in the street.

'No,' Stavros said gently. 'I'm not Ledgerwood. I'm sorry.'

'Zec'tive suite?' The man's accent was so thick he didn't understand. Then he registered and pointed to the door opposite.

'Oh ye-es. Thank you.' The man bowed apologetically and knocked on the other door.

Stavros put out a *Do Not Disturb* sign and padded back to the bed. Christine had taken off her shoes and was looking at her fingernails.

'Who was it, Stavvy?'

'Someone who'd come to the wrong room. It doesn't matter.' They kissed again, with new fervour, new longing. Was five thousand miles too far to come for this? When they paused for breath, her blouse was already off and he was fumbling with her bra-strap. 'I've missed you,' he moaned in a low whisper. 'Why weren't you in Strasbourg?'

Impatient, she undid the bra herself. 'I applied too late. They recruited people locally.'

'But you're coming to Washington?'

'Yes.'

'And Caracas?'

'Yes.'

14

'And the GATT plenary in Lagos?'

'Yes, yes.'

'Won-derful.'

He slithered eel-like out of his trousers and lay on top of her, his lips pressed tight against hers. Their limbs twisted deliriously together and an ecstatic freedom showed in their eyes. Theirs was not the most glamorous of professions: they were mere functionaries, unthinking mouthpieces for the banalities of others. But the love life of a simultaneous interpreter could be a heady nectar, the enactment of an unimaginable fantasy. What other husband could be unfaithful so easily? So often? So far from home? In such undisturbed peace? Then came another knock on the door. Then another. With cold fury, he pulled on his trousers. Greeks took their sex seriously: they were just about the only European people who still preferred it to food.

'If it's that man again, I'll fucking kill him.'

'Why didn't you put out the *Do Not Disturb* sign?'

'I did. He must be blind as well as stupid.'

'Put your shirt on, Stavvy.'

'No, I won't put my shirt on. You're beginning to sound like Monica – I hate it. I've come five thousand miles to get away from that cow and I'm not going to be buggered about by some cross-eyed oriental who can't read simple English. Oh, it's you, Congressman.'

Ledgerwood towered above him in the doorway, a sheepish smile plastered on his face, his right arm half-extended as if for yet another handshake.

'I've chosen a bad moment, haven't I, Stavros?'

He gave him an icy stare. 'Yes, you have.'

'Hell, I'm sorry. I saw the sign and guessed you wouldn't be all smiles to see me. The truth is, I need someone.'

'Why pick on me?'

'Your languages, Stavros. You're an international kind of guy and me, well –' the sheepish smile returned – 'I get a bit out of my depth away from Delaware and DC.' He leant forward conspiratorially and jerked a thumb over his shoulder. 'I've got a guy in there who's told me the most incredible story I've ever heard. At least, I guess it's incredible – the thing is,

I can't make out some of the things he's saying. Have you got ten minutes? I won't forget it, Stavros.'

'Well –'

'Five minutes then. It's just a few words causing problems. And, as a matter of fact' – the Congressman paused while the Congolese delegate passed, followed by a porter carrying two enormous suitcases – 'as a matter of fact, if I've got it right, the man's life could be in danger.'

'Seriously?' Stavros remembered the placard and the frightened eyes and the hand trembling uncontrollably. His shoulders slumped in submission. 'Five minutes. And that's all.'

He went back into the room and put on his shirt. Christine was lying in the bed, with the sheet pulled up to cover her breasts. She watched him anxiously.

'Do you have to go?'

'I'm afraid so. I'll be back in five minutes.' He bent to kiss her. 'I'd have felt bad if I hadn't done anything. I'll be right back. Promise.'

'You'd better be.' She pulled his head towards hers and tugged hungrily at his lips. 'If you're late, there'll be no Addis Ababa' – Addis Ababa because it was where they had first made love, in a steamy hotel-room during a thunderstorm, in the middle of the 1986 plenary of the Pan-African Convention on Population Control.

3

The Executive Suite was bigger than the other rooms. A sofa and two chairs were arranged around a glass-topped table and the bed was draped with an enormous yellow quilt; beside it sat a bowl of flowers and the Congressman's electric razor. The Thai man was sitting in the corner with his face in shadow. He half-rose to his feet in welcome and Stavros held out his hand.

'My name's Stavros. I hope I can be of use to you.'

The man nodded. 'Chiung.' He shook hands gingerly, squeezing only the extremest ends of Stavros's fingers.

16

The Congressman hovered with a benign, all-purpose smile. 'Whisky, Stavros?'

'No thank you.' He scowled. He had come for five minutes, not a bloody cocktail-party. Five minutes of Christine wasn't like any other three hundred seconds: it was the whole world. The digital clock beside the bed said 11-37; it moved forward to 11-38 as he looked at it.

The Congressman got the message.

'Let's get on then.' He arranged the seating in a triangle, with himself at the apex. Stavros remembered – from some long-forgotten source – that Ledgerwood was Chairman of the House Appropriations Committee. Whatever appropriations were – other people's time by the look of things. His Chairman's voice was an octave deeper than his normal voice and he held himself with a stiff kind of importance: he might have been rehearsing for the Oval Office.

'Let me just sum up what Mr Chiung's told me, Stavros. He's some sort of minor politician with a bit of a reputation as a hothead. It doesn't sound like he and I would see eye to eye about most issues, but I don't hold that against him – I'm pleased to think of myself as a democrat.'

Stavros could still taste Christine's lipstick in his mouth. He wondered what the Thai for 'hothead' was – it was years since he'd studied the language.

The Congressman drawled on.

'For the last five years, Mr Chiung's been detained in prison here in Bangkok. On some trumped-up charge, I imagine – we might ask him about that later. What concerns me isn't what he was doing locked up, but how they treated him in prison. You might not know this, Stavros, but Thailand is one of the signatories of the UN Convention on Human Rights.'

Stavros didn't know. He didn't care. He cared greatly for the warm female body waiting for him across the corridor. The clock advanced to 11-42 and he made a gesture of impatience.

The Congressman quelled him with a grim-faced look.

'Show Stavros what you've just shown me, Mr Chiung.'

Chiung took his left hand slowly out of his pocket. It looked quite normal at first – then Stavros noticed the missing index finger and the raw, half-healed stump where the finger had been. It was quite a party-trick. A flicker of pity disturbed him: he took his eyes off the clock and looked Chiung in the face.

'*Bala sa?*'

'*Nit nawy.*'

'What's he saying, Stavros?'

'I asked him if it hurt and he said a little. Do we know how it happened?'

'He told me they did it just before he left prison – as a warning.'

'A warning?'

'To tone down his political views. The bastards.'

'What does he expect you to do?'

'Make a fuss, of course. And do you know what? He's come to the right man. Bill Ledgerwood's known as a hardliner on human rights . . . back home.'

Somehow the added words saved him from sounding pompous. Stavros was able to picture the Congressman on a rostrum, making decent, sincere speeches about the things that mattered – mattered to politicians. He looked at Chiung's finger again and thought about Christine naked in the next room.

'What will you do?' he asked vaguely. He wasn't a political animal: he thought of politicians as a necessary evil, like dentists or estate agents. 'Talk to Ministers? Make a speech?'

The Congressman shook his head.

'I'll need more facts first. If you shoot your mouth off too soon about this sort of thing, nobody takes any notice. But I'm going to get those facts, Stavros. It seems that Mr Chiung and his friends have been preparing a dossier on police atrocities here: names, places, dates, photographs, the works. It's pretty secret stuff and the police are busting a gut to get hold of it – but if he can get it to me and I can get it to Washington, we can raise hell at the UN. This is where you come in, Stavros.'

'Me?'

'It seems the dossier's being kept in a secret hide-out in the centre of Bangkok. It's in a brown, unmarked envelope attached with –'

'Oh no, oh no.' Stavros sprang to his feet and backed towards the door like an animal recoiling from a trap: he stared at the Congressman with fear and loathing and suspicion. 'What sort of sucker do you take me for? I'm an interpreter:

I'm not a stuntman. Go and pick up your own bloody dossier. I can't get involved.'

The Congressman held up his hand like a traffic policeman. 'Sit down, Stavros. We'll talk.'

'I won't sit down. There's nothing to talk about. You've come to the wrong man, Congressman. I'm sorry Mr Chiung's had problems and I don't like police brutality any more than you do – but I can't go chasing round Bangkok for brown envelopes and getting thrown into prison for my pains. Good night.'

As he was leaving, the Congressman barked after him: 'You're a goddam Greek, Stavros.'

He turned back.

'What the hell's that got to do with anything?'

'I thought a Greek might care about human rights. Your lot invented democracy, didn't they? *Demos*, the people, *cratos*, power.'

'Thank you, I know what democracy means. I speak twelve languages and one of them's Greek. That's not surprising because my mother's Greek. She's called Eirene and she weighs fifteen stone because she eats too many pastries. So don't you tell me about Greece – I know more about Greece than you know about being a patronising arsehole, which is plenty. Get stuffed, both of you.' He opened the door.

Over his shoulder the Congressman said: 'I'm disappointed in you, Stavros'; Chiung whispered: 'Good night.' The 'Good night' sounded strange. He turned back.

'Say that again.'

'Good . . .' Chiung faltered.

'You speak perfectly good English, don't you?'

'Yes.' He put his maimed hand sadly back into his pocket, like a door-to-door salesman replacing unwanted goods in a suitcase. 'I read PPE at the London School of Economics.' And, with the admission, even the fear in his eyes seemed to recede, as if that too had been a party-trick, an exhibit to prove that he had really suffered.

Stavros took a step back into the room and looked into the Congressman's eyes. The clock said 12-17.

'You're a devious bastard and, if you ever make it to the White House, I'll have you exposed as a fraud.'

It wasn't a real threat, but then it hadn't exactly been a real conversation. The only real things were Christine waiting for him in bed and Chiung's missing finger – that had been real. The rest belonged to an absurd, inexplicable world of make-believe which he couldn't take seriously – not even on the seventh floor of this, the weirdest hotel in South-East Asia. When he knocked on Christine's door, it was opened by the Congolese delegate, Mr Achapong.

'I'm sorry, I've got the wrong room.' But he hadn't – he'd got the right room: 722 was written in black plastic letters on the door like the Eleventh Commandment. It was Mr Achapong who'd got the wrong room, who didn't belong in the script. Even the pink bath-towel clutched round his waist had the appearance of a stage-prop intended for a different character. They eyed each other suspiciously.

'You're not Miss Golding,' Stavros pointed out coldly.

The African seemed unaware of the *lèse-majesté* he'd committed.

'No indeed. I'm Paul Achapong. I'm attending this conference on behalf of the House of Representatives of the People's Republic –'

'Where is Miss Golding? What have you done with her?'

'Let me see. Was that the lady with the hair?'

Stavros blinked. 'Well, she's not bald. Of course she's got hair.'

'Long hair? Down to her neck?'

'Yes, I suppose you could call it long. Now look here, Mr Appadong.' He clenched and unclenched his fists: the other man was bigger than him. 'What have you done with her?'

'We changed rooms. The hotel had given me the wrong room.'

'What was wrong with your first room?'

'I had booked *this* room. My first room was unlucky.'

'Unlucky?'

'It had a three in it – 732.' He chuckled gleefully. 'You wouldn't believe what that would do to some of the more superstitious people in the Congo. Let me tell you a story . . .'

But Stavros had gone, a whirl of pent-up energy and frustration. Sex wasn't his main motive for being in Bangkok: it was his only motive. At Room 732 he found only a scribbled message. 'Fed up. Gone dancing. Come and get me.' His blood boiled, his hormones teetered ever closer to anarchy. It took him ten minutes to discover that the hotel had a disco and another twenty to find it.

4

In a pool of yellow-green light which seemed to emanate from a revolving aluminium globe suspended from the ceiling, Christine was dancing with the Lufthansa steward. They made a striking couple: tall, blonde, clean-featured, ideally matched. The red of Christine's dress was echoed in the German's shirt, which unbuttoned to reveal a tangle of dark hairs and a gold medallion the size of a soup-plate which bobbed up and down in time with the music. Beautiful, sun-kissed people, they twisted and turned as if in a primitive mating ritual; hips rolling, limbs splaying at fantastic angles, heads performing sudden jerking movements as the music quickened. Stavros wanted to vomit.

He forced his way towards them through the press of heaving young flesh. A girl tapped him on the shoulder and began to dance with him, thrusting her breasts under his nose like a legal document she wanted him to sign. He recognised her as another of the Lufthansa air-crew and turned away in disgust. *'Nein, bitte. Nein, bitte.'* The music got louder, the dancing more frenzied. Christine couldn't hear a word he was saying.

'I'm FREE now. Let's GO.'

She tossed her head and made swaying movements with her hips, inviting him to dance.

'I said, LET'S GO.' He made a grab for her hand and missed; she smiled, mistaking the gesture for a dance-movement. Grimly, to avoid being conspicuous, he started to wiggle his non-existent hips in time with the music. He was a terrible dancer, always had been: at school he'd stayed late in the language laboratory while his friends went to the disco. The German thrust out his pelvis at an outrageous angle and made violent humping movements in Christine's direction. Stavros's whole body shuddered with envy.

The music relented suddenly. Christine shouted: 'This is

Helmut, Stavvy. He lives in Düsseldorf. DUSSEL-DORF.'

The German smiled, the broad, self-confident grin of a winner. Spasms of self-doubt rocked Stavros. Like a man trapping a chicken, he lunged forward, got both arms round Christine and clung to her awkwardly, his mouth sandwiched against her ear.

'Let's go. Please. I hate it here.'

'Don't be such a bore, Stavvy. I've only been here ten minutes. I'm enjoying myself.' She tried to wriggle free of him as the music gathered momentum. He held on doggedly.

'We should be alone. We haven't seen each other for six weeks.'

'You should have thought of that when you disappeared with that stupid American. You said five minutes, Stavvy.'

'I couldn't help it. A man had lost his finger. Chopped off – just like that.'

'His *finger*? For Christ's sake, Stavvy.' She backed off and stopped dancing; her baby-soft features hardened into a sneer. 'Are you being serious?'

'Perfectly.'

'You kept me waiting and waiting because of a man's finger?'

'More or less. Look, I can't explain everything here, Christine. Come to bed.'

'No way.' She stretched out an arm and dragged Helmut to her; she put her arm round his neck and fingered his medallion. Stavros caught a waft of aftershave and the more acrid smell of defeat. He stamped his foot on the floor. The other dancers had cleared a space and were watching them curiously. As the music faded, Christine shouted: 'There's one nice thing about Helmut, Stavros. He isn't *married*.' It was practically a hiss. He stared at her.

'What's that got to do with anything? I've been married as long as you've known me.'

'That's the problem.'

'Problem?'

'Anyone with any balls would have left her by now.'

'Leave my balls out of it. You know perfectly well I can't leave her.'

'Why not?'

'You know why not.' He mumbled the words sadly into the

22

dance-floor, like a man admitting to an incurable disease which the world didn't properly understand: 'Because I'm a Greek.' And because, he might have added, Greeks cared about families; and because they didn't approve of divorce; and because they were decent and old-fashioned and believed in peculiar, inflexible things like principles. A Greek stayed with his wife even if he was unhappy with her – *particularly* if he was unhappy with her. That was the bit Christine never understood. She was English, so she believed in common sense; she thought couples who were miserable should separate – she did have a point. He looked at her mournfully and jerked a thumb at Helmut.

'Are you dancing with that ponce or coming to bed with me?' The question was superfluous. The ponce smiled complacently: he held every card. Christine didn't bother to answer. He went up to the German and slapped him on the face. 'You're a fucking degenerate. No wonder no-one wants to marry you. Get back to Düsseldorf, you arsehole.'

There was a shocked rumbling from the other dancers. As he stormed out of the room, he heard Christine shout: 'You crazy lunatic. I've had it with you.' But he was too incensed to care.

5

When he got back to his room, the telephone was ringing. He dived to catch it, hoping for instant reinstatement, quickfire absolution. The woman's voice at the other end was as familiar as Christine's, but it wasn't Christine. His legs sagged beneath him.

'Monica. Love. I was about to ring you.'

'Stavros, what have you been doing? You checked in two and a half hours ago.' Somehow the telephone managed to magnify her Irish brogue: it boomed down the line like a fog-horn on the Liffey or a Dublin publican shouting 'Time!'

'Did I?' He slumped down on the bed and loosened his collar. His face was flushed and tense with the day's strain. Millions of men married Catholics: alone in the world he had married a Catholic with a vocation as a private detective. He fumbled for an alibi. 'I took a shower.'

'That's a long shower, Stavros.'

'Then all the lights fused.'

'In a five-star hotel?'

'Then a visiting Japanese symphony orchestra started rehearsing on the floor above and I had to go up and tell them to stop. The conductor took a bit of persuading. He said you couldn't make an omelet without breaking eggs – or the Japanese equivalent. I told him that, in Europe, Mahler was revered before midnight and detested after. We had quite a ding-dong. Then the first violin joined in. Anyway, darling, enough about me.' His wildest stories won immediate acceptance – that was the one advantage of living with an Irish woman. He reached deep into his box of voices for the one he was least good at: the concerned husband. 'Is something wrong, darling? You sound upset.'

'I am upset. Stavros, something simply awful has happened.'

'Oh?'

'You know Mr Grandjean on the third floor?'

'The chiropodist with the nose?'

'I think he fancies me, Stavros.'

The words got lost between Geneva and Bangkok and he had to ask her to repeat them. He started to laugh: 'But that's absurd.' The very idea was fantastic: it belonged to a world of childish make-believe, the world of Ledgerwood and Chiung and Achapong. Men didn't fancy Monica: they thought she was a good woman, then discovered she wasn't even that.

'No, it isn't, Stavros. Listen. He passed me on the stairs this morning and gave me a really *peculiar* smile. It was hideous. Then I saw him staring at me from his window when I was out in the garden.' The brogue dropped to a horrified whisper. 'At my body, Stavros.'

'At your body? Good Lord.' He tried to imagine being a four-foot-eleven Swiss chiropodist with cantilevered buttocks and a nose like the south face of the Matterhorn. Would he enjoy ogling a five-foot-ten Irish shrew with a face from a reject china shop and a body which might have been designed by the Vatican as an advertisement for natural contraception? Was sex that ingenious, that ubiquitous? 'I think you're imagining things, darling,' he said gently. He wasn't a violent man: he just occasionally hit people he didn't like.

'I'm not imagining things, Stavros. I know what is. There's no smoke without fire.'

No, he agreed numbly, there was no smoke without fire. But where was the smoke? And how much was this bloody call costing him? He stared out of the window at the city lights and the tree-tops and the rain-clouds banking behind the skyscrapers. Monica said something else he didn't hear.

'Sorry, darling?'

'I said, suppose he *attacks* me, Stavros. What are you going to do about it? I'm five thousand miles away.' Her native logic was at its rampaging, unanswerable best. He reached for a cigarette from his jacket pocket.

'He's smaller than you. He can't do anything.'

'Stavros, he's a man.' The word thundered down the line like a shorthand for everything that was evil in the world.

'He's Swiss. He's programmed to be non-aggressive. You'll be all right.'

'I *hate* it, Stavros. I hate his horrible, lecherous face and his piggy little eyes. I hate being alone in the building with him and you five thousand miles away and no use to anybody. I hate the whole set-up. When are you coming home, Stavros?'

'You know when I'm coming home. Saturday week. After Washington.'

'I don't mean that. I mean, when are you coming home for good? When are you going to stop traipsing round the world and get a job here in Geneva? For good? With me?'

'I don't know.' He remembered the row with Christine and thought: Is there a woman in the world I am capable of living with? For good? From his secret well, he pulled up a few drops of tenderness. 'Maybe soon. I'm not sure. Let's talk when I get home.'

'Now, do you mean that, Stavros?'

'Yes. I mean it.' But then why was his marriage turning out like *The Taming of the Shrew* with the taming scenes cut?

When she rang off, he lay on the bed in his clothes and smoked his way through three more cigarettes. His eyes wandered listlessly round the room and his shirt stuck to him like a wet flannel. His eyelids flickered shut. When he woke, the

sun was streaming through the window and a man called
Günther Boff was shouting at him down the telephone.

'The briefing's started, Stavros. Get the hell over here.'

TWO

I

Günther Boff's position in the World League of Parliaments was broadly equivalent to God's in the Old Testament. More prominent, if anything. The Old Testament God made Man free not to believe in Him, while only a blind man with ear-muffs could deny Boff's massive, omnivorous presence. Boff wasn't a politician: he despised politicians. And he wasn't a democrat. Egalitarianism was an ugly green tide at the periphery of his brain: it lapped against the sea-wall but couldn't breach it. Boff's function in the WLP was simple, his mandate clear. As head of temporary staff, he was the *obergruppenführer* of the clerks and typists and translators and bartenders and security guards who were recruited specially for the conferences. In practice, he ran the whole bloody show.

To the untutored ear, Boff's low growl of warning as Stavros tiptoed into the back of the briefing-room would have sounded like a distant thunderclap or a wave breaking a mile from shore, too far away to matter . . . But that was part of Boff's genius. His tantrums weren't governed by the natural laws, by the same Newtonian principles as the wind and the rain and the sea. When they came, they came with a violence for which there was no possible explanation, no conceivable answer. Boff's fist smashed into the desk and the entire squadron of simultaneous interpreters who had been air-lifted into Bangkok for the conference looked with one accord where he was looking – at Stavros. He didn't need to shout: his audience was riveted.

'I'm paying you nine hundred and fifty Swiss francs a day to sit in a box with ear-plugs on and, for that money, I want a professional. I don't want a short-arsed Greek comedian who doesn't know if it's Monday or Tuesday. *You* knew this briefing started at nine. *You* know I expect discipline and punctuality at all times. *You* try any more tricks and you're finished.' And,

27

as suddenly as it had blown up, it subsided. A final growl, some movement round the mouth (you could never accuse Boff of smiling) and he was back where he'd left off, elucidating a technical problem that might arise if an Arab-speaking delegate raised a point of order while a Spanish-speaking delegate had the floor. Believers in summary justice revered the man: it was his victims who had a way of disintegrating in nervous disorder. Stavros cowered behind the back row of seats and did up his shoe-laces; it was five minutes before he dared pop his head above the parapet to look for Christine.

At first he couldn't see her. Her second language was German, but the German-into-English team was sitting to the left of the room, between the French-into-Italian and the Arabic-into-anything, and she wasn't with them. The Spanish-and-Portuguese-into-German lot were all men and the crack Japanese contingent from Tokyo University were midgets. He spotted several friends from previous conferences: Michael, the Cambridge don, who was in it for the money; Klaus from Heidelberg who was in it for the sex; Vladimir who drank; Maria-Luisa who chain-smoked; poor mad Stefan who didn't have a brain to his name but was the only bilingual Spanish-Pole in Vienna . . . but not Christine. In the end she saw him. She was sitting only a few feet away and got irritated with his clicking teeth – he always clicked his teeth when he was nervous and she always got irritated. 'Shut *up*, Stavros,' she hissed. 'You sound like a stick-insect.' It wasn't the Christine he was hoping for, but he scuttled hopefully across and squeezed into the next seat. Boff was delivering an earnest Wagnerian homily on the importance of not drinking during working hours.

'Look, I'm sorry about last night.'

'I'm not talking to you.'

'You just did: you called me a stick-insect. Some stick-insect. I weigh eighty kilos.'

'Do be quiet, Stavros.'

'Anyway, I'm not any sort of insect. I'm a human . . .' Boff's steely gaze lighted on him and his throat dried. He sat prim and still and breathless and tried seeing how she would respond if he touched her knee lightly and respectfully with his finger.

Boff boomed out: 'People who have had too much to drink

never realise it. But when they are translating at a hundred and fifty words a minute, everyone else realises it.' The Russians and the Dutch laughed. Christine brushed his finger aside. ⸰

'You didn't go to bed with that German ponce, did you?' he slipped in as the laughter subsided. 'Promise me you didn't.' Not many English women enjoyed sex: when you found one who did, you had to pay a price in jealousy. Boff was now asking if anyone had any questions: a Swedish woman asked whether the same duty-rotas would apply if the conference sat after midnight – wouldn't that be rather hard on the people who'd done the first stints in the morning?

'Well, did you or didn't you?'

'I said I wasn't talking to you.'

'That means yes.'

'It means I'm not talking to you. Don't be such a bore, Stavros.'

'Who's being a bore?' He looked at her with injured innocence – the invariable tactic of Greeks in the dog-house – and tried stroking her knee again. Boff droned on. A Frenchman complained that the carafe-water wasn't chilled; a Thai-into-Spanish woman raised a learned point about intransitive verbs. Christine's expression seemed to soften.

'If there are no more questions, I have nothing further to say.' Boff's sign-off had a pleasing Teutonic simplicity. The massed cohorts of linguists rose to their feet in unison and converged on the exit. A sense of urgency was apparent for the first time: there were rumours of Japanese restaurants within striking distance and unbeatable bargains in the shopping mall next to the conference centre. Christine got swallowed up in the crowd and ebbed away. When Stavros lost sight of her, she was descending an escalator between two orientalists from the Sorbonne while he had to disentangle himself from the daughter of the Finnish ambassador to Ecuador. He knew she was the daughter of the Finnish ambassador because he had spent a night of multi-lingual passion with her during the Five Nations Summit on Military Stability in the Philippines in 1979 – which did call for a few words of greeting for old times' sake. He abandoned Christine and went to collect his briefcase.

Everyone who attended a WLP conference was always presented with a briefcase. They were nothing special: the cases were mass-produced locally as an economic spin-off for the host country. But everyone was given one and everyone was always given the same one. No distinction was entertained between American Senators and junior officials from Luxembourg or Lagos: the spirit of democracy infused the ritual with symbolism which people recognised and loved. Never mind that they had a dozen briefcases at home from earlier conferences: the moment they got their hands on the case was the moment they knew they had arrived and the conference had begun. It was like being given your regulation cap on the first day of school.

Stavros tagged on to the end of the briefcase queue at the desk marked RECEPTION/ACCUEIL on the ground floor, where security passes were also being issued. The drill looked simple enough: people handed their temporary pass to the first girl, who smiled and stamped it and passed it to the second girl, who smiled and leafed through a file and produced their permanent pass; the third girl then smiled and handed them a briefcase. After that they queued for their money at another desk, put the money in the briefcase and went off and spent it on a long boozy lunch . . . Stavros had done it all before: he'd queued for briefcases from Copenhagen to Sydney; he'd seen good briefcase queues and bad. The Bangkok queue was only middling: less chaotic than Stockholm, not as slick as Kuala Lumpur. The second girl, the one distributing the passes, didn't seem to be able to spell in the Roman alphabet. The passes were filed alphabetically, but she began her search for each name at A and soldiered through the file till she found it; if she missed the name, she had to work her way back from Z – it was pretty laborious. One or two delegates got impatient, but Stavros was an old hand, he knew better, he had other things on his mind. Just in front of him in the queue was the Congressman.

It could only be the Congressman. The padded shoulders of the jacket, the close-cut hair, the monumental stillness of the head . . . It was like looking at two hundred years of

American history. Stavros experienced one of those moments of moral urgency to which the most lethargic soul is prone; subconsciously he calculated that, if he made enemies and lost friends at his present rate, his wine-women-and-briefcases days would be numbered. Without hesitating he did the decent thing.

'Congressman? I owe you an apology.'

The head lost some of its stillness. The great shoulders wheeled round, like a delicate piece of industrial machinery. Recognition – no more as yet – showed in the steel-grey eyes.

'It was late and I was tired and I didn't want to keep my friend waiting. You know how it is.'

'Sure.'

'We hadn't seen each other for six weeks, so it was quite a reunion – or it was meant to be. I find English women so unpredictable. It's all mood: one minute smiles, the next . . .'

'Sure, sure.'

Anglo-Saxon mating habits didn't seem to form part of the Congressman's political agenda. He shuffled his feet and fumbled for something in his wallet. An Arabic-into-Italian woman passed smoking a cigar. Stavros persevered: it wasn't the Greek way to give up a conversation in the middle.

'Look, I was very rude to both of you: I'm sorry. I felt trapped, out of my depth – I'm just an interpreter, I'm on the fringe of things. I do hope he wasn't offended – Mr Chiung.' At the name, the embarrassed shuffling redoubled. He lowered his voice. 'Anyway, I'm sorry I can't help you with – that business. I'm sure you understand. Good luck with your own efforts.'

'Thank you. Thank you. Ledgerwood, William Ledgerwood.' The Congressman was obviously relieved to have got to the front of the queue. The Thai girl smiled up at him open-eyed.

'You very beeg, mister.'

'Why, thank you.'

'American?'

'That's it.'

'American men all so beeg. John Wayne, Chicago Bears, Ronnie Reagan. Enjoy your stay in Thailand, mister.'

'Thank you. I will. Nobody notices in Delaware,' he muttered over his shoulder. The second girl began looking for LEDGERWOOD in her file; she got as far as CAVALIERE and, for no obvious reason, started again. The Congressman fidgeted. Stavros's height attracted no comment. He handed in his temporary pass: it was stamped and handed to the second girl, the one with the alphabetical problems, who glanced at the name and burrowed into the file again. The Congressman consulted his watch. Stavros looked round the hall to see if Christine had reappeared. The Spanish for 'shit!' boomed out from behind a pot-plant. Two Nigerian delegates ambled past in national costume . . .

A sudden exclamation of triumph issued from the Thai girl, like the tweet of a tropical bird. Improbably she had found both passes at once; she held up DE BATTISTA in her right hand and LEDGERWOOD in her left like a bingo-player shouting 'House!' Everyone smiled: she was a pretty girl, so her enthusiasm was infectious. The passes were pinned to the men's lapels and now the briefcases were as good as theirs. The third girl handed the Congressman a case from the pile immediately behind her, then stiffened as she saw Stavros; avoiding his eyes, she gave a little bow and handed him an identical case, but from a different pile. Stavros thanked her. The cases were navy blue with a rather crude criss-cross pattern on top; the Nicaraguan ones in '87 had been nicer.

'I'll maybe see you around,' drawled the Congressman. He strode off, a grey-suited Colossus in a sea of pygmies. Stavros collected his money – the subsistence allowance was fifteen hundred *baht* a day, barely enough for a decent massage – and sat down at the delegates' bar with a beer. He saw Tight in the distance, struggling under a mountain of documents, and gave a comradely wave. The beer tasted cool and good: it brought a tremendous feeling of mellowness. Suddenly the thought of losing Christine – unimaginable half an hour earlier – could be contemplated calmly, without despair. Boff passed, saw him drinking and scowled. Unimpressed, he ordered another beer. A Japanese delegate asked him the way to the lavatory. He shrugged. Japanese wasn't one of his languages: he could say 'Where's the bar?' and 'Your room or mine?' and that was about it.

Voices were raised in the distance. An argument of some

sort was taking place back at the briefcase desk. The girl who couldn't spell was shouting at the girl in charge of the cases, who was giving as good as she got; a queue of puzzled delegates looked on. The language was getting heated – Stavros recognised one or two expletives omitted from the better Thai dictionaries. He sipped thoughtfully at his beer. One of the girls was gesticulating in his direction – before he knew it, the other girl was gliding towards him across the floor like a delicate insect hurrying to its lair.

'Excuse me, please.' Behind the polite smile lurked an immense, inexplicable terror. Stavros was baffled. He tried to remember how one told a Thai girl – politely – not to get her knickers in a twist. Wasn't there some gracious metaphor involving butterflies and clouds? 'Don't lose your butterflies in a cloud?' That wasn't it. He'd have to find *some* words of reassurance. The girl was staring at his security pass as if the fires of hell were about to enfold her.

'I make mistake,' she whispered. 'I make bad, bad mistake.'

He turned his lapel up to look at the pass. *LEDGERWOOD, Wm., U.S. of A.* 'Ah,' he said, and then again: 'Ah.' There wasn't much else he could say. It seemed a bloody silly thing to get so upset over: perhaps the woman had a psychiatric history. He reached out a calming hand.

'Please. Don't worry about it. Everyone makes mistakes. The last conference I was at, they hired six German-speaking interpreters and no Spanish ones – that was for a symposium on Latin American dialects. The *chef des traducteurs* had to resign on the spot. Don't *worry*.' It was no good. The girl's terrified gaze shifted from his lapel to his briefcase. She wasn't worried; she was a gibbering wreck. Exasperated, he put down his beer and unclipped the pass from his lapel.

'Look, just take this to Mr Ledgerwood – he won't have gone far – and get my pass off him. I'll stay here. And don't worry about security and all that. Nobody's going to take a shot at Mr Ledgerwood if he's wearing my tag, are they? And, if anyone thinks I'm him and tries to kill *me*, well . . . at least my wife will be pleased.' The gallows-humour went for nothing, but the girl regained a little of her composure. She nodded and took the pass, then pointed at the briefcase.

'You get wrong case too. Let me change.' She bent to pick it up.

Stavros got his hand on it first.

'There's no need. All the cases are the same. Just get me my pass from Mr Ledgerwood.'

'Please give. I get you new case very soon.'

'Not necessary. This one's fine.'

'It's Mr Ledgerwood's case. I take it to him now.'

'*No*.' With mounting fury, he wrenched back possession of the case. It was like that shambles over the coffee-dispensing machine at the Tri-Partite colloquy in Bogotá. Why did international conferences always have to degenerate into farce? There were times when he felt like throwing up the whole circus and getting a nice quiet teaching job on a Swiss campus. Now the Congressman was looming over his shoulder, with one of the other Thai girls at his heels. He wore an avuncular smile, but he too had a fussy anxious air.

'It seems there's been some sort of misunderstanding, Stavros.'

'We were handed the wrong passes, that's all. Here's yours. Now you give me mine. That's it. Simple. I really don't know what everyone's getting so excited about.'

'The case, Stavros. They gave us the wrong cases as well.' The Congressman's huge hands descended on the case, next to the Thai girl's; the second girl then got a hand on the handle, making it five hands against two ... But Stavros wasn't to be shifted. He mightn't give a damn about human rights in Thai prisons but, when it came to briefcases he was a hard-liner. Brute strength couldn't be allowed to prevail over common sense: it was the principle of the thing. He did what his mother did in similar situations. He shouted.

'Look here, you dumb bunnies. How often do I have to tell you this? These two grotty lice-infested briefcases are identical. They're the same size, the same colour and I can tell you now they've got the same rubbish inside. *Look!*' With the authority of his anger, he seized hold of both cases and put them down on the table side by side. He clicked the first one open: out tumbled a list of delegates, an agenda for the conference, a signed photograph of the President of the Thai Parliament, two cheap Biros, an illustrated *History and Culture of Thailand*

34

and a more luridly coloured leaflet, *Bangkok After Dark*; inside this was a roneo-ed sheet in eight languages, *AIDS: How to Ensure this not Your Last Visit to Thailand*. There was nothing else. He turned to the second case. The Congressman wore a mournful air, as if his dog had misbehaved.

'OK, Stavros. You've made your point.'

'I haven't finished yet.'

'You can keep your goddam case.'

'I haven't *finished*.' He opened the second case with a conjuror's flourish. A small crowd had gathered, fanning his enthusiasm: it felt good to be in charge of something, good to be the centre of attention. He held each item gleefully aloft like an auctioneer. 'One list of delegates. One agenda. One signed photograph – look, even the signature's identical. *Two* Biros. One *History of Thailand*. One *Bangkok After Dark* – same woman on the front, note – and one leaflet about AIDS. "Condom", for the record, has been spelt "gondom" in both editions. Are you happy yet, Congressman?'

'You're overdoing it, Stavros.'

'*I'm* overdoing it? Who tried to swop the briefcases? Well? Who started this whole shambles?'

'Goodbye, Stavros.'

The Congressman bundled the papers back into the case and stalked off, his shoulders bowed with the enormity of his humiliation. The two Thai girls retreated. Stavros swelled with an absurd, intoxicating pride. He was an ordinary man with ordinary needs: he didn't hunger for the heroic virtues but, when they stirred in him, it was like the rumbling of ancestral gods. He clutched on to the case – *his* case – and ordered a large whisky to celebrate.

3

The first debate of the conference – a light canter through the problems of drug trafficking, unemployment, terrorism and pornography – was scheduled to start at four o'clock exactly, after the opening ceremony in the hotel ballroom in the gracious presence of His Majesty the King. But nobody believed it would start then. Unforeseen delays were part of the fabric of the WLP: parliamentarians were privileged to linger, to spend longer than ordinary mortals, smiling and shaking hands and looking for the bars and lavatories. Added to which, the organisers of the 57th Conference back in Geneva hadn't been notified that the Thai national anthem lasted five minutes; or that it had to be played whenever His Majesty entered or left a room or got to his feet. So four-thirty had come and gone before the delegates assembled for the opening debate. Boff paced up and down on the presidential rostrum, but nobody else seemed to care. They were parliamentarians, so time was on their side: that was what parliament meant.

Stavros sat and waited in the English booth, one of six adjoining glass cubicles at the back of the hall. In the booth with him were Hue (Thai-Chinese-and-Japanese-into-English), Kristyan (German-and-Russian-into-English) and Sophia (Spanish-and-Arabic-into-English); with Stavros taking the French and Italian, between them they were able to cover all the speakers listed for the afternoon's debate. The first French speaker wasn't till third on the list, which would have given Stavros plenty of time to sober up if he'd had his normal lunchtime intake. But he hadn't: he'd exceeded it. He'd trebled, nay, quadrupled it. He was pie-eyed. Legless. Out of his tree.

'Who's that idiot in the silly hat?' he belched.

Sophia was passing round photos of the 56th Conference in Nicaragua to while away the time. He had to hold them three inches from his nose to focus at all.

'That's you, Stavros.'

'God Almighty. Is it? What an arsehole. What an absolute . . . pig-faced . . . arsehole. Hang on. If that's me, who's that cheap blonde with her hand on my bum?'

'Christine. Christine Golding. You know Christine.'

'Oh, Chris-tine. The cheap blonde with the cheap smile. Never forget a face. Forget a name, never forget a face. What happened to her, I wonder, *je me demande?*'

'She's here in Bangkok. Stavros, I thought you and she were –'

'Close? We were, Sophy, old pudding, we were. So close we could almost . . . touch each other. Just like that. Fabulous. *Merveilleux. Wunderbar. Bellissimo.* Why the hell couldn't she come to Bangkok?' His head keeled over: Sophia nudged it back into position.

'She is in Bangkok, Stavros. That's her over there.'

'Where?'

'*There.*'

'Oh, *her.* Why didn't you say?'

A familiar face was watching him sadly from the neighbouring booth. Its sadness arrested him: he had a faint recollection that it could just as easily have been angry as sad and that the sadness therefore represented progress, a few steps along the long road to absolution, reconciliation, peace . . . His face twisted into a foolish smile and he raised his hand aloft, waggling a few fingers in a show of enthusiasm. She smiled back: she *seemed* to smile back. In the chamber the delegates rose to their feet and applauded as the President of the Assembly took his place on the rostrum.

Sophia eyed him suspiciously.

'Stavros, are you going to be all right?'

'Absolutely fine, old pudding. Never felt better.' His eyes rolled in their sockets like sailors crossing a deck.

'You've been drinking. You know what Boff said.'

'Boff can get . . . stuffed. He's a pompous, constipated Kraut who doesn't know the first thing about interpreting. You and I, Sophy, *meine liebe,* have the gift of tongues. Boff doesn't. That's why he needs us, why we're . . . special.' The eyes flickered shut and, with some difficulty, reopened. 'I'll give you an example. The Spanish for constipated is *estrenido.* The Italian is *stitico.* Does Herr tight-arse Boff know that? Of course he doesn't. He's a bureaucrat, he's not smart enough to be a lingpist – sorry, ling*wist.* So sod Boff.' He took off his earphones and laid his head gently on the desk: sleep embraced him like a bridegroom.

Hue was now speaking rapidly into the microphone, translating the President's opening speech.

'. . . and it is a particular pleasure for the Thai delegation to act as hosts at this, the 57th Conference of the World League of Parliaments. Six months ago, in Managua, we were all privileged to be the guests of the Nicaraguan people and enjoy their famous hospitality. Thailand is also celebrated for her hospitality, for the friendly welcome which she extends to

visitors from other countries, especially fellow members of the
WLP. Parliamentary democracy is like a great wind blowing
round the globe: it transcends all national frontiers, all religious
differences, all –'

'Bollocks, I'm trying to sleep.'

It was only a murmur, but that wasn't the point. Stavros had
violated the most sacred rule of simultaneous interpretation:
when a colleague in your booth had his microphone switched
on, you didn't say a word, not one word. Sophia smothered
him with her cardigan and pinched him hard on the leg. Hue
faltered, then continued ashen-faced: '. . . all social divisions,
all ethnic and cultural barriers. It is the wind of life itself.'
Delegates tapped their earphones, puzzled by the extraneous
words. On the rostrum, wisps of steam started to appear from
the top of Boff's head.

Slowly, very slowly, he regained consciousness: Sophia was
holding her hand over his mouth and pointing at Hue. He
nodded, thought sadly about Christine for a moment, then
wrote down on a piece of paper: 'SORY. MUS HAVE FALEN
SLEEPY. WONT HAPPEN TWICE.'

She scribbled back: 'CAN YOU COPE WITH TRANS-
LATING? THERE'S A FRENCH SPEAKER IN ABOUT
TEN MINUTES.'

He stared at her writing and laboriously drafted a response.
'OUI. JAMAIS FELT BETER. FIT AS A . . .' Before he
could finish, Sophia nudged him in the ribs and pointed. Boff
was coming. He sat straight and stopped breathing: without
oxygen his cheeks turned a dull crimson colour.

Like a tiger smelling meat, Boff prowled up and down
outside the interpreters' booths. Twice he pressed his face
against the glass to peer inside: it clouded over and he had to
take a step back. Everybody froze. Stavros's face wobbled like
a nervous goldfish: it seemed to him that he was in the presence
of an infinite evil. Boff stared at him and, by some miracle,
the alcoholic fumes marinading his breath suddenly lifted: he
was able to stare back angelically, as if the word 'bollocks' had
never passed his lips, as if alcohol was a strange narcotic
substance with which he had never experimented. Boff's gaze
passed to Sophia, then Kristyan: with a snarl of frustration,
he returned to the rostrum. The crisis had been averted, Evil

overcome. He glanced at Christine and found her looking at him with a kind of love – no, not a kind of love, the genuine article. You couldn't look at someone like that, with those gentle, smiling eyes, unless you loved them very much, unless you took them for what they were and had no illusions of changing them. In the chamber, a little Frenchman with a moustache started making a speech: it sounded dreadful, the sort of pretentious crap he usually had to interpret ... 'Stavros!' he heard Sophia hiss. 'Stavros!'

He remembered and fumbled for the microphone. Words, any words, spewed uncontrollably out of his mouth.

'The French delegation is pleased, very pleased, to join in the words of, uh, appreciation which have already been expressed to our Thai hosts ... our Thai hosts ... our hosts from Thailand. Thailand is a proudly independent country, *avec une tradition*, with a tradition, of, uh, unfailing, uh, courtesy to visitors, visitors who are ... visiting. At the end of our stay in Bang, uh, cock, Bangdog, Bentcock, we will all carry home with us, *sans aucune doute* at all, the memory of the smiles charming, that is the charming smiles, etched like the most delicate of, uh, oriental paintings on the faces of the Thai people ... the Thai people ... the Thai people ...'

In a single graceful movement, like the launching of a great ship, he had slid to the floor and curled himself into a ball. Sophia snatched the earphones and carried on interpreting. Hue and Kristyan bundled him into the corridor, out of harm's way. An Iranian delegate leapt to his feet.

'Point of order, Mr President, point of order. It appears that one of our esteemed interpreters has been taken ill. Could the delegate who has the floor pause for a moment while a doctor is fetched?' There was a murmur of approval from the other delegations. All eyes turned to the English booth and all eyes but Boff's were touched with the human sympathy, the love of the underdog, which is the most distinctive of parliamentary virtues. Boff hated all dogs, under or over.

'How much did you have to drink?' the doctor asked. He sounded genuinely interested: there wasn't the note of sanctimony you would expect from a European doctor asking the same question.

Stavros sat gingerly up on the couch and shook his head. He was in a tiny pre-fab room with the minimum of medical equipment: a few bottles, some needles, a bag of cotton-wool balls, a canvas stretcher in a corner. A nurse hovered with the inevitable smile and what looked like a half-carafe of retsina – a urine sample, presumably. He shook his head again.

'I'm not sure. It seems so long ago. Two, perhaps three, beers, then whiskies, six, seven . . . I can't be certain.'

'Singles?'

'Doubles. You don't get the benefit with singles. They're very mean with the measures at these conferences: the profits from the bar are what makes the whole thing possible. Make it ten whiskies. I think I must have been . . . celebrating.' An American face flashed into his head, a face sour with defeat, a defeat which he Stavros, the Greek interpreter, had somehow engineered; then a woman's face, younger, ten thousand times more beautiful, smiling at him sadly through a pane of glass. He clutched his head in his hands. 'Or was I drowning my sorrows? I'm not sure, doctor. I remember a bottle of Beaujolais as well – not very good Beaujolais. Is that possible? Can you get Beaujolais in' – he peered around him, at the bare white walls, at the stethoscope, at the kind oriental faces – 'Hong Kong?'

'You're in Bangkok, Mr de Battista, and yes, you can get Beaujolais.' The doctor held the urine sample up to the light. 'Red wine's possible, quite possible. I've never seen this colour anywhere else. I'd like to do a full laboratory test on it, with your permission.' He giggled: he seemed absurdly young and fresh-faced to hold any sort of medical qualification. 'The truth is, we don't have many serious drinkers in Thailand. A few people have too many beers over lunch, but I haven't come across such a – distinctive case before. It's been a pleasure treating you. It really has.'

'Thank you. Thank you very much.' Stavros reached out

and shook him gravely by the hand: he remembered that he was at some kind of parliamentary get-together, where courtesy was expected. 'Very decent of you to look at it that way.' He staggered to his feet and lurched towards the door. The nurse took his arm and said: 'Mr Boff's waiting for you outside.'

He stopped, thought hard and let out a strangulated cry.

'Boff? Günther Boff? The butcher of Stuttgart? Oh my God, oh my God.' He collapsed to his knees and started crawling towards the waste-paper basket.

The doctor helped him to his feet.

'You're not well, Mr de Battista. You need rest.'

'Yes, but Boff, Boff – what am I going to tell Boff? He'd murder me if he knew I'd been drinking. Suppose I tried interpreting in this condition? I'd make a total jackass of myself. I wouldn't be able to tell French from Serbo-Croat. I'd probably . . . Oh my God, oh my God.' More brain-cells came creeping back into motion and an appalling jumble of images flooded his head – earphones, taxi-drivers, a man with a frightened face and a gap where his finger should have been . . . He clutched at the doctor's arm like a drowning man. 'I need your help, doctor. You took the Hippocratic oath, didn't you? You swore to practise your art with integrity, to preserve life at all times. If you let Boff get me, you'll be leaving me for dead, throwing my carcase to the dogs. You can't do it.'

The doctor giggled again. He whispered something to the nurse, who giggled in turn. Their delicate bodies shook with a huge and mysterious glee. Stavros stared at them.

'What's so funny? I'm about to have my head taken off by that demented Kraut and you're wetting yourselves like schoolchildren. What are you up to?' They were laying him out flat on the couch and loosening his tie. He struggled, but the doctor restrained him.

'Lie still, Mr de Battista. I'm trying to help you.'

'I don't want help, I want a police escort. You don't know that man: he could kick down the door any minute.'

'Ask Mr Boff in, nurse.'

'WHAT?'

'Silence. Not one word. Not one word.' The doctor's face was brimming with confidence: where he got it from, Stavros couldn't imagine. Glumly he thought: he doesn't know Boff, he can't conceive the lengths that psychopath will go to, he simply doesn't realise . . . But he had no choice but to do as he was told. He lay back and shut his eyes. There was the sound of heavy German feet pounding the linoleum; then a bone-hard finger prodded him in the ribs.

'Alcohol poisoning. Fucking Greek pisshead. Just wait till he sobers up.'

'I think, Mr Boff' – the doctor's voice was suddenly very grave: there was no remnant of the giggly boy just out of medical school – 'you've failed to understand the situation. Mr de Battista has not been drinking.'

'Hasn't been drinking? For Christ's sake, doctor, where did you learn your medicine? These Greeks will say anything, anything.'

'Show Mr Boff Mr de Battista's urine, nurse.'

Stavros squinted a look. Boff was sniffing at the bottle, his nose wrinkled with disgust; the doctor stood professorially with his hands on his hips.

'If you knew anything about urine, Mr Boff' – a notion which sent Stavros into silent convulsions – 'you would know that the person who passed this sample had virtually no alcohol in their blood-stream. I would be surprised if Mr de Battista had consumed more than one, maybe two, glasses of beer in the last twenty-four hours.'

'Two glasses? But this man's completely legless – just look at him. With all due respect, doctor, I'm calling for a second opinion.'

'Have you heard of *byssinosis toxicara*, Mr Boff?'

'Biss –'

'*Byssinosis toxicara*. It's more common in Asia than Europe. There were seventy cases in Bangkok alone last year. It's hard to diagnose because the symptoms are similar to alcohol abuse and the incubation period is more than a year. Mr de Battista told me he had visited Hong Kong. Perhaps it was there . . .'

A terrible silence descended. Being wrong wasn't part of Boff's universe: it took time to sink in and, when it did, it crushed his spirits like a falling rock. He subsided into the chair beside the couch and stared down at the floor.

'This *byssinosis* – what is it? A kind of virus?'

'That's right. It starts in the lungs. Sometimes it spreads.'

42

'Spreads? That's bad. It's not – fatal?' Stavros seemed to detect an obscene hope behind the question. He heard the doctor say, 'It comes and goes – he'll probably feel normal tomorrow' and Boff mutter, 'So it is just like a hangover?'

The doctor said sternly: 'I beg you, Mr Boff, stop treating this as a moral matter. Mr de Battista is a sick man. He needs all the sympathy we can give him' – at which Boff, incredibly, started patting the back of his hand.

Very cautiously he opened his eyes.

'It's you, Günther.' He enjoyed the 'Günther'. 'How kind of you to visit.'

'It's nothing, Stavros.'

'What happened? Did I black out or something? One minute I seemed to be interpreting normally, and the next . . . I just hope I didn't let any of my colleagues down.'

'You were fine, Stavros.'

'Are you sure, Günther?'

'Positive. Get some rest. We'll hope to have you back with us in the morning.' He rose stiffly to his feet and bowed. 'Thank you, doctor, you've been a great help. Thank you, nurse.' At the door, he swivelled round, checking, just checking . . . The doctor smiled back. Stavros didn't move. He bowed again and left.

When Stavros himself tiptoed out of the room five minutes later, the nurse stopped him. 'Don't forget your briefcase, Mr de Battista.' He looked at the case in confusion: it was so utterly ordinary it hardly seemed to matter whether one forgot it or not . . .

. . . except that it did matter. It obviously mattered. If it hadn't mattered, the Thai girls wouldn't have got so excited, the Congressman wouldn't have put up such a struggle . . . As his brain cleared, he was able to examine the day's events with new insight. He marched purposefully into the nearest gents' and locked himself in a cubicle. The Congolese delegate was standing at a urinal in his national costume. He seemed to be having difficulty – perhaps the costume was only worn at parliamentary conferences.

On close inspection, the briefcase appeared even more ordinary. It was constructed of cheap plywood boards which were beginning to bow in the middle: a thin, navy-blue material was stretched across the boards and held in place at irregular intervals by tiny brass tacks. The handle rattled. The combination lock was jammed at 0-0-0. Even the *pièce de résistance* – Thailand Welcomes Delegates to the 57th Conference of the World League of Parliaments, in gold braid lettering on the inside of the case – had a tawdry appearance, with the braid coming unstitched at the corners. Stavros pondered. It was more than eccentric to covet such an object: it was demented. Washington was a sophisticated city. If the Congressman showed up on Capitol Hill with a naff briefcase, his Presidential hopes would disintegrate as surely as if he started wearing suspenders and stockings. So there must be some other motive . . . He smiled to himself. What a beautiful instrument a good brain was when it had dried out!

He took out all the papers from the inside of the case and put them down on the floor. They were unremarkable and, anyway, he'd seen exactly the same items in the other case. Then he felt his way slowly round the lining of the case. His hand brushed up against a tiny nick in the material; he worked his way into the hole with his fingers and pulled out a folded piece of paper, no bigger than a bus-ticket or a joke in a Christmas cracker.

In some excitement he unfolded it and deciphered the message – the letters were hand-printed in light-green ink. PUSSY'S 403, MY LEFT LEG IS SORE, I HAD AN ACCIDENT PLAYING GOLF. His face creased in disappointment. It *was* a joke from a cracker – there was no other explanation. Was that the punch-line or was there another piece of paper with the punch-line on it? Or perhaps it was a real belly-laugh in Thai but lost something in translation? The whole thing belonged to the childish, madcap world in which the Congressman had tried to involve him – the world of well-intentioned politicians and brutal policemen and fingers that got severed from their owners' hands. He wanted no part of it. He had his own world. He had Christine. He had Boff. The forces of Good and Evil were vying for his soul. Wasn't that enough excitement for one lifetime?

He opened the cubicle to find the Congolese delegate still bent over the urinal – Achapong, was he called? The man turned his head and looked at him. He realised he must have been in the cubicle at least fifteen minutes. 'Bangkok tummy,' he said quickly, pulling a face. 'Watch out for the fish. It hasn't been cooked properly.' The other man nodded politely – though what he'd been doing standing at the urinal for the same fifteen minutes was a mystery . . . Stavros was contemplating the difference between the African and European bladder when the Congressman walked round the corner – with Tight. A mischievous idea occurred to him immediately. As they got within range, he clutched the back of his leg and let out a low cry of pain.

'Are you all right?' Tight asked anxiously, coming to his assistance. 'Looks like a hamstring to me. Here, sit down on this chair, that's it. I had a cricketing friend once . . .'

The Congressman was unsympathetic. 'You should take things easy,' he drawled, thrusting his hands glumly into his trouser pockets. Another small crowd had gathered: a Swede, an Australian, a couple of Venezuelans. He and Stavros seemed destined to act out every scene before a live audience.

'My left leg' – Stavros waited for a moment when the American was looking at him – 'is sore. I had an accident playing golf.' But the words had no impact: a look of blank incomprehension appeared on the Congressman's face, a sour, bewildered impotence at the irrational thought-processes of foreigners.

Tight reacted immediately. 'Do you play? I'd never have guessed you were a golfer. What's your handicap? We might find a course here – if your leg gets better.'

But he wasn't interested in Tight. He saw the Congressman's discomfort – the confused eyes, the air of injured innocence, the residual decency – and felt a tremor of shame. Was it for him to ridicule those who did get involved? Who cared? Who tried to change the world for the better? He reached for reconciliation as if it were a friend from whom he'd been apart too long.

'Here's your briefcase, Congressman. You'll find what you're looking for inside. It's not that I don't care about – those things. I just think the whole business is rather silly. Don't take it personally.' He gave a crooked smile – most of the whisky was still in him.

The Congressman took the case suspiciously, as if a jingle about Greeks bearing gifts was echoing in his head.

'Thank you, Stavros. I'm obliged to you. Where are you going now?'

'Well, I rather thought . . .' He swivelled easily round on his leg, his left leg. Tight stared at it – he was hopelessly out of his depth. 'I rather thought I'd explore the real Bangkok.'

THREE

I

The real Bangkok, it was said, was getting harder and harder to find. You could so easily sweep past it in a taxi and find yourself heading out of town in the wrong direction, on a vast impersonal highway which could have been anywhere in the world. The 'city of angels' had changed beyond recognition since Stavros had spent a month in the Oriental hotel with his mother in 1966. His mother had been between husbands and on the *qui vive*, as she called it, for a millionaire. Probably she had read in *Vogue* or *Paris Match* about an overweight Greek woman being proposed to by a millionaire in the Oriental – she had a very literal approach to fantasy. While Mama sat on the terrace in her billowing silks and outrageous hats, waiting, waiting, waiting, the boy Stavros ventured out of the hotel and explored the canals and the temples and the long dusty streets lined with food-stalls and wizen-faced women peering over balconies. Already he was a linguist. He learnt that a canal was a *klong* and a temple a *wat*; he learnt how to say please and thank you and how much of that green soup with noodles will you give me for five *baht*. He grew up a lot in that month while, back at the hotel, his mother grew old and heavy with failure. It was his turn to fail in Bangkok now.

His taxi cruised slowly down the Larn Luang Road and past the Democracy Monument. 'Just drive,' he had said. 'Just drive.' He'd had enough adventure for one day – a moving taxi in a sea of traffic seemed like a kind of peace. On either side of the car, swarms of *tuk-tuks* – Bangkok's tiny three-wheeled taxis, the cheap local alternative to the air-conditioned limousine – buzzed angrily past, veering from lane to lane, hurtling into the narrow gaps between the vegetable trucks. He remembered the *tuk-tuks*. It used to be joked that they were driven by trainee stunt-drivers – none of the drivers ever completed their training.

By the time they got to the river, it was after six. The sun had already set and the great Temple of the Dawn in Thonburi was just a silhouette against the skyline. A few lop-sided boats bobbed up and down in the water; there was a smell of festering and decay. The taxi turned left, right, left again. A big modern building loomed on the left-hand side. 'What's that?' he asked. 'Prison,' the driver said. He told him to stop.

It didn't *look* like the sort of place where people had their fingers chopped off. The walls, the windows, the little front lawn, were almost antiseptically clean: it could have been a maternity hospital in Lausanne. Even as he watched, an inmate walked slowly out of the main door swinging a small canvas bag. His girlfriend was waiting in an orange blouse and white silk trousers. They hugged each other and jumped up and down and hugged again. As the man's hands met behind the woman's back, Stavros was able to count his fingers. He smiled with relief. This was the real Bangkok – not Chiung, not Ledgerwood, not that hotel filled with lunatics. He said to the driver: 'What are the police like here? Do they give you much trouble?'

The driver shrugged. 'I'm an honest man.' He pointed to the meter. 'This is legal.'

'I'm sure it is. That wasn't what I meant. How would the police treat you if you . . . weren't honest?'

The driver shrugged again.

'Maybe not so good. It's better not get caught. Police a bit stupid here. If you say right things, you not get caught.'

'Do you have anything to do with politics?'

'Politics?' The man's body convulsed with laughter: he rocked forward, sounding the horn by mistake. 'Mister, I drive taxis. Politics!' The whole car seemed to shake at the absurdity of the suggestion. When he'd wiped his eyes, he became sharp and serious and rather sour. 'You in trouble, mister? Why ask about police?'

'I'm just curious.'

'You look for drugs? You American big-shot? You try make quick buck selling heroin?'

'No, it's not that.' He smiled. 'I'm an interpreter.'

The driver didn't smile back. Perhaps he didn't know the word; perhaps interpreting wasn't such an anaemic profession here; perhaps Thai interpreters got their hands dirty in the real world . . . Again Stavros got that unwanted feeling. There were six million people in Bangkok – wasn't there one, just one, who did want him? He gave the man a hundred *baht* and got stiffly out of the taxi. A police car roared past and turned into the prison. From the direction of the river a cooling breeze drifted down the street, past the multi-storey car-park and the cinema showing *Mad Max III*, and took away the worst of the heat. He started to walk eastwards, towards the Oriental, towards childhood, towards the world he knew . . .

It wasn't there. Or, if it was there, he couldn't find it. He looked around him with a lost, pained expression, the pain of a man ambushed by middle age when he thought he had ten years to go. Where had they gone, the naked children playing in the streets, the fresh-faced girls peeping through bamboo shutters, the man riding a bicycle with a sewing-machine on his head? The children were in T-shirts and jeans. The girls sauntered confidently down the middle of the pavement with French cigarettes in their mouths. The sewing-machine had become a Sony Walkman. It was as if a world war had been fought which he hadn't heard about, sitting in his glass booth with his earphones and his microphone and his thirteen languages and his dreams of Christine. And he hadn't seen Patpong yet.

He'd heard about it, of course. Sex was one of the things Bangkok was famous for – that and the floating market and the reclining Buddha at Wat Po. What ingenious tourist board had devised that troika of attractions? In the guidebooks, the Patpong district between the Silom and Suriwong roads – not so very far from the Oriental, though further, light years further, than he had ventured as a boy – was marked simply 'sex and sin centre'. It was a cunning designation: it conjured thoughts of sex that wasn't sinful and sin that wasn't sex-ful and exotic, unimaginable cocktails of the two . . . Patpong was a must for most visitors – and he was most visitors. In his head, a silly riddle was still revolving. Pussy's 403 . . .

He turned right by the Sheraton, into the heart of the area ringed on the map, and waited like a prim spinster for the real Bangkok to hit him. It did so with a suddenness and a savagery for which he hadn't been prepared by the language-laboratories. Immediately a hand gripped his right arm. 'This way, mister. Most disgusting show in Bangkok.' Another gripped his left. 'One man, two girls, all action, hundred *baht*.' A girl with a missing front tooth and too much make-up thrust her face into his. 'I make you so happy, mister.' On the pavement a one-legged man was selling T-shirts. Stavros, cautiously, purchased a T-shirt. That felt better – he had an excuse for being here now. It was navy-blue and had a small green alligator on the front. It cost a hundred and ten *baht*. What comfort a simple object could provide . . .

He walked on, more confidently, with a greater air of purpose. The hustlers eased off, gave him up as a bad job. They had probably decided he was English – lecherous but poor. He made his way anonymously down the middle of the street, past the cheap bars with the obvious names: Moulin Rouge, Arabian Nights, Crazy Horse Saloon, Suzy Wong's Place. The happenings inside seemed pretty obvious too. Padded doors opened into smoky rooms filled with tourists; strippers danced listlessly on top of the bars; there was the smell of joss-sticks and stale beer. He felt numb, disorientated: he couldn't imagine what he was doing there at all, unless perhaps Christine . . . Then a more palatial, less sleazy, establishment came into view. *Pussy Galore's – For That Sensuous All-Over Massage.* And he remembered.

2

An escalator took him up to the first floor and he was standing in what looked like an aquarium at a zoo. The room was in darkness except for a brightly lit window at the far end, behind which women, young women . . . It was too much, the imagery was too disturbing. He turned to leave, but a firm masculine hand gripped his arm.

'Come choose, mister. No hurry. Best girls in Bangkok.'

'I really don't think . . .'

'Just come look, mister. You tired after long day? We show you real good time. These girls do anything, never stop smiling. Very clean, best price. Where you from now? American? English?'

He blushed. 'Bulgarian.' His mother couldn't be implicated – they hadn't even heard of this sort of place in Athens. The man grinned: his teeth were black from some indeterminate vice.

'From Bulgaria? Get that. First Bulgarian we ever have at Pussy's – I give you fifty *baht* discount. How long the flight from South America? You like tall girl, short girl?'

'Just let me look for a minute. On my own. Please.'

'OK, mister, OK. I get you beer. Best girls in Bangkok. You see.'

His companion disappeared into the shadows, towards a dingy bar where a middle-aged man in a white jacket was talking to a younger man in jeans. 'That one's got tits like water-melons,' came an Australian voice; a subdued, raucous laugh crackled with hate and nicotine across the room. As his eyes got used to the light, Stavros noticed other men lurking in the dark corners, in alcoves, behind pillars, looking, waiting, choosing ... A small figure crouched on a bar-stool had Tight's glasses, Tight's dull grey suit, Tight's tense, nervous manner. Was it possible? Nothing seemed impossible any more.

At least fifty girls, row upon row of them, were sitting in the window. They wore long silk dresses in bright colours, with numbers pinned to their shoulders like competitors in a beauty contest. They were young and they were pretty – or they should have been. Their bodies were too tense, their smiles too desperate: as men ventured up to the glass to inspect them, they indulged in an auction of flirtation, pouting their lips and eyes into the darkness. One girl was summoned over the intercom, bobbed to her feet and stalked out of the side-door as if she had won first prize in a TV game show. The economics of the market-place operated with a magnificent, brutal simplicity.

Girl 403 was shorter than the rest. She was dainty, demure even: you could imagine her peeling the skin off grapes or perched on a piano-stool picking out a nocturne by Chopin. Her smile was sad and wispy, less aggressive than the others; legs like matchsticks showed through the slits of her dress. Once she coughed – the room was air-conditioned, it catered to the customers, not the staff. She shouldn't be here, Stavros thought angrily, she doesn't belong. But then nobody in Bangkok belonged, did they?

His companion rejoined him, holding a bottle of Singha beer in one hand and a cracked, dusty glass in the other. 'On the house,' he said, with a strange smile of apology – as if he hoped that a great evil could somehow be redeemed by a little good. He nodded in the direction of the window. They might have been fine art dealers strolling round a museum.

'227 very good girl. Speak good English, very friendly, lots of tricks. Father a judge. 326 shy but kind. From Burma. 72 very popular with Americans. Long legs, big –'

'I want that one.' He pointed awkwardly – he couldn't bri g himself to use the number. Disbelief was choking him. What mad impulse had led him to this place?

'403? Good choice. Young, clean, very gentle. Father a banker, mother used to work here. What service . . . ?'

'I want a massage. Just a massage. That's all. You understand?'

'Sure, mister.' The man looked downcast: he seemed to take it personally, like a chef whose food had been returned uneaten. 'No extras? Nothing?'

'Nothing.' Stavros gulped down his beer and made a wry face. 'Bulgarians have a very low sex-drive – it's a by-product of the communist system. How much is it?'

'One hour massage, no extras, four hundred *baht*. Fifty *baht* discount for being Bulgarian, three hundred and fifty *baht*. You pay at bar.'

'Thank you.'

The man escorted him to the bar, where another man wrote out an invoice. He handed over a five-hundred-*baht* note and was given change. A string of credit card signs was pasted to the cash-register – 'extras' seemed to be expensive. Girl 403 was summoned and introduced. 'My name's Kim. Good evening, mister.' She was told mister didn't want any extras and showed no disappointment – was her commission that small? She led Stavros out of a side-door and into a lift, then offered him a cigarette from her white leather shoulder-bag and lit it for him smoothly. They smiled. They might have been on their way to a film premiere together.

The lift stopped at the third floor. An older woman in a

white coat was sitting at a desk. Ward sister, Stavros thought. The woman handed Kim a key and two bath-towels.

Kim said, in Thai: 'I think this one must be queer. He only wants a massage.'

The older woman said: 'You're lucky, girl. It saves effort.'

They laughed in unison, a long, rolling peal of the gentlest, most innocent merriment Stavros had ever heard.

He said quickly, in Thai: 'It's all right. I'm perfectly normal. I'm just too tired – I've got a headache.'

They looked at him, then at each other and blushed. The laughter started again, louder, merrier, echoing in relays down the corridor – until a man in a suit appeared and it stopped like a light going out. Stavros thought: senior consultant. The man scowled and tapped his watch. Kim nodded. She took Stavros down the corridor, away from the laughter, into the unknown. She unlocked the fourth door on the left and showed him in. He had an uncomfortable feeling that his wife or his mother was going to be waiting in an armchair and he wouldn't have an excuse ready.

There was no armchair: just an enormous bed and, beyond it, a sunken bath set in a floor of terracotta tiles. Mirrors lined every wall and half the ceiling. Stavros could choose from half a dozen images of himself, each more shabby and forlorn than the last. He saw the white cheeks and the bloodshot eyes and remembered all the drink he'd had at lunch-time – perhaps a massage would help, make him feel less fragile. He carefully straightened his tie in the mirror. Kim sat him down on the bed and removed the tie. More Bangkok logic . . .

'You sweat,' she said, pointing to the damp patches on his shirt. It wasn't an accusation: it was a student nurse being frightfully keen.

'Yes, I'm sorry. Shouldn't drink in this weather. Here, let me.' He peeled off the shirt, then the rest of his clothes. She took off her dress; underneath she wore only a white triangle of material held in place by a tiny thread. She took this off too and folded it neatly on top of her dress. Then she bent to undo her shoes. Stavros remembered that women's bodies had pleasant biological effects on men's bodies; and that, as well as his mother in Athens and his wife in Geneva, there was an English interpreter called Christine who would probably rather he was browsing in a second-hand book-shop than admiring another woman's bottom. He tried not thinking about Christine and found it surprisingly easy – the volume of alternative stimulus was considerable. Kim turned on the television set next to the bed. He peered at the screen. The Ohio Buckeyes seemed to be leading the Pittsburgh Steelers 17–14. She switched channels. J. R. Ewing was telling Sue-Ellen – in perfect Thai – not to make such a goddam spectacle of herself. She switched channels again. A young Japanese couple with no clothes on were doing something vaguely familiar . . . She adjusted the set. The woman's buttocks reared into focus like a catamaran looming out of the fog. He settled back to watch. Kim bowed and went to turn on the bath. He wished she wouldn't bow like that – it spoiled the naturalness of the situation.

'You like water hot?' she asked.

'What? Oh, yes please. The hotter the better.'

She poured in something from a bottle and the bath steamed and bubbled with a yellow-green foam: the foam overflowed and inched towards him across the carpet. It was like appearing in a low-budget science fiction film – what alien creature was about to emerge from the suds? She took him by the hand and helped him into the bath, then got in herself. Her legs intertwined with his and her hands worked at his shoulders, kneading them, stroking them, taking away all the stiffness, all the awkwardness, all the tension . . . He smiled. She smiled back. He wondered if Günther Boff had experienced half as much pleasure in his entire life.

'This nice, mister?'

'Wonderful. Won-derful. Thank you.'

'What I call you?'

'Stavros. It's a Greek name.'

'Greek?'

'From Europe.' He thought: she knows I speak Thai, but she's not going to talk in Thai unless I talk to her in Thai first. That's called manners, better manners than I can begin to understand. He thought: You're a lovely woman, Kim, and said, in Thai: 'How old are you? You're a very pretty girl.'

She smiled. *'Yii!sip.saam?'*

He did his sums and nodded. Twenty-three. She looked five

years younger, perhaps she was five years younger – but he liked her far too much to doubt her. He wished he had enough Thai to say: 'I've only been here twenty-four hours and everyone else has been horrible to me. I've been rejected and bullied and cold-shouldered and involved in ludicrous happenings I want nothing to do with. You've restored my faith in human nature and I love you for it.' But he didn't.

He said, in English: 'My left leg is sore, I had an accident playing golf.'

And the smiling stopped.

3

Kim got out of the bath, put a towel round her waist and went over to the door to turn off the light. The room was plunged into darkness, all except for the flickering Japanese bodies on the television screen – their moans punctuated the silence like a child crying in the nursery or the distant lowing of animals. Stavros lay immersed in the green foam, not daring to move. He wished he had his clothes on. He wished he'd stayed at home in Geneva, with Monica and the cats. He wished he'd read medicine, not languages, and got a nice quiet job as an obstetrician in Belgium. He preferred Belgium to Thailand: you could drive through it in an hour and a half without anything nasty happening . . .

Kim was crouching down beside the bed. She appeared to slide open a concealed panel and pull something out. Then she tiptoed back to the side of the bath and showed it to him – it was a brown unmarked package the size of a small briefcase. Someone had even wound sellotape round it – had they anticipated it would be handed to a man having a bath and might get wet? It seemed unlikely, but then the whole thing seemed unlikely, Stavros thought glumly: at least his hangover had improved.

He smiled at Kim. 'Thank you. That was what I was after.'

She bowed and put the package down on a chair – but there was no answering smile. He recognised the same fear he had seen in Chiung's eyes, in the eyes of the girl who'd given him the wrong briefcase. His brain churned in confusion. What did they mean, those kind, frightened faces? Was Ledgerwood a fool or a hero to get involved? Kim slid off her towel and joined him in the foam: she started to massage his shoulders again.

'So you Mister Ledgerwood,' she whispered. 'I thought Mister Ledgerwood big man.'

'He is big man. I'm not Ledgerwood. I'm a friend.' He nodded at the package. 'I will take that to him. Everything will be all right. Don't worry.'

She said nothing and scrubbed his chest with soap, picking at the hairs like a chimpanzee de-licing her young. He smiled appreciatively. She said: 'You so nice man. Be careful. There are police . . .'

'I know.' The lovers on the TV screen had spent their passion and put their clothes on. A Tom and Jerry cartoon was showing. Stavros caught a glimpse of a mouse being squeezed into a food-processor, about to be chopped to pieces . . . He knew how the mouse felt. He stood up in the bath, still covered in foam. 'I know the police.' If only he had . . .

Kim draped him in a bath-towel and patted him dry. The mouse escaped from the food-processor at the last minute and was chased around the kitchen with a meat-cleaver. Stavros sighed from the depths of his being: deeper than the whisky, deeper than Christine, deeper than Mama back in Athens. He looked sadly at Kim's frail body.

'You shouldn't be working here, Kim. You're a nice girl. All this' – he made a vague sweep of his arm, taking in the bed, the mirrors, the copies of *Playboy* piled neatly on the table, that mysterious sellotaped package – 'is wrong. It's not you. You're better than this.' As he pulled on his trousers, a spark of moral vigour ignited in him: he felt like Gladstone haranguing the prostitutes, Christ with Mary Magdalene . . . 'Sex, politics – it's the same messy, brutal business. It's tragic to see a beautiful young girl like you involved in . . . this way. You need to get out of here. I'll help you get out. Somehow.'

He didn't mean it – not really, not the least bit. Which was just as well, because she didn't believe him for a minute. She pretended she had no English and handed him the package.

'Here. Go. Be careful.'

He put it in his briefcase and left. At the bottom of the

escalator leading to the street, he ran into Tight. Tight recognised him and started hopping up and down like a headless chicken.

4

'Tight. Hullo.' He couldn't remember his Christian name. Walter? Godfrey? Did it matter? The surname was perfect on its own. 'What are you doing here?' He seemed absurdly agitated, even by his standards: when they reached the street, he adjusted his glasses and dug his chin deep into his chest as if terrified of being seen. Stavros suppressed a smile. The poor man didn't belong in a red-light district: his habitat was the mahogany desk, the filing-cabinet, the wad of departmental minutes, the middle-aged secretary in a dowdy skirt.

'Enjoy your massage?' he asked blandly – it was impossible not to squeeze some mischief out of the situation. He wondered if there was a Mrs Tight. Was there a woman in the world . . .

Tight scratched his ear. 'I'm sorry – what did you say?'

'Your massage. I saw you in there just now. Nice place. I got a fifty-*baht* discount for saying I was Bulgarian – did you think of that? Best girls in Bangkok, the man said. I reckon he was right.'

Tight scratched his other ear. He started to stammer – a whole edifice of respectability was crumbling round his ears. 'Ye-es. Except that I'm, I'm, it's not . . . what you think. I was meeting someone. B-business.'

'Sure.' Stavros looked at him and thought: when you're five foot one and English, your dignity is everything, it's all you've got. He took pity and changed the subject. 'How was the conference? Are they still sitting?'

'Till ten, I think. Are you going back to the hotel now?'

'Yes.'

'Perhaps we could share a taxi?'

'Certainly. Shall we try the local speciality?'

They crossed the street to where a *tuk-tuk* was waiting. A motorcycle revved up to their left: it bore down on them and they had to side-step into a puddle to avoid it. The rider made a grab for Stavros's briefcase, but he held on to it successfully.

The motorcycle disappeared down a side-street in a cloud of dust; a prostitute shouted an obscenity after it; some German tourists shook their heads. Tight looked down at his wet shoes and said: 'Christ Almighty. What was all that about?' Stavros rather wished his mother was with him.

'A thief, I suppose,' he said thoughtfully, more to himself than to Tight. 'He tried to make off with my briefcase. I wonder how . . . ?'

'Should we tell the police?'

'What's the point? I've still got my case, so there's nothing to report. We don't want trouble.'

'No.' Tight looked at the prostitutes on the kerb, the smoky bars, the bright neon lights. 'We don't want trouble.'

Stavros went up to the *tuk-tuk* driver.

'Did you know that man? The man on the bike?'

The driver shook his head. He was an immensely fat man, with a worldly air: a lifetime's experience seemed to be crammed into the broad chest, the exorbitant stomach, the cavernous grey trousers. He offered to take them to the Europa for eighty *baht*. Tight started to bargain, but had lost the will – one whiff of the underworld had demoralised him. What was twenty *baht* in a world turned cruel and sour?

They squeezed into the passenger-seat together. It was a rickety contraption, open on all sides and covered only with a plastic canopy. The engine started with a bang, like a gun going off. The driver grinned. There was a strange innocence in his face, the trust in Providence you see in people who are either very religious or very fat. He swerved to avoid a pedestrian, shaved a lamp-post and roared the wrong way up a one-way street. The speedometer passed sixty – Stavros couldn't remember if that meant miles or kilometres. Two vans and a police car approached at speed from the opposite direction. There was a jam of brakes followed by a flurry of horn-blowing. The driver turned left, pushed the accelerator into the floor and lit a cigarette with one hand; with his other, he made a V-sign at another driver. The steering-wheel wobbled and he had to use his enormous stomach to steady it.

Tight shouted something at Stavros.

'What did you say?'

'I said, do you believe in God?'

'Oh really.' Stavros made a gesture of annoyance. Why was the English sense of timing so appalling? The *tuk-tuk* veered right over a narrow bridge: a canal loomed, then receded. 'Of course I bloody don't.' A temple whizzed past on the left-hand side, then another.

'I find it helps . . . at times like this.'

Stavros glanced at him: the tense, scared face, the knees pressed together, the hand clutching the side-rail. It did make a kind of sense – for who but a God could love such a man? 'Are you a Catholic?' he asked hopefully – perhaps he could pair him off with Monica.

'Methodist.'

'How interesting.' Were they the ones who didn't believe in drink or the ones who thought Jesus was a scientist? He had the vaguest notions of religious sects. The *tuk-tuk* came to an abrupt stop at a traffic-light: the driver threw his cigarette into the gutter and scowled at the red light as if he were the victim of a monstrous miscarriage of justice. Stavros shouted something at him in Thai. The man gave a sardonic laugh and shouted something back. His belly wobbled against the gear-stick like the underside of a whale.

'I hope you asked him to slow down,' Tight said miserably.

'You can't. They take it personally. It's like saying their mother slept with a donkey. Thais are very sensitive about donkeys. I just asked him how long he'd been driving this thing.'

'What did he say?' The question was drowned in the roar of the exhaust as the light turned green.

'Three weeks. He used to be a typesetter on the *Bangkok Post*.'

They careered up the Sukhumvit Road; a motorcycle closed behind them and came alongside. Stavros glanced at the rider and recognised the man who'd tried to snatch his briefcase in Patpong. He wedged the case between himself and Tight and told the driver to go faster. The speedometer reached ninety; the motorcycle fell back slightly, then caught up. Tight swore – a simple Anglo-Saxon expletive he probably hadn't used in years. Stavros shouted something to the driver, who shook with laughter: he did a U-turn, grazed the side of a bus, went.

through a red light and headed back down Sukhumvit the way he had come. There was a slight bump as the speedometer passed a hundred.

'What was that?' Tight asked, white-faced.

'I think we ran over a dog.'

Tight groaned and put his head between his knees in the brace position used for crash landings in aircraft. Stavros heard him mutter 'Wake me up when we get to the hotel' and somehow the joke was the oddest thing that had happened all day – jokes and Tight just didn't belong together. He glanced over his shoulder. The motorcycle was trailing by about a hundred yards. He said to the driver, in Thai: 'How long to the hotel?' The driver shouted: 'Five minutes' and did another U-turn. A bus jammed on its brakes and a chauffeur-driven Rolls with an ambassadorial flag screeched into the back of it. Shouts of fury followed them on the wind.

At the intersection just before the hotel, there was another red light. The driver gestured hopelessly at the stream of traffic and braked. Stavros strummed his fingers on his knee. He looked back. The motorcycle was coming up at speed, getting closer, closer ... The rider took one hand off the handle-bar and reached into his pocket. As the lights changed, the *tuk-tuk* roared forward with a loud bang. Tight lifted his head.

'What was that? Exhaust?'

'No.' Stavros stared at the blood trickling from the gash on the back of his hand. 'A gun.'

When they got to the hotel, Tight keeled over and vomited on the shoes of the nearest porter.

5

The Congressman was lying on his bed in pale-blue boxer shorts reading the *International Herald Tribune*. One of his socks was under the bed, the other next to the minibar; his suit was hanging outside the wardrobe, waiting to be pressed. On the table were the remnants of his dinner: a soggy lettuce-leaf, a trail of brown sauce, a can of Budweiser. Out of the limelight he looked ten years older, like a woman without make-up: it was a tired, care-worn face, the face of a man who'd been running all his life and was beginning to feel his legs. He greeted Stavros with weary familiarity, as if he were a neighbour for ever borrowing torches and screwdrivers. 'What can I do for you?' Behind the question lay supreme indifference: his eyes barely strayed from the paper.

'Nothing.' Stavros put his briefcase down on the edge of the bed. 'I've done something for you.'

The Congressman stirred slightly: he noticed the handkerchief bandaged round Stavros's hand.

'What the hell's that?'

'A scratch. Nothing serious. All in a good cause.'

'Good cause?'

'Democracy. Like you said, Congressman, I'm a Greek – I'm lazy but I have my moments. That riddle intrigued me. Pussy's 403 . . .' He clicked open the briefcase with a flourish and produced the package. The Congressman slid off the bed and seized it in both hands; a gleam of the purest excitement lit up the tired, middle-aged face. Stavros blushed – he wasn't used to giving so much pleasure to anyone.

'Well, you goddam . . .' The excitement faded: anxiety took its place. The Congressman raised a warning finger to his lips and padded round the room switching off the lights.

'What are you doing?'

'Not so loud. This place is crawling with them.'

'Them?'

'Police. The bell-boy, the lift-man, the laundry-girl, that guy with a squint at reception.'

'Not the laundry-girl surely? She's a Hindu. How do you know all this?'

The Congressman took on a lofty air. 'I've got a nose for these things – I'm a politician. If the police get hold of this dossier, Stavros, we're done for. Chiung said it was dynamite. Thirty men are named – senior police officers. Just wait till I get it to Washington. Bill Ledgerwood's known as a hardliner on human rights' – he stretched for the final light-switch – 'back home.'

Stavros remembered him using exactly the same words before: it was like a tape that had got stuck in the middle of a corny tune. He made a gesture of protest.

'Leave one on, for Christ's sake. We'll look like complete idiots sitting in the dark together.'

'Do you reckon?'

'Thais don't like homosexuals. It's a criminal offence.'

'I thought that was Iran.'

'I can't risk it. My wife's a Catholic.'

'Is that right?'

They sat in silence on the floor, with their faces in shadow. The tiny bed-side light beamed fiercely down – on the ashtray, on the hotel notepaper, on the regulation Bible, on the Congressman's chunky filofax, open at a page giving baseball statistics. The sellotaped package lay chastely in the middle of the carpet: it was hard to imagine one object generating so much excitement, so much fear . . . Stavros passed the Congressman a cigarette. He wished he could make up his mind if he was dealing with a hero or a raving schizophrenic. He felt a twinge of pain in his hand and remembered the bullet. A hero, probably.

'How did that happen?' the Congressman asked.

He told him about the *tuk-tuk*, the chase, Tight vomiting in terror . . .

'How come you were with Tight?'

'We ran into each other in Patpong. He'd been sampling the local talent.'

'No kidding?' The Congressman turned away his face and chuckled. There was a knock on the door. He froze. Then another knock. He kicked the package under the bed, hustled Stavros into the bathroom and put on a dressing-gown – it had been made for a smaller man and barely covered his shorts. Stavros heard the door open and a rather stilted conversation take place.

'Your dinner, Mister Ledgerwood.'

'I didn't order dinner.'

'You ring room service ten minutes ago?'

'No, I didn't.'

'You want this meal? Soup very good. Spicy. Only made in this hotel.'

'Thank you, no. There's been a mistake.'

The door closed. The Congressman slipped into the bathroom and put his finger to his lips again. He raced round turning on everything that moved – the shower, the taps in the basin, the transistor radio on top of the toilet. Beethoven's Third Symphony swelled above the running water.

'What did I tell you?' he hissed. 'Crawling with them.'

'Perhaps he'd just got the wrong room?'

'Jesus Christ, Stavros. Did you see his eyes?'

'How could I? I was locked in here.'

'He was on to us all right. He looked at me like I was some kind of criminal – a goddam criminal. Who saw you come to my room?'

'Nobody. At least, I don't think . . .'

'Shit.' The Congressman subsided on the bidet, where he perched like an enormous vulture laying an egg. He seemed to be pondering various options: he had the harassed look of a committee chairman summing up a heated discussion. Beethoven's violins swept majestically on. A cockroach struggled for life in the basin. Two toothbrushes – one red, one blue – leant against a bottle marked Husky After-Shave Lotion – The Call of the Wild. Stavros noted every detail. If the man on the bidet was their next President, the American voters had the right to know.

'Have you thought of the diplomatic pouch?' he suggested, as the orchestra rested between movements. He revered Beethoven – it was tragic to confuse the Eroica with the plumbing. The Congressman looked at him quizzically.

'How do you mean?'

'Get the dossier sent to Washington in the diplomatic pouch. It will be quite safe: the ambassador will probably think it's a huge joke. I sent my dirty laundry from Strasbourg to Geneva in the pouch every Friday for three months. Nobody minded.'

The Congressman shook his head vigorously. 'You obviously don't know our man in Bangkok, Stavros. Young, Ivy Leaguer, wants to keep his nose clean. Nice guy, but a stickler for protocol. It's no good, Stavros: I'll have to handle this one myself.' He rose to his feet, his mind made up, his shoulders squared, his face set in an altogether more resolute mould. Stavros admired the decisive profile, the unblinking eyes. Perhaps the man was a hero after all – a sort of hero. The taps were turned off, Beethoven silenced in the middle of a bar. A reassuring hand rested on his shoulder – it was like being taken under Santa's wing and asked what he wanted for Christmas.

'You've done your bit, Stavros. Leave the rest to me. Why not go and have a good time with that girl of yours?'

Yes, he thought, why *not* go and have a good time? He could almost believe he'd earned it.

FOUR

I

He didn't even have to look for her. She had somehow talked
or bribed her way into his room and was lying waiting on the
bed. Her hair was down, her white linen jacket discarded on
a chair, her sandals placed neatly under the table. In her hand
was the book he'd left open beside the bed – an escapist
pot-boiler in which couple after couple managed to commit
adultery in five-star hotels without being disturbed. He felt
like a bit of escapism himself – Bangkok's gritty naturalism
could pall after a few hours. Christine put down the book and
smiled. They looked at each other with fond amusement, like
travellers who had agreed to meet on a prearranged mountain
in the Andes but never quite believed the other would make
it. Her smile faded as she saw his bandaged hand.

'My poor love. What have you done?'

'It's nothing. The bleeding's stopped now – it doesn't hurt
any more. An . . . accident.'

'What sort of an accident?'

'Well, a bullet actually.'

'A *bullet*? Stavvy, dearest.' She clung to him as if nothing
could separate them again. A desperate longing seemed to
spark in both of them at once: they weren't Christine and
Stavros, they were one person, one flesh. With his lips to her
ear, he told her everything that had happened to him, the
whole absurd, bewildering story, everything but the massage
bit which had to be toned down slightly – in the expurgated
version, Kim was a middle-aged waitress in a chop-house in
the Chinese quarter. Then the telephone rang.

'Leave it,' she whispered. He was only too happy to leave
it. They waited for the ringing to stop, undoing each other's
buttons, giggling with the deliciousness of anticipation.

It didn't stop. On and on it went, bleep-bleep, bleep-bleep,
as if some tiny but determined insect had got trapped inside

the receiver. He picked it up and put it down again, but the ringing resumed with new urgency, new insistence. Outside, the nightly downpour had just begun: the rain streamed down the window-pane; the clouds loured behind the skyscrapers; there was a flash of lightning from the direction of the river. Christine said with a sigh: 'You'd better answer it.' She reached into her handbag for a cigarette and stared up at the ceiling.

'Monica,' he said, without emotion. 'It's you.'

'Of course it's me. Who else would ring you at this time of night?' There was something merciless about her logic: it bumped and screeched down the line like an aeroplane landing on a runway. She said something quite unbelievable. He put his hand to his ear.

'What did you say?'

'I said, you must get the next plane home.'

'How can I? I'm under contract here.'

'Stavros, you have to. The man's got a history. This is a crisis.'

'What's a crisis? Who's got a history? Why do you never tell me things in the right order?' There were times when he could have had fifty languages and not understood a word she was saying. Christine disappeared into the bathroom with a look of exasperation, despair, contempt . . . He knew how she felt. He gripped the receiver and wished every Catholic in the world eternal damnation. The Irish brogue persisted.

'It's Mr Grandjean again.'

'The chiropodist?'

'Do we know any other Grandjeans? Stavros, he *touched* me.'

'Ah.'

'On my – bottom.' The boom diminished to a coy whisper. 'In the lift. At three in the afternoon. I was holding four shopping bags. Stavros, are you my husband or aren't you?'

'I'm your husband, Monica.' The words limped from Bangkok to Geneva like a criminal confession. He tried to remember when he'd last put his hand on her bottom: it certainly sounded like the act of a depraved mind. A demon of mischief stirred in him.

'Did you enjoy it?'

'Stavros!'

'I was joking.'

'What sort of joke's that? Men.' Then again, with greater vehemence: 'Men.' Then a third time: 'Men.' Why couldn't she find something else to hate? Dogs, golfers, estate agents – there was so much scope.

He said wearily: 'What did you do?'

'What do you think I did? I told him to keep his filthy hands to himself.'

'And?'

'He said he was sorry, he was just trying to be friendly. Friendly! How does he behave when he's being unfriendly? It's obscene.'

'He did apologise. I shouldn't think he'll give you any more trouble.'

'Stavros, he's got a *history*.'

'Oh yes, you said.' Why could her brain never get from A to B by the simplest route? It kept veering off at tangents, like a knight on a chess-board. He looked out of the window: the rain pelting down, the tops of the trees blowing in the wind, the still, dark office-blocks stacked against the skyline. 'What sort of history? Has he touched other women's bottoms? There are worse . . .'

'Stavros, he *kissed* a woman in the next street.'

'She lives in the next street or he kissed her in the next street?'

'Both.'

'Ah.' He started to laugh. He couldn't help it. His body convulsed with a demonic pleasure; his mirth swept back down the line like a rushing wind. He heard a sharp intake of breath at the other end, then, as she put down the receiver: 'Stavros, if he rapes me, you'll go to Hell.'

He stopped laughing. It seemed more logical than her other propositions, intellectually sound, morally sobering – like reading your own obituary or being harangued by an Old Testament prophet. Christine stepped naked out of the bath-room.

'I don't want to hear, Stavvy.'

'I don't want to tell you.'

He took off his clothes, turned down the air-conditioning, closed the curtains, put out the lights. The great storm outside reduced to a low, rhythmical throb; there was no other sound.

He took her hungrily in his arms. What Hell could ever subtract from this pleasure, this peace? He devoured her whole body, reached for something primitive, hallowed, ultimate . . .

She said: 'Stavvy, don't you have a condom?'

2

He stared at her through the darkness. 'Did you say what I thought you said?'

'You do have one, don't you?'

'No. Does it matter?'

'Times have changed, Stavvy.'

'They haven't changed that much.'

'My love, they have. Oh, Stavvy.'

'Oh, Christine.'

'Oh, Stavvy.'

The action had stopped at an awkward moment. His left leg was twisted round her upper torso; her right arm was taking the full weight of his body. They lay there in silence, heavy with defeat, resentful of the universe, crushed by the intricacies of modern life . . . then Stavros got cramp. He hopped smartly off the bed and stubbed his toe on the table. An old Greek expletive came out, last used by Herodotus in the 5th century BC. Christine said: 'I came off the Pill.' Stavros used another expletive, from Aristophanes.

'Why the hell didn't you tell me?'

'I couldn't. We were five hundred miles apart. I thought all men carried condoms nowadays.'

'Not Greeks, they don't. It's like asking a great artist to wear a glove. We're a proud people, we've got our dignity. We, we . . .' He made a frantic clawing gesture, raging at everything in the room – the purple curtains, the black bananas in the fruit bowl, the *batik* painting of a tiger, the puce carpet . . . 'I suppose you don't trust me. Is that it?'

'Stavvy, of course I trust you.'

'The only other woman I've slept with since the Dark Ages is Monica. Monica is entirely decontaminated: she's a one-woman exclusion zone. If Monica's got it, everyone's got it. The Pope's got it. Mother Theresa's got it. There'll be no human life on this planet by the year 2000. Why do we have to go through this charade?'

'Everyone else is doing it, Stavvy.'

'Not Greeks, they're not. I suppose you screwed that German ponce. Is that why you're scared?'

'*No*, Stavvy. Please don't get so mad. It's nobody's fault. Come here.' She took his head gently in her hands and ran her fingers through his hair. He simmered down. 'It's quite simple. There's a twenty-four-hour pharmacy on the mezzanine floor. Next to the newspaper shop. You'll be back in five minutes.'

'Are you sure?'

'Stavvy, please.'

He pulled on his trousers, still sulking – Greeks were quick to think of themselves as tragic heroes, even when their habitat was bedroom farce. The sufferings of his ancient compatriots began to seem like whingeing. Did Prometheus have an Irish wife? Did Oedipus have to make awkward inquiries of pharmacists? At the door, he stopped and turned. His face softened suddenly: he could have been a small boy looking back at his mother from the school gates.

'You'll still be here, won't you?'

'Stavvy, of course.'

'What I mean is . . . don't pick up the telephone, don't answer the door. This place is a mad-house. You never know what's going to happen.'

He stepped gingerly into the corridor, half-expecting to be shot at from behind the aspidistra or mown down by a runaway *tuk-tuk*. Nothing happened. He walked to the lift. The thick pile of the carpet brought a further sense of reassurance: it was soft underfoot, like a tropical beach; it carried no threat. The Congolese delegate passed, clutching a wad of papers for the next day's sitting; he gave a solid, friendly, parliamentary smile. The lift descended smoothly from the twenty-first floor. The doors opened. Inside were a young couple in jeans – and Boff. Of course, Stavros thought blackly, of *course*. Who else?

'Good evening, uh, Günther.'

'You should be in bed.' It wasn't a casual comment: nothing Boff said was casual. It was a High Court judge pronouncing sentence. Stavros nodded nervously at the couple in jeans and cleared his throat. 'I am in bed – in a sense. The thing is . . . I have to pick up something from the pharmacy.'

Boff's eyes narrowed dangerously. 'Do you have a prescription?'

'I don't need a prescription.' The lift stopped at the third floor and a middle-aged woman got in holding a Pekinese. 'It's a commonly available product.' He indicated the flimsy slippers he was wearing. 'For God's sake, Günther: you don't think I'm off on the razzle, do you?'

Boff erupted.

'I don't know what you're fucking doing. Do excuse me.' At the expletive, the woman had taken fright and clutched her dog to her bosom. 'Just make damn sure you're there on time tomorrow.'

'I will be. Don't worry. What's the debate?'

'Human fucking rights,' Boff snarled. The dog yelped and fastened on to his trouser-leg; Bavarian expletives were flying as Stavros slipped out of the lift. He found the pharmacy, sauntered past it three or four times, then made a dash inside. Unfortunately what he thought was the family planning section was entirely devoted to the bowels: remedies for diarrhoea and gastric influenza stretched as far as the eye could see. He looked in bewilderment at the loaded shelves and an assistant came to help him. Female – of course. Young and virginal – naturally. With very little English – it went without saying. He fulminated at Christine, at the medical profession, at his aged mother. Why had she brought him into a world like this?

'What I'm looking for . . .' He sensed his hands creeping in front of him, about to perform an obscene mime. He stuffed them back into his pockets. 'I have a friend. She does not want baby. Do you understand?'

'Why she not want baby? Babies beautiful.' The girl smiled the shy, confused smile of the innocent. The young couple who had been in the lift wandered into the shop and browsed among the shampoos and shaving-creams. Stavros grabbed a packet at random from the shelves and gave it to the girl.

'Here. This is what I want.'

She looked at the label. 'Mister eat something funny? Fish? Curry?'

'Fish. Look, go and wrap this. I may . . .' She glided over to the cash-register. 'I may want one other thing.' He rummaged desperately through the shelves: Tampaxes, cotton-wool balls, make-up remover, films, razor-blades, depilatories, lots of depilatories . . . When he got to PERSONAL HYGIENE, he was cornered by the couple he was trying to avoid. He felt his cheeks redden.

'Can we help?' The man sounded Dutch. He had a fresh, friendly face. His companion was cool, slightly superior – a modern woman to her finger-tips.

Stavros shook his head. 'Thank you, I'm just looking.' He sounded like a retired schoolmaster browsing in an antiquarian book-shop.

The man persisted.

'I can guess what you're after.' His left eyelid drooped mischievously. 'They don't stock them.'

'I'm sorry?'

'Thais prefer their sex simple. They like big families – it's a way of life. The Government's only just got wise to the benefits of contraception. I've got plenty in my room if . . .'

'I really don't think –'

'Oh come *on*.' The woman joined in with ominous enthusiasm. 'Don't be so silly. There's no need to be embarrassed. You're not English, are you?'

'Greek.'

'From Athens? Yes? We were in Rhodes last year. Come upstairs and we'll fix you up. You have a friend waiting? Yes?'

'Sort of. Look . . .' He saw the Thai girl bearing down on him with his earlier purchase. Her face shone with pleasure at helping him, and he thought: is it better to corrupt innocence or rub shoulders with experience? He shrugged. 'All right. Why not?'

They got into the lift together and went up to the thirteenth floor. Another long impersonal corridor, door after door looking exactly the same – 1312, 1313, 1314 . . .

'We travel light. Yes?' The woman anticipated his question as he looked doubtfully around the room. It was all so pristine: the fruit-bowl, the duvet-covers, the neat stack of leaflets beside the bed – *Eating Eastern at the Europa, Your Room Service Explained, Day Trips to Ayuthaya and the River Kwai, Avis Car-Hire* . . . They might have just arrived and been waiting for the porter to follow with their bags. The man disappeared into the bathroom and made various rummaging noises. Stavros hovered nervously. He wasn't going to be asked to choose, was he? Gossamer, ribbed or black with red spots? He wandered over to the window and looked out. The rain lashed the roofs of the tenements; the lightning raked the city like an avenging God.

'Better in than out. Yes?' Close to, the woman's eyes were glazed, unfocused. Drink? Pot? Stavros couldn't imagine.

He said: 'It's quite a storm.'

In the bathroom a cork popped. What the hell . . .? The woman said quickly: 'You're a businessman, I think?'

'An interpreter.'

'Here for the big conference. Yes? Your friend – also an interpreter?'

'Yes.'

'A girl? A boy?'

'A girl. Definitely a girl. Look, I wonder . . .' He looked at his watch, at the woman's coarse, inquiring face, at the door into the bathroom where nothing – or everything – was happening. Why did sex have to carry this terrible price-tag of embarrassment? What had happened to spontaneity?

The woman gave a lewd wink, enjoying his discomfiture.

'She must be some girl, your friend. A real – how do you say? – *goer*. You can't wait to have her. Yes?'

'Well, we've been apart a long time. It's perfectly normal . . .'

'What *are* you going to do to her? You naughty, naughty boy. Now I am jealous, I think.' Her lips pouted and she seemed on the point of thrusting her body against his. He looked desperately towards the bathroom. The man emerged carrying a tray: on it were a bottle of champagne and three glasses.

'I'm sorry to keep you. The cork was stiff.' He bore serenely down on them with the tray before him. The glasses were arranged in a neat semi-circle, so that one of them was nearer Stavros than the others. Behind them, protected by them, was a condom-packet. He couldn't reach the condoms without first accepting the champagne – it was a vicious little conundrum. In some resentment he took the glass. The man handed the woman another glass, took a glass for himself and put the tray down on the table. He clinked glasses with the other two and said: 'Bottoms up.' The woman giggled. The whole thing had the mesmerising quality of a conjuring-trick. Stavros kept his eyes rooted to the condoms throughout – as if that silly pink packet was his only access to sanity, freedom, peace . . . He raised the glass to his lips, then withdrew it. He wasn't completely stupid.

'Excuse me – what are we celebrating?'

'Do you not like champagne? We have some gin.'

'No, it's not that. I just find this whole situation a bit . . . odd.'

They looked at him anxiously. The woman said: 'Sex, champagne – it's just good fun. Yes?'

'Oh I see that link. It's not that I'm a killjoy. I'm a Greek: we know how to enjoy ourselves. It's just . . .' Perhaps he *was* completely stupid. Or his brain was tired, lacklustre: it took him for ever to make the simplest connections. 'What I'm getting at is, isn't it more normal to share the champagne with the person with whom you're . . . doing the other thing? I'm sorry. I put that badly.' He reassured himself that the condoms were still there and took a sip from the glass. It tasted slightly bitter – made in Taiwan probably.

The man watched him closely.

'Are you in a great hurry? We didn't mean to keep you waiting. You have all night, don't you? Perhaps your friend could join us?'

'No, I really don't think –'

'We're only being hospitable. It's hard making friends when you travel – don't you think? There was no intention . . .'

'Of course not, of course not.' He gulped down the rest of the glass. 'Please excuse me if I sounded rude.' He bent to pick up the condoms and felt unaccountably dizzy, as if he'd drunk the whole bottle. Halfway to the door, his knees buckled under him. As he lost consciousness, he heard the man say in Dutch: 'You get his room-key. I'll ring . . .' But the final word was drowned.

A man's voice broke through the oblivion. It seemed to be saying, in Thai: 'Shall we throw the body at the tractor or give it to the sewing-machine?'

Another voice said: 'The sewing-machine is too dangerous. There are stewed clams in every shirt-sleeve.'

A third voice said simply: 'My aunt is an engine-driver.'

Stavros chafed with incomprehension, the brilliant linguist out of his depth. Thai was such an elusive language: a lot of words sounded just like other words until you had mastered the inflections. What had become of the simplicities of the phrase-book – 'My mother takes me to the market on Saturday', 'A room for three persons with a bath and shower'? He opened his eyes.

He was lying on a hard wooden floor in a simply furnished room. There was a calendar on the wall and a couple of pin-up girls; a big old-fashioned fan throbbed and rattled in the centre of the ceiling. Three men, young, unshaven, leanly built, were sitting at a table playing cards; a fourth stood by the window looking down into the street. Stavros saw the rain streaming down the window-pane and remembered a thunder-storm, a Dutchman with a champagne-bottle and – long, long ago – a woman called Christine who wanted him to wear a condom. He groaned aloud: at foreign travel, at being a Greek, at the unrelenting cruelty of the universe. The men playing cards sprang to their feet. The fourth man disappeared into an adjoining room and returned with an older man: he wore a prosperous grey suit and was smoking a cigar. He said something to the card-players, who dragged Stavros to his feet and propped him up in a chair; then he sat down himself. He had a scar on his right cheek and an air of irritated authority: there was a touch of Boff in the eyes. Stavros had a feeling they weren't going to get on together.

The man tapped the ash of his cigar on to the table. 'What did you do with the packet?' His English had an American drawl, as if he'd learnt it from Hollywood. When Stavros didn't answer, he reached across and slapped his cheek with the back of his hand. 'I said, what did you do with it? It's not in your room.' He raised his hand to hit him again. Stavros cringed.

'I won't be treated like this. I demand to speak to the Greek ambassador.' The words rang hollow as a drum. Was there a Greek ambassador to Thailand at all? 'I am here as the guest of the Thai government. I have diplomatic status. I am a parliamentarian.' Each protest seemed more irrelevant than the last, like thunder-claps fading into the distance.

The man said: 'Don't play games, mister' and hit him again – the back of his hand was hard and rough, as if he'd been using it for this purpose all his life. The other men watched quietly. Stavros rubbed his eyes with his hand.

'Who are you? Police?'

The man raised his eyebrows and gave a dark chuckle. He said something in Thai to the others, who laughed nervously. One of them lit a cigarette. Stavros noticed that his index finger was missing, just like Chiung's, but the man wasn't Chiung – he was too tall. He rubbed his eyes again.

'I don't understand. Who are you? What do you want? What happened to that Dutch couple? I never meant to get involved in any of this. I'm only here to be with my girlfriend. You must believe that. I'm a simple, sex-loving Greek who happens to be good at languages. That's all. Really.'

He gave a sheepish, moussaka-wouldn't-melt-in-his-mouth grin. He was rather proud of his sheepish grins: in Europe it was how he made friends. The man watched unmoved, expressionless, then hit him a third time, harder than before. 'I don't want to hear about your woman problems. I want the packet. Where is it?'

Stavros whispered: 'I gave it to Mr Ledgerwood,' and lowered his head in shame. No true-born Greek would have caved in like that. Odysseus would have had his guts dragged out before betraying a friend; Achilles would have killed the man with his bare hands . . . But the world had shrunk since then.

The man said: 'That's better,' and left. Stavros heard him talking on the telephone in the next room; he made out the word 'American' a couple of times, not much else. The other men returned to their card-game. The storm redoubled, rattling the window-pane.

The man in the suit returned. He was angry and the scar on his cheek seemed to smart with fresh pain. He said: 'Mr Ledgerwood is an American Congressman.' Stavros nodded. He shouted: 'Are you telling me you gave that packet to an American Congressman?' Stavros nodded again. The man crashed his fist on the table.

'Mister, I don't like people playing games with me. You tell me what you did with that packet or I kill you right now.'

'I told you. I gave it to Ledgerwood.'

'Why did you give it to him? Are you crazy?'

'Because he wanted it. What's so crazy about that? He's a politician: he cares about this sort of thing. He was going to make speeches in Washington.'

'Speeches? What is this? Now I know you're playing games.' The man shouted an instruction to the others. One of them bent down and pulled a knife out of his sock. The others pinioned Stavros's arms behind his back. He shouted: 'There's been a terrible mistake.' The knife flashed in front of his face. He screamed: 'All right, I'll tell you. It's in a blue bag in the laundry-room of the hotel. On the second shelf from the top.'

They let go of him and the man in the suit smiled. He said to the others in Thai: 'They always talk in the end.' Congratulations were exchanged. Stavros prayed that the hotel had a laundry-room and passed out with shock. When he came to, he found that someone had tied his arms and legs together – and that whoever had tied his arms and legs had also just thrown him in the river. He wriggled his way to the surface and shouted for help in eleven languages, but the water overwhelmed him.

4

'You could have drowned, you know,' pronounced an English voice, in a tone of mild rebuke. 'If I hadn't been watching the water, nobody would have seen you.'

'Why did you have to tie yourself up?' came a woman's voice. 'It seems rather silly. Were you trying to prove something?'

He opened his eyes and saw a group of people in formal dress gathered around him. They were drinking champagne from long-stemmed glasses; a waiter moved among them with a tray of canapés; there was the distinctively glassy good humour of the English getting drunk. A woman with voluminous breasts whispered: 'I think he was trying to *kill* himself.' Her companion muttered: 'Why do you have to reduce everything to psychology, Celia?' Another woman hovered with a towel, while two younger men undid the ropes with which Stavros had been tied. He got shakily to his feet and addressed himself to the stout man in glasses who seemed to be the leader of the group. He wore a badge saying 'Chairman' and his trousers were dripping wet, as if he'd somehow been instrumental in Stavros's rescue.

'I can't thank you enough, sir. You've saved my life. They tried to kill me, you know.'

'You've had a bad shock,' the man said briskly, not listening to a word. 'A large whisky will see you straight. I've sent someone for a change of clothes.'

'They wanted me out of the way because I knew too much. They didn't believe me when I told the truth. I think they were police of some sort – *secret* police.'

'Yes, yes, you've had a rough time of it.' He thrust a whisky to Stavros's lips and steered him towards a chair. 'Sit down and get your breath back. Keep your story till later. Steady on, Madeleine' – this to the woman with the towel, who was rubbing Stavros's hair with unnecessary vigour – 'our friend's had a bad shock.' That phrase again: flat, automatic, irritating in its inadequacy. Stavros shivered.

'Excuse me – where am I?'

'You're in Bang-kok,' said the woman called Madeleine, with tiresome precision. She sounded like a prison visitor or a speech therapist, someone used to talking down to people. 'In Thai-land.'

'Thank you. I know that. But where is this place? What time is it? It was dark before. There was a storm . . .' He shielded his eyes against the sun, which was low in the sky on the left. It was early morning. The river in front of them was as still as a picture and a faint chorus of birds could be heard above the chatter of the champagne-drinkers. He looked at his watch, which had somehow survived the night: it said 7-17. But then why . . .?

'We're giving Bunty a champagne breakfast,' Madeleine explained. 'Don't worry – we don't normally start knocking it back this early in the day.' She gave a giddy laugh, throwing doubt on the accuracy of the statement.

'Bunty?'

'He's sixty today. Hard to believe, isn't it?' She nodded in the direction of a white-haired man in a grey suit who was trying to prong a prawn with a cocktail-stick; a waiter held the tray steady for him. He looked nearer eighty than sixty: the prawn was dead, but still looked capable of evading capture. Stavros shook his head. They seemed to be on the terrace of a grand, old-fashioned hotel: everything else was a mystery.

'Excuse me – who is Bunty?'

'Didn't you know that was his nickname? Nobody calls him Rufus, not even the other side. Bunty! Bunty, come and say hello to our friend.'

'Who is Ru . . .' Stavros began, then noticed the man was wearing a badge. '*Sir Rufus Barnacle MP, Hon. Vice-Chairman, UK delegation.*' He'd never heard of him. Madeleine announced that Stavros was the poor man who'd had to be helped out of the river and Sir Rufus nodded sagely. Ignoring Stavros, he looked out across the river like a retired admiral surveying the Solent.

'Wouldn't take a swim in that stuff myself.' A segment of prawn followed the words out of his mouth and disappeared down his shirt-front.

'I wasn't swimming. I was thrown in.'

'Crowing?'

'*Thrown in.* To the water.'

'Larking about, were you? I don't understand you young, you young . . . Turks.' It wasn't the most tactful way to address a Greek, but he gave a little chunter of pleasure as if he was the first person to associate youthfulness with Turkishness. 'Ah well – you'll know better next time.' A passing tray of drinks caught his eye and he shuffled after it, his pendulous belly wobbling before him. Madeleine touched Stavros's forearm.

'I think he's worried about his speech. He's normally such a friendly man. Considering.'

'Speech?' Considering what?

'He's opening for us on human rights. The debate starts in a couple of hours. He's been in politics for thirty-five years, but he still gets nervous when he has to stand up and perform in public. It's like acting, politics. Wouldn't you agree, Mr . . .'

He nodded slowly. He remembered now. There was a man called Boff who was going to tear him limb from limb if he missed the debate and a woman called Christine who was going to make love to him if he could find a condom. Or was it the other way round? Was it Boff who wanted the condom and the woman who was going to tear him limb from limb? It all seemed so long ago, like something that had happened in childhood. He recognised the hotel now too. Where but the Oriental was Dom Perignon served at seven o'clock in the morning? Where else did the waiters glide about their business like so many champion ice-skaters?

'I've found you some dry clothes,' came a voice behind him. He turned to see a tense, breathless figure holding a newly pressed suit and a clean white shirt. Where but the Oriental . . . ? Then he recognised him.

'Tight. How good to see you. I haven't seen a familiar face since – it seems like hours. I should have guessed you'd be with the British delegation. You just wouldn't believe what's been happening to me since I last saw you. I really don't think I've ever –'

'It's you,' Tight said, with Anglo-Saxon economy: he sounded as if he wished Stavros had been left in the water. Stavros was beginning to feel the same way himself.

5

Nobody who stayed at the Europa hotel had got their money's worth until they had tried complaining to Mr Lo. Mr Lo was the assistant manager in charge of customer relations: he sat at a separate desk in the corner of the lobby and handled any whingeing guests. He was shrewd and tenacious, a past master of stonewalling. Getting a refund agreed by him was like discovering a Rembrandt in the attic or making love in a moving vehicle: many aspired to it, but few succeeded. His genius was to listen to the most vitriolic outburst without losing his air of concerned beneficence. He smiled incessantly: he *never* answered back. In time the vitriol would burn itself out, the plaintiff retire exhausted, the life of the hotel go sweetly on. The Great Wall of China – Lo's parents had fled from Peking during the cultural revolution – was never breached.

When Stavros arrived in the lobby – after another hair-raising *tuk-tuk* ride from the centre of town – Lo was already occupied. It was only 9-15, but a queue of a dozen guests had formed in front of his desk and the mood was militant. A German man stamped his foot on the floor and an Australian woman was on the verge of hysterics. 'You try wearing the same pair two days running in this heat,' she shouted, at nobody in particular. 'You try!' Even Lo's habitual smile was fraying around the edges.

'What's wrong?' Stavros asked a man dressed in pyjamas and dressing-gown. Three sobbing women joined the queue as he spoke. There was an air of complete unreality about the situation.

'The laundry's gone,' the man said laconically. He had a slightly shell-shocked air, as if he didn't quite believe his own story.

'What, all of it? For the whole hotel?' Stavros twitched guiltily: he had a vague recollection he was somehow responsible for . . .

'Every last thing. They didn't leave a single pair of socks.'

'They?'

'Three men with guns. Guns! Would you believe it? Why do you need guns to steal clothes? Why clothes? Why this hotel? Why me? I give up.' He wandered off in a daze.

Stavros pushed his way to the front of the queue.

'Mr Lo, what's going on here? Who were these men? When did this happen?'

Lo shrugged: shrugging was one of the trump cards in his arsenal of delay. 'They said they were police.'

'Were they?'

'They said yes. The police said no. The real police,' he added without great confidence. Stavros caught the note of perplexity in his voice.

'You don't seem certain. Did they look like police?'

'I don't know. I didn't see them.'

'Who did see them?'

'The laundry-boy. They threatened him with their guns.'

'Do police normally carry guns?'

Lo gave a dry smile. 'Not when they're picking up the laundry.' It was almost a joke. 'One of them had a finger missing.'

'Yes, I know.'

'How do you know?'

'I was . . .' Stavros stopped. There was an ugly mood among the guests: it wasn't the time to launch the latest volume of his autobiography. 'Someone told me,' he muttered.

Behind him an English woman wailed: 'If I don't get my skirt back, I'm not going to any bloody British Council do – I'm sorry, Roger.'

He remembered Christine and shuddered.

'Do you have any Dutchmen staying in this hotel?'

Lo blinked. The shift was too sudden, too baroque. 'It happens,' he said cautiously, as if being asked about a cholera outbreak among the kitchen staff.

'Are there any here at the moment?'

'I don't think so.'

'Then who was staying in Room 1315 last night?'

'Excuse me a minute.' Lo consulted his computer.

The guests behind Stavros rumbled mutinously. An American shouted: 'How long is that man going to sit on his arse? I can't sell securities in this shirt.'

Lo smiled impassively. 'Room 1315 has been vacant for two weeks.'

Stavros nodded: he'd expected no different. He sprinted towards the lift.

Christine's room was empty. So was his, very empty. Someone had been through it with an axe and a sledge-hammer: it looked like a bomb-site, not somewhere where something agreeable and adulterous had been about to take place. The mattress had been ripped open, the panelling torn from the cupboards, articles of clothing scattered to every corner. One of Christine's shoes was wedged beneath the overturned television: there was no other remnant of her. He looked desperately out of the window. Way, way below, by the swimming-pool, a woman in a blue bikini was stretched out reading a book. She looked for all the world like Christine, but no somersault of the imagination could convince him that it was, that she had escaped the devastation. He said a hastily composed prayer in Greek – praying and swearing were his only calls on his mother tongue – and stopped abruptly. The telephone was ringing. He waded through what remained of the duvet-cover and picked it up. He needn't have bothered.

'Stavros, I've decided to forgive you.' For reasons of her own Monica had adopted her Mother Superior voice: its stilted, syrupy calm numbed him into silence. He knelt on the floor making little gulping noises, while a woman five thousand miles away tried to patch up her marriage the Irish way.

'You were probably a wee bit tired when we last spoke. I understand, really I do. But Stavros, you're a man. Your life's so simple, sitting there in your smart hotel room with room service at your beck and call and not a care in the world.' Still kneeling, Stavros vomited quietly on to the pillow. 'How can you know what it's like to be alone in a flat with a fellow like Grandjean on the floor above? He's not safe, Stavros, he's sick – and that's being kind to the dirty bastard. Stavros, I'm telephoning to let you know that I've hired a private detective till you get back. He charges eighty francs an hour – I hope that's all right. Stavros, are you listening to what I'm saying? Stavros!' He was already in the lift, halfway to the ground floor.

'I'm looking for Miss Golding,' he shouted at the reception clerk, another smiling procastinator in the Lo mould. 'Where is she? Someone has broken into my room and abducted her. I'm holding the hotel responsible. Do something, damn you.' He felt like hitting him: the sense of powerlessness was overwhelming.

Another man was sent for. He appeared with a file open in his hand. 'Miss Golding checked out two hours ago,' he announced, blinking nervously: there was a suppressed terror in his eyes, as if someone were holding a gun to his head.

Stavros banged his fist on the desk.

'I don't believe you. She was staying here a week. I've never heard such an absurd story. Did anyone see her check out?'

The file was consulted. 'Only Hue.'

'Hue?'

'The night clerk.'

'Can I talk to him?'

'I'm sorry, sir.' The blinking intensified, like a monstrous nervous disorder. 'He's been called away. He's taken a train to Chiang Mai.'

'What for?' he asked mechanically: he was too demoralised to care.

The file was snapped shut. 'A family funeral.' It sounded half-plausible – in the circumstances.

FIVE

I

Günther Boff looked up from his desk and grunted. If the sound hadn't come from the middle-aged man in a grey suit, one would have looked behind the filing-cabinet for a rhinoceros. 'Good morning, Stavros.' Such simple words, such measureless evil behind them . . . But Stavros was too agitated to be frightened.

'I must talk to you, Günther.'

'Not now, Stavros.'

'Christine Golding's been –'

'Not *now*.' He indicated the other people in the room – a meeting was in progress. Stavros recognised three of his fellow interpreters: Carlotta (English-into-Spanish); Jean-Claude (anything-east-of-Baluchistan-into-French) – and Barry. Barry was one of the worst linguists ever to be given a passport: not so much a simultaneous interpreter as a one-man Tower of Babel. With a heavy Birmingham accent and a Latin 'O' level to his name, he relied for employment on his secretaryship of the EPGU (UGPE in French, EPUG in Spanish, something indecipherable in German), the international interpreters' trade union. Carlotta and Jean-Claude were also active in the union – as was Stavros when he wasn't being shot at, threatened with knives and condoms and thrown into rivers. Curious in spite of himself, he sat down next to Barry.

'What's all this about?' There was really no need to ask. All EPGU ever demanded was money: suitcases full of it.

Barry brandished a type-written list. 'There are a hundred and twenty speakers on human rights. Eight minutes a speaker, questions to the Minister, points of order . . . We'll be here till midnight.'

'For the second night running,' Carlotta added. 'Who do they think we are? Robots?'

'It's worse than Islamabad,' moaned Jean-Claude. None of them ever forgot Islamabad: it was written like Calais on every interpreter's heart. The air-conditioning had broken down; the bartender had cerebral palsy; an elderly German-into-Spanish woman had collapsed with exhaustion and been carried out of her booth on a stretcher . . . 'If there were proper overtime payments, colleagues might perhaps accept some inconvenience for the sake of the conference. As it is . . . We're trying to talk some sense into Herr Boff . . . *mais c'est difficile.*' He gave a Gallic shrug.

Boff grunted again: the rhinoceros behind the filing-cabinet was getting very angry indeed.

'I don't pay you jokers overtime. It's not in your contracts. The WLP doesn't work like that: it never has. You get paid by the day and, if you have to work late, you have to work late. It's too bad.'

'Not after midnight,' Carlotta shouted. 'Not two nights running. We agreed that in Manila.'

Boff's eyebrows shot up imperiously.

'Who agreed? I didn't agree. Do you have it in writing? Your contracts –'

'Our contracts are neither here nor there. It's the principle of the thing.'

'Contracts *are* principles.'

'And interpreters are human beings. Do you agree with *that*, Herr Boff?'

There was a fractional pause. Boff muttered something under his breath in German, touching on the humanity of the interpreting profession. Carlotta went purple and asked Jean-Claude in Spanish if Boff had just said what she thought. Jean-Claude replied in French that his German was rather rusty but, *oui*, he did think Boff had used that word. Barry asked if they could talk in English. Stavros was consulted and said in his Swiss French that, from what he remembered of German slang, Boff's comment was particularly abusive. Carlotta screamed in a heavy Basque *patois* that she wasn't going to be spoken to like that by a two-bit Kraut pen-pusher. Barry repeated his plea for English. Boff grunted something inaudible in a language unknown to man. And Jean-Claude said *'merde!'* which everyone understood perfectly – except for

Barry, who twiddled his finger in his ear. Then came a knock on the door and a familiar face.

'Say, is there a Mr Boff here?' Congressman Ledgerwood's easy courtesy brought order out of chaos.

Boff rose smoothly to his feet. '*Ya*, I am Boff.' The others composed themselves.

'Are you the guy I talk to about the debate this morning? I have to know what order people are speaking.' He caught sight of Stavros and nodded uneasily: they might have been clandestine lovers, out of their depth away from the privacy of the bedroom.

Boff showed him the list of speakers and he ran a practised eye over it. 'Looks like we'll be here late again. Tough on you fellows who have to interpret. Still' – he smiled, not noticing the outrage in Boff's face, the glee in Barry's, the wounded self-righteousness in Jean-Claude's – 'I guess they pay you for it.' He looked at the list again. Carlotta gabbled something in Basque. 'I'd like to speak before eleven if possible, but there are quite a few ahead of me. How long do we each get to speak, Mr Boff?'

'Eight minutes.'

He clapped his hand to his forehead. 'Is that it? Everything you know about human rights in eight minutes? I call that a tall order, Mr Boff. How do you get people to care what's going on in the world in eight minutes?' He stalked out of the room and Stavros followed: the others carried on shouting at each other in an assortment of languages.

'Have a good evening with your girl?' the Congressman asked Stavros drily as they ascended an escalator. His shoulders were tense with misery, as if the Greek's very presence imposed an intolerable strain.

'No,' said Stavros emphatically. 'I didn't. Can I tell you about it?'

The Congressman growled: he seemed to be bracing himself for a disquisition on Greek shortcomings in bed. When he heard the real explanation, his face went very grave.

'Who else have you told about this?'

'Nobody. Not the whole story.'

'We must be very – careful.' He paused to nod at Mr Petersson, the leader of the Norwegian delegation, who was holding forth about acid rain to a bemused group of Africans. 'I don't know what the hell's going on here, but it's no good shouting our mouths off. Not yet.'

'But what are we going to *do*? I have to find Christine. If that means going to the police, I'll go to the police.'

The Congressman shook his head emphatically. 'I wouldn't, Stavros. What makes you think they're on our side? Do you see that guy over there?' He indicated a man in uniform at the entrance to the hall. 'What do you notice?'

'He's carrying a gun.'

'Anything else?'

'He's four foot six with glasses.'

'He's been *watching* us, Stavros.' As he hissed the word, a glint of pure paranoia appeared in his eyes, the same unhinged quality Stavros had noticed the night before. 'He hasn't taken his goddam eyes off you the whole time you've been talking.'

'Seriously?' Stavros glanced across. The man seemed half-asleep: he surveyed the toings and froings of delegates with complete indifference, as if they were a species of insect unworthy of his attention. It made no sense at all to think . . . A bell went off, signalling the opening of the morning session, and the Congressman gave his hand a quick squeeze. 'I must get along, Stavros. Don't do anything I wouldn't do.'

He laughed miserably and trudged round to the interpreters' booths. Never mind not doing anything the Congressman wouldn't do: he couldn't think of anything to do at all. He'd come five thousand miles to get well and truly laid and he wasn't even going to get a refund.

2

It was the practice of the World League of Parliaments for the Chair to be taken in rotation by the leaders of the national delegations; for the human rights debate it was the turn of M. Berbizier of the Cameroon. Berbizier was a French-speaker, which meant Stavros had to interpret his opening announcements into English; but the French he spoke was like no language Stavros had ever heard. No sooner had he settled into his booth and put on his earphones than he was bombarded by a series of sing-song noises which made as much sense as the proceedings of a Welsh eisteddfod. It was every interpreter's nightmare. Normally in such situations, you imagined what the speaker *might* be saying and regurgitated it in a convincing form; but Stavros wasn't feeling very imaginative. He twined his fingers miserably round the microphone and cleared his throat.

'Good morning, dear, uh, colleagues. Today we are debating ... human rights, a, uh, subject dear to all of us parli-parlia-parliamen*tarians*.' He caught Sophia's eye. She didn't seem to have forgiven him for the previous day's drinking: the exasperation on her face was tangible. Drily, she pointed out a piece of paper sitting in front of his nose: a text of Berbizier's speech translated into English. He pounced on it gratefully and read it out in tempo. A smell of fresh croissants wafted across from the French booth.

'There are a hundred and twenty speakers on the list for this debate. This means that, if we are to conclude the debate at a reasonable hour, the time allocated to individual speakers must be limited to eight minutes. I must ask all delegates to adhere to these limits strictly and to take their place on the rostrum as promptly as possible. Human rights is a matter which concerns all of us. Let us set the outside world a good example by respecting each other's rights to contribute to the debate on a fair and equal footing. I thank delegates for their co-operation in this matter.'

He stopped and squinted at the presidential rostrum, only to find that Berbizier was still reading from his French text. There was no English text left for him – he had gone through it too quickly. To avoid a hiatus, he said more slowly: 'Courtesy is a quality which all parliamentarians should try to practise' – that sounded uncontroversial enough. Berbizier read on. He scoured his desk for a second sheet of English translation: there wasn't one, so he had to carry on improvising. 'At all times. Wherever they are. Be it here in Bangkok ... or in their own count-ries.' By now he was sweating and Sophia was looking daggers at him; there were signs of an imminent explosion from Boff's corner of the rostrum. All the simple things in an interpreter's life – condoms, missing fingers, massage parlours – seemed worlds away ...

Berbizier stopped and put down his notes. Stavros breathed out: his ordeal was over. Berbizier added a few words not in his brief. Stavros froze, not attempting an interpretation: with any luck it was just a little grace-note which nobody but a Frenchman would understand anyway. Berbizier stopped. Stavros relaxed. Then pandemonium broke out. It *hadn't* been a grace-note.

'*Monsieur le Président!*' shouted a Belgian delegate, leaping to his feet. '*Monsieur le Président!*' He started expostulating in French.

Stavros understood every word and wished he hadn't. Glumly he provided the interpretation.

'I think your last suggestion is outrageous, Mr President. With all due respect, I do not think I have heard such a bizarre proposal in the thirteen years I have been a delegate to this Assembly.'

'*Absolument! Absolument!*' A Canadian Senator made the same point, in even stronger terms. Stavros interpreted. The non-Francophone delegates looked bewildered: there was a buzz of confusion around the Chamber. Sir Rufus Barnacle of the British delegation tottered to his feet and made a series of puffing and wheezing noises which slowly formed themselves into a speech.

'Forgive me, Mr President, fellow delegates, but it seems there has been a, ah, misunderstanding. Nothing you said seemed to me in any way outrageous, indeed your final words – and I too have been a delegate to this Assembly for many years, very many years – your final words, Mr President, about the importance of courtesy, of courtesy in parliamentary life, seemed to me to sum up, with your customary skill, if I may say so, those ideals which I would hope united all of us, whoever we are, wherever we –'

'*Non, non, non!*' The Canadian Senator was on his feet again. He didn't have any quarrel at *all* with what Mr Berbizier had said about courtesy. Of *course* parliamentarians should be courteous, he screamed, gesticulating at an Iraqi delegate to sit down and stop trying to interrupt – that was common ground among all of them. It was what Mr Berbizier had said *after* that which was so disturbing. Perhaps he could repeat what he had proposed, so that everyone could be absolutely clear what they were being asked to agree?

M. Berbizier repeated his proposal. He did so slowly and clearly, in a sentence of about twenty words of which Stavros could decipher just one: '*necessaire*', three words from the end. He leant forward nervously.

'I say it again. That is . . . what I said and I hope it will not be, uh, *necessary* to repeat myself.'

The pandemonium intensified. The Canadian Senator shouted '*Voilà!*' and threw his order paper in the air; the two-man Monaco delegation stormed out of the Chamber; the French group to a man chanted '*Fasciste! Fasciste!*'; the Irish and Australians raised points of order; so did the Russians, so did the Chinese. Only the Polish delegation had the nous to work out what was going on. They formed a posse in front of the interpreters' booths and peered at the faces behind the glass, looking for the culprit: one of them pointed at Stavros and shouted an expletive. From what he remembered of the language – and he only really had pillow Polish, garnered during a fling with a girl called Maria at a regional economic conference in Buenos Aires – the insult embraced his mother as well as himself. He quaked and tried one of those sheepish grins which had used to stand him in such good stead; the Polish man said something even more insulting and banged his fist on the glass.

'For Christ's sake!' Sophia hissed. 'Pull yourself together, Stavros.' She scribbled something down on a piece of paper. He read it numbly.

'WHAT M. BERBIZIER SAID WAS, THE DEBATE SHOULD CONTINUE THROUGHOUT THE DAY WITH NO BREAK FOR LUNCH.'

Then she seized the microphone and took over.

3

The debate proper started twenty minutes later. A statesman-like compromise had been agreed through the good offices of Monsignor de Ste Croix, the chubby-cheeked papal nuncio in Singapore who was attending the conference as an observer. The Assembly *would* break for lunch, but for one hour instead of the normal three; to make up for the time lost, speaking time would be cut from eight minutes a delegate to seven and a half. Everyone applauded the ingenuity of the arrangements – except the interpreters, who groaned in protest. They knew what was coming. Delegates wouldn't actually deliver shorter speeches: they would deliver the same speeches at a faster speed. It recalled Strasbourg in '86, when a Spanish-speaking Turk had delivered a twenty-minute speech on Cyprus in five minutes flat and reduced the finest linguists in Europe to gibbering impotence.

At least the first speaker was Australian, which took the pressure off the English booth. Sophia switched off the microphone and glared at Stavros.

'You've been drinking again, haven't you?'

'No. Definitely not. I'm sorry, Sophy – I just couldn't cope with that man's French.'

'It wasn't that bad. *I* understood it.'

'It was dreadful. I'm not up to that sort of stuff at this time of the morning.' He touched the sleeve of her dress in contrition and mumbled: 'Look, I'm sorry, Sophy – really. Something terrible's happened. Simply terrible.'

Her glare relented a little.

'What's the matter?'

'It's Christine.' He explained what had happened – some of what had happened, the believable bits.

In the Chamber the Australian delegate was waxing emotional about Aborigines; other delegates read newspapers or sidled out to the bar; the entire Spanish delegation shook hands with the entire Mexican delegation . . . Sophia listened to his story and tossed her head.

'You *have* been drinking, haven't you?'

'That was yesterday. I learnt my lesson – really. I know all this sounds a bit strange, Sophy, but –'

'Stavros, I've had it with you. I'm not working with you again.'

'Why not? What's wrong? Why don't you believe me?'

'Christine's sitting over there. She looks perfectly all right to *me*. Now shut up, for God's sake.' She snapped on her earphones and bent forward over the microphone: an Iranian delegate had taken the floor.

Stavros looked where she had pointed and saw Christine bent over *her* microphone in the German booth. He trembled with excitement. Never mind how she had got there: that sweet, gentle face offered fresh hope amid the chaos. He glanced back at the proceedings in the Chamber. The Iranian speaker was slagging off the Iraqis, who were sitting in the same part of the hall; other delegates put down their newspapers to listen; Sophia interpreted with meticulous care. He turned disdainfully away. If he heard any more glib pronouncements on human rights, he was going to vomit. It was *his* rights that counted, his inalienable freedom as a Greek citizen to get into bed with the woman of his choice. Anywhere. At any time. With or without a condom.

Simmering with militant hedonism, he slipped out of his booth and tiptoed into the back of the German booth. Christine carried on interpreting with her back to him; the other two interpreters looked outraged and gestured to him to leave. He looked over her shoulder and saw a small envelope marked STAVROS on the desk in front of her. She nodded at him to take it and he tiptoed out again. The Iranian delegate had had his seven and a half minutes and was about to be followed by a Frenchman. He hurried back to his seat and took over the microphone from Sophia.

'*Chers collègues, délégués distingués, citoyens du monde . . .*' After Berbizier it was a doddle: the language of Racine and Corneille spoken as it was meant to be spoken, by an old, white-haired Gaullist MP who articulated every word as if he were using it for the first time. Stavros untensed. 'Dear colleagues, distinguished delegates, citizens of the world . . .' He could do it in his sleep.

Christine's letter was in front of him. He eased his finger into the flap and pulled out a piece of paper: he recognised it as the writing-paper provided in the hotel. There was a short, two-sentence message. 'We are both in danger. I have been instructed to make no contact with you till the conference is over.' It was her handwriting: in the same graceful script he'd once read sentiments of the purest love, locked in the bathroom in Geneva while Monica cleared away the breakfast. How long ago that seemed.

'Instructed by who, for fuck's sake? You're not somebody's slave. You don't have to do what some crackpot tells you.' He said the words aloud because he felt them deeply: indignation welled up within him, mingling with the pain, the fear, the confusion ... And they would have been rather eloquent if they hadn't been so out of place in their context – a patrician French discourse on human rights. Delegates tapped their earphones: 'crackpot' was too colloquial for this speaker's style; 'fuck' was an ugly gatecrasher at the banquet of words. Sophia's knuckles went white with fury. Stavros needed all his ingenuity to recover.

'. . . and, uh, *because* we are not slaves, we must stand up to bullies. We must be ferocious in our defence of human rights, even if it means using strong, uh, *very* strong language. Dear colleagues, distinguished delegates . . .'

The French speaker swept majestically on, in love with the sound of his voice, oblivious to the bowdlerising of his words by the interpreter – and the crisis passed. Delegates returned to their newspapers; business picked up at the bar; the subtle rhythms of parliamentary life were restored. Stavros stole a glance at Christine, but she looked studiedly away – then Barry walked unannounced into the booth and took the microphone.

'This is Barry Balderstone, secretary of the EPGU. I regret to have to inform delegates that, because of unresolved contractual problems, the simultaneous interpretation service has been suspended. If the WLP authorities can be persuaded to negotiate with us in good faith, the delay should be only temporary. Thank you very much.' He switched off the microphone and winked at Stavros. Carlotta was making the same announcement from the Spanish booth, Jean-Claude from the French, a red-haired man called Karl-Heinz from the German. It was a brilliant piece of stage-management: the announcement of a bomb in the Chamber couldn't have had a bigger impact. Delegates made gestures of outrage and disbelief; Boff sprang from his seat as if he'd sat on a burning poker; there was a flurry of points of order, meaningless without the interpretation. Stavros surveyed the scene spellbound.

'I'm not with you, Barry. Why are we doing this?'

'Boff.'

'What about Boff?'

'He's a pig-headed Kraut fascist.'

'I know he's a pig-headed Kraut fascist. He's been a pig-headed Kraut fascist since 1975. He's also a tight-arsed, bird-brained bureaucrat and a paranoid schizophrenic. But we haven't gone on strike about it before. Did he say something to Carlotta?'

'She was practically in tears. We've got to show solidarity.'

'What did he say?'

'He called her a Lesbian bitch. She thinks it was that. Jean-Claude thought it was left-wing troublemaker. It was in Kraut-speak. Either way, we've got to do something.' He looked proudly out at the pandemonium in the Chamber: he could have been a gardener admiring his delphiniums. 'Marvellous, bloody marvellous. All those political big-shots and without us they're nothing, eunuchs. Boff will *have* to meet us.'

'What are we asking for?'

'Overtime rates after midnight and a written apology to Carlotta. In *English*.' He grinned satanically.

Stavros glanced across at the German booth: Christine's place was empty. He ran out into the corridor, but she was nowhere to be seen. Boff appeared from the opposite direction, breathing fire. All his previous tantrums had just been play-acting, rehearsals for the real thing.

'I want to see you and you.' He stabbed his finger at Barry and Stavros. Carlotta came out of the Spanish booth. 'And *you*. In my office. Now.' He turned on his heels.

They followed, staying close together. Solidarity was no longer a cliché of the trade: it was a prerequisite for survival. As Boff's door slammed behind them, Barry took a piece of paper out of his pocket and laid it gently on the table. It read:

'(1) On behalf of the World League of Parliaments, I undertake to facilitate the payment of overtime rates, at twice the normal EPGU rates, for all interpretation work carried out after midnight. (2) I apologise to Carlotta Marquez for my foul and abusive language. (signed) Günther Boff.'

None of them dared look Boff in the face as he read it.

4

'Dear colleagues, I am pleased to announce the resumption of our debate on human rights. Because of the time lost, I regret that speaking time will have to be reduced to five minutes per speaker – five minutes, gentlemen. I now give the floor to Señor Valdes of Guatemala. He will be followed by Sir Barnacle of the United Kingdom. Señor Valdes, please. You have five minutes.'

Stavros handed the microphone to Sophia and took a sip of water – a very tiny sip. He had learnt a new philosophy of life in Bangkok: trust nothing; believe nobody; expect anything. Things might appear normal, but they were never normal – they were pregnant with danger. Even when Fate was kind – as in the latest incident with Boff – it was kind only to tease, to pave the way for something monstrous, diabolical ... It can't last, he thought, looking round the Chamber – at the delegates sitting in their places, at the Guatemalan speaker talking quietly and earnestly into the microphone, at the national flags fluttering outside the window ... It can't *last*.

He would have bet all the money he had against Boff signing on the dotted line. Boff never signed anything, he never surrendered: he was a primitive animal locked in a life-and-death struggle with the human race. Stavros remembered his roar of anger as he read the document; the veins bulging on his neck; his hands twisting with violence ... and then the Congressman's appearance and its incredible, quite incredible, sequel. 'I believe I would sign that chit if I were you, Mr Boff ... It doesn't do to dig your heels in at a time like this ... I think some kind of apology to Miss Marquez would be in order, don't you, Mr Boff – in the interests of parliamentary democracy? ... Dammit, Boff, we're talking human rights out there and you're monkeying us around as if you owned the place ... That's better, Mr Boff – I respect a man who listens to reason ... You must come to Wilmington some time – we have quite a flourishing German community ... Don't worry about that overtime now – the American delegation will pick up the tab ... Is that acceptable to you, Mr Balderstone? Good. Now, let's get on with the business in hand, shall we?'

Stavros looked across the Chamber to where the Congressman was sitting: that great head stood out among the rest like a rock in the sea. Never mind human rights. Never mind the Presidency. Never mind Kim and Chiung and the larger struggle. The man who could tame Boff was already a hero: to such a man belonged honour and renown all the days of his life.

'. . . which is why the American delegation should be ashamed to be sitting in this Chamber – ashamed, I say. They pay lip-service to human rights, but in reality . . .' The Guatemalan delegate was getting emotional: he trilled his indignation like an opera-singer and made chopping gestures with his hand as if he were dismembering a chicken. Sophia's perfect diction was inadequate to the occasion: she sounded as if she were reading an annual report to shareholders or asking a child what it wanted for Christmas – with the result that the Spanish-speaking delegates got excited and the English ones read their newspapers, unaware that their withers were being wrung. The French got excited *and* read their newspapers; the Italians passed round salami sandwiches. Stavros looked over to Christine's booth, hoping to catch her eye and share his amusement at the proceedings; but her eye wasn't to be caught. She sat still and tense in her place, with her head turned away and an air of impenetrable aloofness. It was as if they had quarrelled. Perhaps . . .

'Stavros!' Sophia thrust the microphone into his hands – M. Berbizier was speaking again. He cleared his throat.

'Thank you, uh, Mr Valdes. The Assembly has listened with great interest to your speech, but I must deplore the fact that it has lasted for five minutes and seventeen seconds. I remind delegates that the time limit for speeches is five minutes – five minutes only, gentlemen. I now call Sir Barnacle from the United Kingdom. Sir Barnacle.'

Sir Rufus staggered to his feet and made his way to the podium, a slow, statesmanlike progress, with pauses to shake hands with the leader of the Zambian delegation and with Mr Achapong, who seemed taken aback by the honour. There was an appreciative round of applause, such as might greet an old theatrical knight who had done a marvellous Hamlet in 1938 and nothing but sherry ads since. A sense of expectation combined with feelings of pity: the medical auxiliaries at the back of the Chamber stubbed out their cigarettes and took up positions by the stretcher. If the clock had started as soon as he'd been called, Sir Rufus would have used up four of his five minutes before he'd opened his mouth – then a further thirty seconds clearing his throat and evacuating the remains of his breakfast on to the microphone. But for Sir Rufus the normal stringencies could be relaxed. He was, as he might have said himself – for Englishmen of his generation had only one second language – *sui generis*.

'Mr President, fellow parliamentarians, I shall be brief, very brief . . . very – brief.' For Sir Rufus to repeat himself was so commonplace that none of the delegates noticed anything amiss. It was Stavros, fellow traveller on the banana-skin trail, who divined what was wrong: the elder statesman of the WLP had mislaid his speech. Smiling copiously and clutching on to the microphone like an ageing rock star, he fished in the left-hand pocket of his jacket with his right hand and the right-hand pocket with his left, then stuffed both hands down the front of his trousers and carried out a vigorous trawl of his lower anatomy. Nothing materialised – certainly nothing connected with human rights. When his hands resurfaced, one of them was holding an elastic band and the other what appeared to be an old-fashioned corkscrew. But no speech. Thrown back on improvisation, he rose gamely to the challenge – but two of his five minutes had already gone.

'What is there to say about human rights that hasn't been said already, or that won't be said in the course of this debate by parliamentarians of far greater, ah, experience' (cries of 'No!' from the younger members of the Dutch delegation, who were always happy to take part in any slapstick) 'wisdom' ('Never!') 'and insight' ('Impossible!') 'than myself? I don't intend to deliver a great oration about matters which – if we're honest with ourselves, as I believe we must be – do not so much divide us as, ah, unite us in a common cause, the cause of *Parliament*.' A sudden vigour flared in his voice, as momentary and unexpected as a top C from a diva past her prime; then the shoulders sagged again. 'I'm going to tell you a story – a simple enough story, you may think, but an instructive one.' A red light flashed on the rostrum, indicating that Sir Rufus had one minute left. He ignored it.

'This morning I talked to a young chap I'd never set eyes on before. Turkish, I think he was.' Stavros stirred uneasily: it wasn't possible, was it . . . ? 'We sometimes complain that the youth of today are a pretty lazy lot, a bit, ah, undisciplined, a bit, ah, lacking in *spunk*.' The Spanish interpreters looked blank and shrugged their shoulders: one of them reached for a dictionary. 'And sometimes we're right. When I think of my son-in-law having to stand up to Hitler or go back to bed, I know which he'd choose.' He paused. M. Berbizier tapped the desk to indicate time. He scowled: he didn't like his punch-lines being interrupted. With a sly look, he added: 'Handsome woman, my daughter' and waited for the laugh. When it didn't come, he looked baffled – the gag had worked well enough in Manila, in Nicaragua, in San Francisco . . . He stumbled on. 'Well, let me tell you something. This chap this morning had spunk all right – a good deal of spunk. Spunky chap – from Istanbul.'

The Spanish interpreters had located the word in their dictionary: now it was the turn of the Spanish delegates in the Chamber to look confused. They tapped their earphones and looked round at the interpreters; one of them made a rude gesture of inquiry at which the others giggled. M. Berbizier banged the desk again. Sir Rufus summoned his strength for a final effort.

'And do you know what he'd done? This chap from Istanbul? He'd *swum* fifty miles, with his arms and legs tied together, to raise money for charity. I call that pretty spunky stuff – what?'

He stopped. Delegates started to applaud. Every speech Sir Rufus ever made ended with 'what?': it was like the floor-manager's placard saying 'CLAP'. He waddled back to his place, shaking hands to right and left like an elderly penguin making free with its flippers, then dispatched Tight to the bar to fetch a pink gin. The Congressman took his place on the rostrum with a face like thunder. Stavros knew how he felt. He had five minutes to expound his most heartfelt political convictions – to an audience who had just been transported into the heyday of the Victorian music-hall.

5

But he did not flinch. If heroism can be expressed in mere words, then there was heroism in what the Congressman said. 'Today, gentlemen, we are debating the most important issue facing the human race.' In a sentence he had imposed his own gravity on the proceedings. The chuckling stopped. Newspapers were abandoned. Discarded earphones were picked up again. Delegates *listened*. Stavros watched mesmerised. He had already caught glimpses of the man's true stature – the toughness behind the affability, the determination behind the decency, the shrewd good sense behind the moments of paranoia. Now, on the rostrum, the whole man was revealed: masterful, eloquent, committed . . . he glanced at Christine and felt a sudden surge of confidence. With such a colossus to protect them, how could their lives be threatened?

'We who between us represent the majority of the people in the world owe those people one particular debt. We owe them our determination to protect their rights as human beings. To extend those rights. To fight for those rights. If necessary, to *die* for those rights.' A wave of applause rippled through the Chamber, quite different in feeling and intensity from the clapping that had greeted Sir Rufus. The Congressman raised his arm to quell it. 'And if we are to do that, if we are to pay that debt and win that struggle, we must begin with a far more painful process than the making of speeches, the denouncing of evil, the drafting of resolutions. We must consult our own consciences. All of us. We in America and you here – in Thailand.'

The hairs rose on Stavros's neck. He looked over at the Thai group – sitting in a prominent place at the front – and saw the shoulders stiffen, the hands shoot up to the earphones. There was complete silence. The Congressman's light, folksy baritone rang effortlessly through the hall.

'I believe they call this the city of angels. Well, we've got a city called the city of angels in America, and I'll tell you something – there's nothing angelic about either of them. I've seen one or two things here in Bangkok that have shocked me, gentlemen – and I use that word advisedly. I hope that parliamentarians can always talk frankly to each other, so I'd like to say something frank to our Thai friends right now.'

He paused. Stavros stole a glance at Christine: she was as tense as he was. A Thai official scuttled across in front of the rostrum and said something to another official, who left the

Chamber. The Congressman bent closer to the microphone, gently, painstakingly, as if it were an old man's ear-trumpet. 'This may sound discourteous, but I don't mean it in that spirit. I mean it as a constructive comment on what I believe to be the situation here.' He paused again, cleared his throat, looked directly at the Thai group – and every light in the place went out. 'What the hell . . .?' But the power to the microphone had also gone. His was no longer the voice to which everyone else listened: it was one sound among many, lost in the babble of outrage and bewilderment.

'*Chers collègues, chers collègues!*' M. Berbizier appealed for calm but, with the interpretation lost, only the Francophones heard him and they were incapable of being calm at the best of times. Not that it was possible to see who was being calm and who wasn't. The Chamber of Peace and Tranquillity had been designed by an architect with no affinity with natural light. His concept had been a symphony in neon: two one-foot-by-eight windows were the only means for daylight to enter. Near-total darkness enveloped the hall. A Swiss delegate produced a candle from his briefcase, round which other delegates gathered; a Turk used it to light a cigar and it flickered out. Not a single face could be identified. The spoken word – in forty-two languages – was sovereign.

Stavros stumbled out of his booth and went looking for Christine. A solid wall of people separated the two booths. Delegates were stampeding to the exits. Someone had said something light-hearted in Urdu which in Spanish meant: 'The bomb's about to go off. Mind your heads!' A German appealed for people to move in single file, which the Rumanians mistook for an announcement that oxygen masks would be made available. An Italian asked the way to the *uscita*: an Englishman shouted that there was no need to get personal. A Spaniard pinched a Danish woman's bottom, only to find that it belonged to Señor Sanchez, the burly six-foot-eight leader of the Argentine group . . .

'Christine!' Stavros shouted. 'Chris-tine!' He had an uneasy recollection that in Swahili the word meant 'Kill the pig!', but he had to risk it.

'Stavvy, I'm *here*!' she shouted back, from what sounded like a long way off.

'Where's here?' he shouted, then tripped over something, a frenzied dwarf of a man who was trying to elbow his way back into the Chamber.

'I have to find Sir Rufus Barnacle. Let me through, please. Sir Rufus has a serious heart condition. I have to find Sir Ru . . .'

'Tight,' said Stavros, relieved to hear a familiar voice. 'It's like a battlefield, isn't it?'

Tight recognised him through the gloom.

'Absolutely bloody. Can't you say anything to calm people down?'

'What did you have in mind?'

'Say there's an emergency generator and power will be restored soon. Can you manage that?'

'I'll try.' He tried. He tried in French. He tried in German. He tried in pidgin Serbo-Croat. There was no effect: the stampede only quickened. He gave up and looked for Christine. Tight brushed past him towards the Chamber. The lights – finally – came on again. Christine was standing on the opposite side of the corridor with her back to the wall, trying to avoid being swept away by the crowd. Sir Rufus was being sick into the window of the Spanish booth. Other delegates were frozen in absurd, ungainly, terrified postures . . .

All this he took in later. His eyes fell first on a man in a blue suit lying face down on the carpet, not moving a muscle: something looking like a bronze paper-knife was sticking out of his back. On the floor beside the body was a badge. '*J.-M. Arnoux, Belgian delegation.*' Stavros had never heard of him.

'*Il est mort,*' whispered a Tunisian delegate. '*Absolument mort.*'

Tight nearly fainted. 'Oh my God! Oh my God!' He was no insular, monoglot Englishman: he'd got a distinction in French 'O' level at Harrow.

6

After that, human rights didn't get a look-in. The Belgian delegation moved that the Assembly observe two minutes' silence in M. Arnoux' memory. The leader of the Japanese group moved the adjournment of the debate until the following morning. Sir Rufus Barnacle moved that the condolences of the WLP be conveyed to M. Arnoux' wife Mariette, whose *soirées* would be remembered with affection by many delegates. A Belgian delegate begged leave to point out that M. Arnoux' wife had been called Françoise and had been dead for many years. Sir Rufus withdrew his motion and apologised to the Chair. He hadn't meant to speak out of turn at such a solemn moment, but he was sure . . . A Kenyan delegate, on a point of order, asked if it was true that M. Arnoux had been murdered and if the villains had been apprehended. The President said that the police had been summoned but that, notwithstanding the knife protruding from M. Arnoux' back, it would be dangerous to leap to conclusions; he believed that this Assembly in particular would wish to see proper inquiries made, without the issue being prejudged. Another delegate pointed out that M. Arnoux was a former chairman of the prestigious External Relations Committee and should therefore be accorded particular honour by the Assembly. A further two minutes' silence was observed. Finally, a Cypriot delegate moved that a sub-committee be appointed to oversee the power supply to this and future conferences, so that another tragedy could be averted. The motion was carried by a hundred and ninety-seven votes to six, with the Austrian delegation abstaining. The Assembly adjourned at 11-42.

'*Monsieur le Président! Monsieur le Président!*' A delegate at the back of the hall jumped up and waved his arm. The President remonstrated with him: the Assembly had just adjourned under Rule 26, so no further points of order were possible. The interpreters knew Rule 26 backwards: they had switched off their microphones and formed an orderly stampede to the bar. Stavros lingered, curious. The delegate ran forward to the rostrum.

'*Mais je ne suis pas mort, je ne suis pas mort! C'est Arnoux qui parle!*'

'*Arnoux?*'

'*Arnoux?*'

'*Arnoux même!*'

The President quickly consulted an official and announced that he was using his discretion under Rule 11(4): M. Arnoux could have the floor for thirty seconds, although his intervention would not be minuted as the Assembly had adjourned. Arnoux shouted that he didn't care if his intervention was minuted or not: he just wanted everyone to know that he was alive and well and the body was not his.

'Whose is it then?' asked an English delegate, with a nose for detail. 'Can you make inquiries, Mr President?'

The President promised to do so and the Assembly adjourned for the second time at 11·51. A pack of reporters was waiting at the entrance to the conference centre: locals mainly, with a leavening of foreign correspondents. The death of a delegate had caught them unprepared: they had expected only pageantry, the same platitudes recycled in different languages; most of them had been drinking since breakfast. 'Can someone help me?' groaned a pot-bellied Australian: his shirt hung out of his trousers, his eyes rolled wildly among the delegates. 'Was Mr Arnoo thirty-six or sixty-three? I have to know these things.'

Another reporter made straight for the Congressman. 'Frank Baker, *Des Moines Post*,' he shouted, forcing his way through the crowd.

The Congressman beamed and reached over a Japanese delegate to shake hands.

'*Frank!* How are you doing? Biggest asshole in the mid-West,' he muttered to Stavros.

The two Americans talked rapidly in what appeared to be English.

'Bill, can I ask you about the big one?'

'Just shoot, Frank.'

'Are you still declaring this fall?'

'I'll take a rain-check on that question, Frank.'

'But you could be pitching in there at Iowa?'

'Sure, Frank.'

'And you haven't done a flip-flop on the budget?'

'Bill Ledgerwood don't do no flip-flops, Frank. I'll be jaw-boning through Super Tuesday.'

'What are you doing on a boondoggle in Bangkok? Shouldn't you be on the stump?'

'This ain't no boondoggle, Frank. I've been networking so hard I'm tuckered out.' The Congressman drew himself up to his full height and put on a solemn air. 'Don't quote me on this, Frank, but you're talking to the next President of the United States.'

For half a second, Stavros believed him.

SIX

I

Now the last taxi had gone and Stavros was left standing with Tight on the steps of the conference centre. They looked at each other with grim affection, like the only survivors of a nuclear holocaust. Everyone else had returned to the hotel or ventured downtown – shopping, lunching, sightseeing, risking their lives in massage-parlours. Christine had vanished with the rest: he'd watched her squeeze into a *tuk-tuk* with a Japanese interpreter, Mr Achapong the Congolese delegate, and a man looking like an estate agent. Perhaps he *was* an estate agent – it would be no odder than other things he'd seen in Bangkok. Where were they going? What were they doing together? Why was the Japanese interpreter holding hands with the estate agent when they appeared to be the same sex? What sex were they? Why did Mr Achapong put an avuncular arm round Christine's shoulder? Why, why, why? Maybe one day a team of historians would explain in words of one syllable what had gone wrong with his quiet, orderly world. But it wasn't going to be this day or the next. It lay far in the future, like those childhood fantasies he'd confided in his mother – wealth, fame, success, living with a woman who brought him croissants in bed on Sunday mornings . . .

Tight looked at the empty taxi-rank and announced: 'We'll have to walk.'

'Walk?'

'Aren't you coming downtown?'

'I hadn't thought about it.'

'There's nothing to do here.'

They fell into step together along the muddy, unpaved verge of an eight-lane highway: ahead the city's squat, congested skyscrapers; overhead the sun, harsh, ubiquitous, unrelenting. Tight said: 'It's rather warm.' Stavros took off his jacket and draped it over his arm. Tight hesitated, then did the same. The cars and lorries roared past without pity.

A golf course – implausibly – came into view on the right-hand side. Two Japanese men strode down the middle of the fairway: a pair of local women followed carrying their clubs. An English voice shouted 'Fore!' from behind a tree.

'Bunkered it,' said Tight with an air of authority. Stavros looked blank. Tight explained. 'He swung back too quickly.'

'I'm sorry?'

'I would have used a wedge from there. It's real tiger country.'

'Tiger country?'

'The rough. I played similar courses in Africa as a boy. You need a machete to get through it, particularly when it's rained. If you use a long iron, the head of the club gets tangled.'

'I suppose so,' said Stavros doubtfully. 'I don't play the game,' he added, finding limited possibilities in the conversation.

'I thought that's how you did your leg?'

'My leg?'

'"My left leg's sore, I had an accident playing golf" . . .' He quoted the words with gleeful precision and Stavros looked at him in alarm. 'I never did believe that story,' he added mysteriously.

Stavros blushed: he had underestimated the man. He had assumed things would pass over his head as they passed over a child's: he had forgotten the hard-nosed scepticism of childhood. They walked on in silence, past a canal, past a food-stall, past a minor temple festooned with flowers, past a one-armed beggar who took one look at them and gave them up as a bad job.

'Isn't it bloody?' Tight said with sudden vehemence, as they waited to cross at a traffic-light. Stavros looked up and down the street. When the brain works slowly, it works literally: he expected to see a child with a nose-bleed, a headless chicken spattering blood on the pavement . . .

'This whole business,' Tight explained. He waved his stumpy little arm in the direction of West Bangkok. 'I'll be happy to get home.' He sounded distraught, as if he were labouring under a great burden he was about to ask Stavros to share. Stavros remembered that he had religious tendencies.

'Yes,' he said hurriedly – though how he envied a man for whom home and happiness were synonymous. The light turned green and they crossed the street. Above the roar of the traffic Tight appeared to say: 'I'm sorry, I haven't been very nice' – and he had to grapple with a new riddle. No, Tight hadn't been very nice – but then he didn't seem the sort of person who was very nice to anyone. Niceness and Tightness were as alien as Boff and subtlety. And who anyway apologised for not being nice?

'Will you excuse me a minute?'

'Of course.'

'I promised my wife I'd buy her some silk.'

Tight darted into a small shop. There was a printed sign in the window, SARUDA FABRICS; then below, in handwritten red letters, BEST PRICS IN BANGKOK. Rolls of material were stacked around the room like enormous children's crayons: their strong, simple colours gave the place a cheerfulness with which Tight was immediately at variance. He did a perfunctory browse, then selected a bolt of violent yellow material. Stavros watched through the window. It was hard enough imagining a Mrs Tight – but a Mrs Tight dressed as a banana? And the comedy was only beginning. The young salesgirl was used to customers bargaining: she wasn't used to them treating buying and selling like the opening exchanges of World War III.

'Two hundred *baht*. Five hundred *baht* a metre no good price.'

'Four hundred fifty *baht*. Mister's missus look so beautiful in it.'

'Don't talk about my wife like that. I'm buying seven metres, so I expect a decent discount. Two hundred *baht* a metre.' He was starting to shout: the girl was in danger of buckling under the sheer weight of decibels.

'Mister not offer enough. Top quality silk – best in Bangkok.'

'Two hundred *baht* or I go somewhere else.'

'Four hundred twenty. Mister's missus –'

'Two hundred.'

'Four hundred. Last price. Mister pay with Visa, American Express?'

'Neither. I don't believe in that rubbish. You can have fifteen hundred *baht* for seven metres, but that's your lot.'

The girl did some sums on a pocket-calculator, then disappeared behind a row of shelves and returned with a man. An American couple came into the shop and closed the door behind them: Stavros had to watch the comedy without a sound-track. He saw Tight point from the material to the calculator and strike a determined, boy-on-the-burning-deck pose. His glasses were crooked, though, and there was something not quite right in his manner: his acting was more well-rehearsed than convincing. The Thai man wrote down a figure on a piece of paper which Tight greeted with a shooing gesture, like a man being pestered by photographers. The man conferred with the girl and wrote down a different figure. The American couple lost patience and left. The door swung open again and the sound-track returned.

'I'm offering you sixteen hundred and fifty *baht*. You should be bloody grateful. It's probably not real silk anyway.'

'Does mister know about silk?'

'I know a rip-off when I see one. And don't mister me.'

'Three hundred seventy *baht* a metre. Very last price.'

'Two hundred and fifty.'

'Three hundred sixty. Mister being greedy.'

'Oh –' Tight used an English expletive which Stavros hadn't heard before. He took a step into the doorway to catch the word – and escaped death by inches. Even as he moved, a car swerved on to the pavement behind him and swept past where he'd been standing. He ran back into the street, followed by Tight and the shopkeeper. The car was back on the road and heading towards Siam Square. The shopkeeper shouted an obscenity about women drivers. Stavros wiped his brow. Of course, the whole thing could have been an accident – the sinister explanation just seemed more plausible.

Tight wore a distracted, professorial air. 'I got the number if you're interested. DR 177. I did a bit of train-spotting as a lad.'

'Train-spotting?'

'Didn't boys do that sort of thing in Zagreb?'

The sun had reached its zenith and he was still walking: he
was quite alone now. Tight had disappeared into a department
store, muttering something about cheap tapes or cheap shirts
– he couldn't remember which. He trudged past five or six
market-stalls under simple canvas awnings and bought some
satay on a skewer at a street-corner; a small child smiled
approvingly as he threw the skewer in the gutter. He crossed
streets with care and made a point of facing the oncoming
traffic, but he took no other precautions. In thirty-five years
he'd never cared less whether he lived or died.

Three blocks ahead, Patpong beckoned dully, teasing what
was left of his brain and it wasn't much. Patpong mattered:
he was certain of that. Before he'd gone there, his life had been
simply chaotic, an absurdly protracted hard-luck story: from
the moment he left, death or the threat of death had followed
him like an angry insect. The two were connected – they *had*
to be connected.

Pussy's was closed and a type-written sign pasted to the
door: FOR RELIGIOUS REASONS NO MASSAGE BE-
FORE LUNCH TUESDAY. He winced. It reminded him
of Monica and her stolid, literal Christianity. 'For religious
reasons, no sex before 1997.' But he didn't want a massage.

'Where are the girls?' he asked the old man lolling in the
doorway. 'I must see the girls.'

The man threw him a look of amused pity: he must have
heard the same inquiry every Tuesday for thirty years. He
pointed at the sign. 'No girls.' It wasn't an apology: it was a
gloat of triumph.

'Why not?'

The man tapped his watch and repeated: 'No girls before
two.'

Stavros said: 'I can't wait till then,' and the man's smile
broadened. He had missed his vocation: he should have been
a Jesuit priest, tongue-lashing his parishioners for their sins of
the flesh.

'For Christ's sake, I don't want a massage. I just want to
talk to one of the girls. To *talk* – do you understand me?'

'I understand you.' The man gave a slow wink: he had

heard that one before too. 'Mister can "talk" at two. Not all days are holidays.' It sounded like a proverb of some sort.

'Two isn't good enough.'

'It will have to be good enough.'

'Well, it isn't. Here.' He thrust a thousand-*baht* note into the man's hand – an enormous bribe in any circumstances. Tight would have been horrified: to give so much, free, on the off chance . . .

The man folded the note in four and put it in his top pocket. 'Time changes everything.' He seemed to have a quotation for every contingency, like a Jehovah's Witness.

'I'm not after sex, you know. I just have some questions. If I want sex, I don't have to come to this dump.'

'A man can ask, a woman can say no.'

'Frankly, the way I'm feeling right now, I couldn't make love to a woman if you paid me. I feel like a beer more than anything – I've had a rough time and I'm tired.'

'A sleeping tiger wakes quickly. Come, mister.'

He led him down an unlit corridor, through a door into a courtyard and up a flight of wooden stairs. Another door opened into a small anteroom, where a middle-aged woman was sitting at a desk reading the horoscope page of a newspaper. She stood and bowed. The man said something in Thai of which Stavros could only make out the words 'rich American'. The woman gave him the once-over with her small, venal eyes. His suit was crumpled and dirty and he was wearing the cheapest of Japanese watches – he didn't look the part at all. The man handed her a hundred-*baht* note and winked at Stavros. 'Mister can talk now.' He padded off, his whole body creaking with amusement.

The woman conducted Stavros into another, larger room. About twenty girls – none of them were women yet – were gathered round a table having lunch. They were in different states of undress: some wore little make-shift G-strings, others were naked. Their working clothes – the brightly coloured dresses with numbers clipped to the front – hung on hooks beside the door. Almost all the girls had cigarettes in their mouths – and somehow the smoking shocked more than the nudity: ash dribbled freely over the food and a pall of smoke hung above the table as if a volley of cannons had been fired;

an orange lantern brought a fierce glow to the girls' faces and shoulders. It was like walking into a medieval inferno.

The older woman introduced him. Again the only words he caught were 'rich American'; and a sea of young smiles greeted him like a slap in the face. 'Greek with a wife and mortgage' would have injected a better sense of realism – but what the hell was the Thai for 'mortgage'?

'Where is Kim?' he asked instead, before rumours of his wealth could be further exaggerated. The girls looked mystified. 'Mister want q'im?' one of them asked, wrinkling her nose in disgust. He remembered that a q'im was a kind of farm-animal.

'No, no. Look.' He took out a piece of paper from his wallet and wrote down '403' in big figures. The girls clustered round and a ripple of anxiety passed between them; the older woman glanced at the number and took him aside.

'403 not here. Sorry, mister.'

'Where is she?'

'At home. Bleeding.'

'*Bleeding?*'

The woman made a coy gesture. 'Back tomorrow.'

He nodded, understanding. It was quite possible – but then why the fear? He glanced at the dresses hanging by the door: Kim's was still there, number and all. He touched it with a sudden intensity, as if her memory were tremendously precious to him, as if that simple blue dress were the last remnant of a better, saner world. The girls murmured in protest. A rich American was allowed his quirks, but fondling their dresses . . . The older woman said firmly: 'Mister must choose.'

'I'm sorry – I really was only interested in 403.'

'403 is bleeding. Mister must *choose*. 78, 207, 181 – very pretty girls, very clean.' 78 pouted her lips to order. 207 peeled off her G-string. 181 rubbed the front of his trousers as if she was pounding pastry-dough.

He recoiled: he'd remembered he had only five hundred *baht* in his wallet. 'I really must be going.' He sounded like a social misfit leaving a party after one tomato juice.

'Mister can't go, mister must choose.' The woman locked the door to emphasise the point. 'Mister pay double Tuesdays,' she added, in case he was missing her drift. 'Mister must perform now.' The words carried extraordinary menace, like a sentence of death.

'There's been a misunderstanding,' he protested, with a tight, scared smile. None of the girls smiled back: they closed on him like a pack of animals, their eyes trained on his wallet, their teeth bared in hatred. He capitulated with his usual alacrity. 'How much?'

'Ten thousand *baht*.' The woman's voice was as clear as a bell – there was no point in arguing.

'Do you take American Express?'

'Of course. This is a decent place.' She took his card and left the room. The smiles returned to the girls' faces as if they had never been absent: some of them flirted outrageously, vying for his custom. He looked mechanically from girl to girl: the pretty ones, the less pretty ones, the ones with too much make-up, the ones with glazed eyes who looked as if they were on drugs. Unless they meant to share the proceeds and take him together on the table – among the noodles and the chopsticks and the little paper cups filled with tea – he would have to *choose*. Decisions, decisions . . .

The older woman returned with his card and a chit for him to sign. Ten thousand *baht* had been translated into eighteen thousand *baht* by the addition of something called PLUS-PLUS CHARGE – an ingenious piece of accounting. He wondered what Monica would make of it back in Geneva: she opened his bills as a matter of course, on a variety of pretexts. ('Don't I have more time than you, Stavros?', 'Wasn't my father the second best-paid accountant in Dublin?', 'Isn't it right for a wife to know what her husband's spending money on that she might be spending herself?') He shuddered at the prospect. It was like a bad night's sleep: one nightmare following another with no waking between.

The woman smiled for the first time. 'Mister can choose now.'

'Thank you.'

'Mister can take his time.'

'Thank you very much.' For eighteen thousand *baht* he had bought a moment's peace: it wasn't cheap, but it was worth it. He felt as if he had regained control of a horse that had bolted a long time before: the reins were back in his hands and there was a sense of order, of life passing normally, without hurry. He looked among the smiles for one he could trust: a tall, rather Western-looking girl provided it. She was older than the others and had a chipped tooth which gave her face a quality of humour. Sex he could do without: a good laugh might restore him.

'Her,' he said, pointing gauchely. The older woman looked surprised.

'82? Mister sure?'

'Positive.'

'Mister feeling tired?'

'A little.'

She shrugged. 'Mister has paid.' He thought: if I hadn't had my American Express card, even 82 would have been too good for me. The woman took a blue towel from a pile in the corner and handed it to the girl. 'Be good,' she said in Thai: it seemed a strange choice of word.

The girl took his arm and led him to the door. The other girls stood up and clapped, flicking tea-leaves at the happy couple – a local custom, presumably.

'They're jealous,' the girl whispered, surprising him with her good English. The accent was a bit odd, but the inflections were right – perhaps she'd visited the States . . .

In the bedroom the truth came out. 'Glad you went for me,' she said, unstrapping her bra. 'Name's Tilda, by the way. I'm from 'uddersfield.' She held out a tiny clammy hand and explained that it was in Yorkshire.

3

For nearly four hours, nobody tried to kill him. Perhaps killing, like whoring, was off limits on Tuesday mornings; or perhaps the people who were so anxious to see him dead had lost track of him, snug in that little room with Tilda and then, later, having lunch on his own in the back room of a restaurant on the Surawong Road. Even the fear of death, of the inevitability of death, lifted; and like colour returning to pale cheeks, his faith revived that life was the better option. A local beer slipped easily down his throat, as cool and refreshing as a *gelato* in his favourite café in Geneva, and then another. He felt – nearly – happy.

Tilda hadn't helped him much with his inquiries. Ay, she said, there was a girl called Kim who worked at Pussy's. Ay, she had been caught up in summat strange. Ay, she had gone missing the day before – and, nay, it wasn't t'curse because she'd had t'curse Friday week. ''Tween thee and me,' she whispered, flooring the brilliant linguist, 'the *pigs* have been round' – whereupon his brain stalled and he puzzled for an eternity why the rotundity of pigs should be discussed in such confidential terms. They crossed wires again when he asked about a secret packet and she told him there were condoms in the drawer – and after that it seemed easier not to ask questions, not to probe, not to behave like a 'pig' himself. He explored instead how good a massage eighteen thousand *baht* could buy in Pussy's on a Tuesday morning. Very good, was the answer, very good indeed – he now knew why rich Germans were always smirking when they came out of such places.

He had another beer and paid his bill. The sun dipped down behind the skyscrapers and the temperature dropped. Business was picking up in the market on the other side of the street: stall-holders took down the awnings and lit little kerosene lamps in preparation for the evening; boys and girls sauntered past in American jeans, with school-books under their arms; there was the smell of vegetables sizzling in woks. It was like a replica of the Bangkok he'd despaired of seeing again. He crossed the road . . .

'Mister want watches?'

'No, thank you.'

'Mister want T-shirt?'

'I don't think –'

'Mister looking for map of Thailand? Mister feeling hungry? Mister want sexy white trousers? Mister –'

'*No.*' He accelerated his stride: he had forgotten the relentlessness of the Third World's demands on the First. The hustlers receded and he was able to drift more anonymously from stall to stall, inspecting the wares, smiling at the shopkeepers. He had two hundred *baht* left: it cried out to be spent flamboyantly, like the last hour of love before the dawn parting. He stopped at a jewellery stall and bought a pair of earrings

– for Monica. It was when he was miserable that he resented her so much: forgiveness came more easily at times of peace.

A new and stronger urge assailed him. It was six hours and as many beers since he'd visited a bathroom: his bladder was the size of a water-melon. He walked faster, with his hands stuffed deep in his pockets, and looked for a hotel – a public convenience was too much to hope for. A small side-street beckoned: it was free of people and there was a damp patch at the bottom of a wall where others had had the same idea. He glanced over his shoulder and steadied himself. There were times when a devotion to foreign travel could wear perilously thin . . .

'STOP!'

A uniformed policeman was standing at the end of the street with a baton in his hand. Stavros tried to obey the order, but the jet he was discharging was like a cruise missile: once launched, it couldn't be recalled. He turned to explain his difficulties in his best Thai and redirected the jet on to the policeman's shoes. It wasn't a good omen for his first encounter with the Bangkok police.

The policeman had a magnanimous quality. He could easily have done something nasty with his baton: instead he looked in the other direction until nature had taken its course and Stavros had zipped up his trousers. Then he took out a large notebook from the top pocket of his shirt.

'American?'

'Greek.'

'*Greek?*'

'Yes.' Stavros struggled with a familiar problem. How *did* you explain Greekness to the uninitiated? In Oslo he'd once impersonated Zorba dancing on the beach – and been immediately understood. But Bangkok was light years from the Aegean, from the rosy-fingered dawn and the wine-dark sea; the ghosts of Agamemnon and swift-footed Achilles didn't stalk among the *klongs* and the *wats*. He said: 'I speak English.'

The policeman took a piece of paper out of the back of his notebook and unfolded it: it appeared to be an idiot's guide to Thai criminal law in six different languages. He drew Stavros's attention to the penultimate entry. 'PUBLIC URINATING THROUGH ACT OF PARLIAMENT IS INHIBITING.

CONVINCED URINATERS ARE FIND 200 BAHT.'

Stavros nodded solemnly. There was probably some Thai colloquialism for 'It's a fair cop', but he'd forgotten it. He said: 'Guilty. But I'm afraid I don't have two hundred *baht*.' He opened his wallet to demonstrate. 'I do have an American Express card.'

Here the policeman's sense of humour failed. He snatched the wallet and burrowed through it, then made him turn out his pockets: Monica's earrings were the only thing to emerge.

Stavros said: 'Actually, those are worth two hundred *baht*. I didn't get a receipt, but perhaps if you came with me . . .'

The policeman pulled out his whistle.

'Mister does not laugh at policemen.'

Stavros agreed enthusiastically. He *never* laughed at policemen; the officer had been quite right to arrest him; if he'd had the money, he would have paid two *thousand baht*, nay, twice two thousand . . . It was all a bit academic by now: a police car was conveying him through the Chinese quarter at ninety miles an hour.

4

Bangkok central police station practised a familiar form of racial discrimination. Locals were herded together in the main hall like third-class passengers at an Indian railway station; visitors were ushered into a separate office. The only other detainees when Stavros arrived were a young couple in jeans and a grizzle-haired man looking the worse for drink. A smiling receptionist told him he would be seen shortly and his police escort retired. He sat down in the corner: a shaft of late afternoon sun fell across his face, bringing an odd feeling of contentment. The whole room was so *clean*, like a dentist's waiting-room – there was a bowl of flowers on the table and Western magazines. In some disbelief, he picked up *Country Life* and looked at three-hundred-thousand-pound houses in Gloucestershire.

'What yer in for, Jimmy?' The grizzle-haired man had come to his senses, disturbing his idyll. Stavros looked hopefully towards the man in jeans, but he was no more a Jimmy than he was. Per or Olaf probably – there was a Scandinavian seriousness in the cheekbones. No, the question was directed at him.

'A small misdemeanour,' he said, with a smile and a shrug. The Scotsman cackled.

'Jimmy, yer didna piss in the street too?'

He nodded unhappily; the Scandinavian couple exchanged looks of pure disgust. The Scotsman lurched across and put a huge, marauding arm on his shoulder.

'Jimmy, yer me friend for life. Why dinna we piss on the carpet too, to show these yella fellas whoo's whoo?' He made as if to suit the action to the word, then slumped back into his chair and closed his eyes.

Stavros turned to the other two. 'It's hot, isn't it?' It was the sort of remark one made without thinking in the tropics: he'd forgotten the air-conditioning was on. The woman shivered and said something sarcastic to her companion: Nordic languages weren't Stavros's forte, which was just as well.

'Are you in some sort of trouble?' he asked, with that very Greek reluctance to abandon an unpromising conversation.

'*Yo*,' said the man, then changed his mind: '*Ne*.'

'*Ne*,' said the woman, then immediately: '*Yo*.'

They were going to have to work out a better story for the police. Stavros tried his luck in German. He explained that he was a Greek living in Geneva and had been arrested because he didn't have two hundred *baht* to pay an on-the-spot fine: the woman nodded and said in much less good German that she and Sven had been caught copulating in a temple. Stavros laughed and said that must have been fun and the man said yes, but Thais took a hard line on drugs. Stavros opened his mouth and stopped. What was the point – unless there was a Norwegian-into-German-into-Greek dictionary hidden under the *Country Life*?

A police officer came into the room. 'Which is the naughty man, please?' He had a pleasant, hail-fellow-well-met look about him.

Stavros took his chance.

'Me.'

'Follow, please.'

He followed: down a corridor, up one flight in a lift, down

another corridor, into a small room with a desk and two chairs. The officer took a printed form out of the drawer and a badly chewed Biro from somewhere behind his ear.

'Your name, please.'

'Stavros de Battista.'

'Again.'

'Stavros de –'

'*You* write.' He handed him the form and the Biro.

Stavros printed his name and glanced down the list of questions. No. 27 was 'MARRIAGE STATE' – he was going to be there quite a time. He returned the form: the man looked at the name and repeated it slowly to himself, one syllable at a time. He stopped, puzzled by something – then he gestured to Stavros to stay where he was and went into the next room to make a telephone call. Stavros craned his head to listen. It sounded as if the man was saying 'I have caught a big fish' – but if people who pissed in the street were big fish, what did they call the murderers? Glumly he followed him up another floor, along another corridor and into another, larger office. A middle-aged man was sitting behind the desk: his front teeth protruded slightly, like dentures that hadn't been pushed in all the way.

'Sit down, Mr Battista. My name's Ukrit.' He had an American drawl: possibly he'd been seconded at some stage to a police department in the States. 'We've been looking for you.' It didn't sound as if his sense of humour extended to Greeks with frail bladders.

Stavros grovelled.

'Look, I'm terribly sorry about this. I'd had a few beers, so I was genuinely desperate, but there's no excuse for that sort of behaviour, no excuse at all – particularly when you're a guest in another country. I'm a Greek. From Greece,' he added. 'It used to be famous.' He felt ashamed, as if he were disowning a senile relative. 'I've got the money back in the hotel.'

'Money?'

'For the fine.'

'What are you talking about, Mr Battista? There's no question of a fine in this situation.' He looked annoyed and suspicious, as if his leg were being pulled.

Stavros hurried to placate him.

'You do know that I urinated?'

'*Urinated?* Somewhere serious? In a temple? In the presence of the King?'

'In a side-street.'

'Were there women under eighteen watching?'

'I don't think so.'

'And nobody complained?'

'Oh no. It was quite an out-of-the-way place. Not very sanitary, I know, but I was partly hidden by an advertising hoarding. You see . . .'

'Mr Battista, *please*.' Ukrit dismissed the charge with an imperious wave and leant urgently across the table. 'That is *not* what I wanted to talk to you about.'

'No?'

'I'm afraid I have some bad news.' He stopped and pulled a packet of cigarettes out of his pocket. His hand was shaking and signs of embarrassed decency showed on his face, as if to say: no policeman, no man, should have to do such things. He said: 'They've got your girl.'

'Got her?'

'Yes.' He made a crude gesture of death.

The light-bulb hanging from the ceiling was suddenly very bright; the air-conditioning was audible for the first time. Stavros's chest was as tight as a drum.

'When? This afternoon?'

'Can you come, please? A formal identification is necessary.' Ukrit sprang to his feet, his duty done, an unpleasant moment negotiated without fuss.

Stavros followed numbly: along a corridor, down three floors in a lift, through a maze of passages in the basement, into a small cold room with an unmarked door. Half-smiling faces greeted him all the way, as if they knew but couldn't quite express . . .

Four bodies were laid out under sheets on a single slab of stone: the room's coldness explained itself. Ukrit directed him to the final corpse and pulled back the top corner of the sheet. He faltered. Pity and joy rose in him at once, each as strong as the other.

He said: 'She's called Kim. She gave me a massage on Monday.'

Ukrit pressed him. 'Are you sure?'

'Positive. She worked at Pussy's. Number 403.' There was a sickly smell coming from her mouth and he had to put a hand on the slab to steady himself.

Ukrit had a brisk, unsentimental quality. He pressed him again. 'Is something wrong?'

'I was expecting someone else.'

'Another Pussy's girl?'

'A friend.' And he wished he'd used a different word – for wasn't Kim a friend too? He gazed at her marble-smooth face with a tenderness out of all proportion to the time they had known each other. 'How was – how did she die?'

'Her throat was slashed. By an amateur. Do you want . . .?' Ukrit offered to pull back the sheet like a wine-waiter presenting a label for inspection – it was all in a day's work for him.

Stavros shook his head. It had been a woman's body, now it was just a body – the declension was too sudden, too brutal. 'The bastards,' he said, with cold fury. 'They should be shot on sight.'

'They?'

'The man who did this.'

'You said "they".'

'I don't know what I said.'

'But you were with this woman on Monday?'

'Oh yes, I was "with" her.' He redirected his fury, like a man lashing out in the dark. 'How do you know, Ukrit? Were you watching us? Are there cameras in those rooms? What sort of sick joke's that?'

Ukrit pulled the sheet back over Kim's face. 'We must talk.' He shepherded Stavros back to the lift, up to the third floor and along a corridor: an elderly woman passed with a bucket and mop. They went into yet another office, the biggest and most imposing so far. A picture-window stretched across the room: Stavros could see the grey outline of the river through a gap in the skyscrapers and a red belt of sky where the sun had just set. Still angry, he lit a cigarette. 'So this is where the fingers get chopped off,' he snapped, careless of any danger to himself. He'd given up trying to understand: he just wanted to *feel*.

Ukrit said nothing and left the room: he returned with a buff folder and a smile that looked as if it had been stuck on by someone else. 'I have some questions. They won't take long.'

'Who says I'll answer?'

'Mr Battista, *please*. You are not being charged. The fingerprints on the girl's handbag were not your fingerprints.'

Stavros stared.

'How do you know?'

'A simple forensic test.'

'But I haven't given you my fingerprints.'

'You used a napkin at lunch today. The owner of that restaurant is the brother of the Deputy Chief of Police. The arm of the law is big,' he added, missing the idiom by a whisker.

'Are – you – telling – me –' Stavros began, shaking with outrage. Appalling thoughts assailed his very soul: he seemed to be hemmed in by an evil so far-reaching, so comprehensive, that there was nothing to do but crawl into a hole and die. A telephone rang in the corner: Ukrit picked it up.

'It's for you,' he announced. It was his turn to look surprised.

'For me?'

'Your first name is Stavros?'

'Certainly.' He picked up the receiver and a familiar voice started talking nineteen to the dozen about Mr Grandjean's drinks party. 'Monica, how did you know I was here?' For a moment admiration quite superseded annoyance. Others were going to fantastic lengths to make his life hell – she at least did it because she loved him.

'How do you think I knew? I *asked*.'

'Asked who?'

'The police, of course. Stavros, will you sober up and tell me what I'm supposed to do?'

'The problem being . . . ?'

Ukrit offered to leave, but he gestured at him to stay – without a witness, how could he convince himself the conversation was happening?

'The problem *being*, Stavros, that my detective hasn't been invited and it will look mighty queer if I turn up with some fellow nobody's clapped eyes on before.'

'Invited?'

'To Mr Grandjean's party. If I didn't have to say everything twice when you'd been drinking, I'd be five years younger. So do you mind if he goes as your brother?'

'Who? Goes where?'

'To the party. François.'

'François?' He shook his head. Ukrit's face was a study in bewilderment: he'd been ushered into a strange, twilit world for which his police work hadn't prepared him.

'The *detective*, Stavros. Mother of God, will I ever get you back on orange juice next week.'

'But Monica, I don't have a brother.'

'Does Mr Grandjean know that? We thought Xerxes would do.'

'Xerxes?'

'As a name for François. At the party. It's a Greek enough name, isn't it?'

'It's a bit *passé*. How Greek does he look?'

'Greeker than you do.'

'That's not saying much.'

'He's your *brother*, Stavros.'

'Of course he is.' He suppressed a smile. 'Should he bring a bottle of retsina? It would help his credibility. Some olives perhaps, a bowl of taramasalata . . .'

'Stavros, I've told you about sarcasm. I won't have it when you're five thousand miles away.'

'I'm sorry, Monica.' He looked at Ukrit in embarrassment: Thai men didn't apologise to their wives, it just didn't happen. He scribbled down 'DR 177' on a piece of paper and whispered: 'Could you trace this car, please?'

Ukrit retired with a shrug. Monica was incanting a sermon about sarcasm and drinking and how the two went hand in hand like the two whatsits in the Apocalypse. He interrupted.

'Monica, there's something I don't understand. Why are you going to this party at all? I thought Grandjean was about to attack you, so you were locking yourself up in the flat with the detective till I got back. Have I missed something?'

'Stavros, am I a fool?' The question was rhetorical: she swept on. 'If he thinks I'm frightened, he *will* attack me. If he has to attack me in front of forty people, he may have second thoughts. The dirty little so-and-so.'

'Forty? Is it a big party?'

'Am I psychic? How should I know?'

'You could be the only guest.'

'There's François.'

'You mean Xerxes?'

'Have it your way, Stavros – I'm not arguing on the telephone. Has the weather been good in Bangkok now? I wish *I* could enjoy some peace and quiet and a wee bit of sun – chance would be a fine thing.'

He slumped into a chair: Ukrit had returned with a serious look on his face, like an emissary from the real world. 'Monica, it rained yesterday,' he said and put down the receiver. After ten years he'd learnt to contradict her gently, like a father disillusioning a child. He turned to Ukrit. 'Well?'

'That car you asked about. It belongs to Mrs Kalugin.'

'Who's she when she's not trying to mow down innocent pedestrians?'

'You don't know Mrs Kalugin?

'Of course I don't. What is she – a stunt-driver?'

'She's the Russian ambassador's wife. Now, Mr Battista – suppose you tell me what's going on?' He clicked his fingers and, with ominous promptness, a man and a woman appeared. The woman seemed to be a stenographer: she sat down next to Ukrit and balanced a notebook on her knee. The man's function was obscure.

'Let's start at the beginning,' Ukrit said crisply. He seemed unaware of the scale of the undertaking: he should have telephoned Mrs Ukrit first and told her not to start cooking the rice.

Stavros shook his head.

'I'm not answering your questions. I don't have to.'

'You'll be released sooner if you do.'

'I don't want to be released. I want a lawyer.' A poisonous rhetoric suddenly flared in him. 'You do have lawyers in this crappy country, don't you? Or did all that go out of the window with human rights? How many lawyers are there in Bangkok? One for every hundred policemen?'

Ukrit sighed and waited for the stenographer to catch up. 'Yes, we have lawyers.' He sounded more sad than angry at the belligerence.

Stavros kicked back his chair and paced up and down.

'I'm fed up with being pushed around like this, Ukrit. A girl's dead and all you do is fire a lot of stupid questions at someone she saw two days ago. It won't do – I have some very important friends in Bangkok.'

Ukrit's eyebrows rose.

'Who are your friends, Mr Battista?'

'Do you know Mr Ledgerwood?'

'Of course.'

'Well, he's one of them. Friends don't come much bigger than that.' He felt faintly ridiculous, like a man boasting about the size of his penis.

Ukrit smiled.

'He's your friend, is he?'

'Certainly.'

'Are you sure?'

'As sure as I'm standing here. One of my best friends in the world.' The penis had reached eighteen inches: he had graduated from fiction to science-fiction.

Ukrit said something to the other man, who crossed to the table next to the window and switched on a tape-recorder. An unmistakable voice rose above the crackling.

'I want that Greek faggot dead, do you hear?'

'Is he dangerous?'

'He's a loose gun on deck. Can't trust the guy further than you can kick him.'

'Don't you think . . . ?'

The voices were drowned in static. Stavros listened hypnotised. The Congressman's drawl was so vivid he might have been standing in the room. The other voice was less distinct, barely rising above a whisper.

The static faded. '. . . total goddam comedian. I'm a dead man if he shoots his mouth off again. No wonder they lost the war.'

'I didn't think Greece . . .'

'Screw that. He's a dago, isn't he? Talks like a cockatoo and keeps his brains in his ass. I never should have trusted the faggot – biggest goddam mistake I ever made. That guy couldn't get a burger and fries from a carry-out without ballsing it up. I want him out of the way . . .'

The static drowned the name and the other man's reply. Stavros glanced at Ukrit.

'Are they on the telephone?'

'In Mr Ledgerwood's bathroom. Yesterday afternoon. We have ways and means . . .' Ways and means, ways and means: the phrase had an odd ring of parliament and fair play.

The crackling stopped. '. . . thousand dollars. And there'll be another ten grand if you get rid of the girl. Do you have her number?'

'403.'

'That's it. Throw her in the river if you get a chance – nobody misses a whore in a town like this.'

'I'll try. Listen . . . Bill.' The name was used tentatively, as if for the first time. 'I don't like all this k-killing.'

'No more do I. But dammit, there's a war going on out there. When guys on our side louse things up, we've got to kick their asses into touch. Do human rights matter or don't they?'

'They matter – Bill.' And the second 'Bill' was even more tentative: the man didn't sound as if he'd kicked an ass into touch in his life.

Ukrit crossed the room and pressed the off switch. 'The rest's inaudible, I'm afraid.' He seemed to be resisting a temptation to gloat.

'You win,' Stavros mumbled. His head was throbbing with the pain of it all. 'I'll answer your questions.'

Ukrit gave a small bow. 'In fact we only really have two. It's the first one that's important.' He glanced to see that the stenographer was ready. 'That man Ledgerwood was talking to – do you know who it was?'

'No, I'm sorry.'

'Are you sure?'

'Positive.'

Ukrit shrugged. 'A pity. The other thing that puzzled us . . .' a thin smile appeared '. . . what is a faggot exactly? He called you that twice. In your own words, please, Mr Battista.'

Stavros snarled: he was too tired for jokes. 'You have them with gravy.'

'Gravy?'

'I guess you'd say soy sauce here.'

6

But he did know the other voice. It came to him when the man talked about 'k-killing': after that he could almost see the lines of his face as he spoke. Tight's anxiety, Tight's fastidiousness, Tight's scared servility: they were as familiar in their way as the Congressman's 'goddams' and his breezy certainties.

He tracked him down at a reception given by the German delegation in the hotel ballroom: he had a gin and tonic in his hand and was struggling to keep up a conversation with a man twice his size. It was an effort simply to reach him through the press of delegates. There must have been over a thousand people in the room: waiters in national costume circulated with trays of drinks: a Finnish woman complained of the heat; there was a run on the *satays* and the curried meat balls . . . Tight greeted him with obvious alarm – as if violence and retribution were already written on his face.

'Stavros, this is Señor . . .' he swivelled expertly, avoiding eye-contact '. . . Dom*in*guez, the leader of the Mexican delegation.'

The Mexican smiled beneficently from an enormous height.

'*Buenos días, Stavros.*'

'*Buenos días, Señor.*'

'*¿Que le parece su estancia en Bankok?*'

'*Es una ciudad encatadora.*'

'*¿Es usted Aleman?*'

'*Griego.*'

'*¿Griego? Extraordinario.*'

'Will you excuse me?' Tight disappeared behind Señor Dominguez and darted through a small gap that had opened up between two Indian delegates.

Stavros followed, but the gap closed before he reached it:

one of the Indians leant forward to say something and the other wagged his finger in disagreement. 'But your argument is defective, Mr Pandit. Amendment 16 is *prima facie* unconstitutional.'

Stavros veered to Mr Pandit's left, side-stepped a drinks-waiter, wriggled between a woman with large breasts and the back of a man with a large bottom and caught up with Tight in conversation with a group of French secretaries.

'I have to talk to you, Peter.'

'What about?'

'A private matter.'

'Can't it wait? I'm enjoying myself.' Nothing could have been further from the truth. All sense of pleasure had shrivelled in him as soon as Stavros appeared. His eyes twitched; his shoulders were stiff with misery; he held his glass in both hands as if frightened of dropping it. One of the secretaries had to rescue him.

'*Qui est votre ami?*'

'*Il s'appelle Stavros. Stavros parle beaucoup de langues. Il fait là, uh, traduction contemporaire dans l'Assemblée. Stavros, laissez-moi introduire Bernadette, Marie-Claire, Françoise, Justine . . .*'

Stavros shook hands grimly. '*Ravi, Bernadette. Marie-Claire, enchanté de faire votre connaissance . . .*' His superior French brought no feeling of triumph. Nothing is nearer humanity than incompetence – and mightn't it actually be harder to kill a bad linguist than a good one? Yet he did mean to kill Tight. He meant to kill him summarily, without pity, as Tight had killed Kim. A death for a death . . . He had ransomed his neutrality to that one holy purpose.

But Tight proved a cunning adversary. He waited until Marie-Claire asked Stavros if he thought Thai women were more beautiful than French women, waited until Stavros said, well, that was a fascinating question, waited until four very presentable French women were hanging on his verdict – then excused himself again. This time he got a head start: by the time Stavros extricated himself, he was twenty yards and fifty delegates away. Stavros followed, but Tight's shortness gave him the advantage: his head kept disappearing in the sea of faces and he was able to burrow through openings Stavros had to use elbows to negotiate. Chance intervened with scrupulous fairness, once on each side. Tight was buttonholed by Sir Rufus and made to hold his drink while he tucked into a bowl of noodles. Stavros gained ten yards, fifteen yards . . . then a man in a white dinner-jacket barred his way.

'Stavros! How are you?'

'Fine, fine. I'm sorry, I –'

'Malta 1981? Hotel Bristol?'

'Malta – of *course*.' He put on a happy, those-were-the-days smile and cranked his brain into action. He remembered Malta, he remembered 1981, he remembered the Hotel Bristol . . . But the man? A fellow interpreter? A politician?

'You were right about Helga, Stavros.'

'Was I?'

'You saw the whole thing coming.'

'Did I? Look . . .' Total amnesia enveloped him: the man's kindly smile only aggravated the misery. 'I'd like to hear the whole story – some other time perhaps.'

Tight had slipped away from Sir Rufus and was making for the exit. He followed doggedly. Two Danish interpreters greeted him, but he didn't even risk a hand-shake; smiling waiters plied him with canapés; a woman swore in Spanish as he knocked her drink out of her hand. Tight still had the advantage: he was only feet from the door when a wizened little man in glasses intercepted him. Stavros made a final spurt and joined them.

'Stavros, this is my uncle.' Tight's face plumbed new depths of pain: he could have been admitting possession of a miscreant dog.

'Pleased to meet you, Mr Tight.'

'Gravel, actually. I'm Cecilia's brother. Do you know the family?'

'I'm afraid not.'

'The Gravels go back further than the Tights. Sir Walter G lost a leg at Naseby fighting on the wrong side: it took us four generations to recover from that. We're an odd lot – mavericks, I suppose you'd say, though there's no harm in that. Peter gets his puckishness from his mother's side – don't you, Peter my lad?'

Tight shifted position and looked longingly at the exit – but he'd misread the situation. His eccentric uncle was like his bad French: it humanised him, gave him an obstinate individuality it would be hard to brush aside. Stavros's resolve faltered. In five minutes he'd be seeing the puckishness himself. He took a deep gulp of gin.

'What are you doing in Bangkok, Mr Gravel? Are you a politician?'

'Shit, no. Wouldn't dirty my hands with that shower – if you can dirty your hands in a shower, that is. Well, I say that – you're not a member of the Bundestag, are you?'

'No, I'm an interpreter. A *Greek* interpreter.'

'I *knew* you weren't German. It just didn't make sense. I'd have read Greek at school if I'd had the brain for it: of course, I imagine the language has changed since Virgil. Fancy you and Peter being so thick – all his other friends are actors. Will you excuse me? That man with the stomach was in Egypt with me.'

Stavros watched him go. 'What does your uncle do?'

'He's a professional bloody gate-crasher,' Tight said with unexpected venom: he seemed to have shed some of his nervousness. 'Doesn't have a job, doesn't pay his way, just turns up when it suits him. God *knows* what he's doing in Thailand. And all that balls he was talking about the Gravels – they're the biggest charlatans in England.'

'Even your mother?'

'Particularly my mother.'

'You're not close to her?'

'God, no.' It was as if he'd been asked if he were a freemason.

'And *are* all your friends actors?'

'A lot of them. I do two productions a year with the local theatre group.' They were out of the lobby now, away from the crowd and the smoke and the chatter: the water glistened in the fountains and there was a wave of balmy air from the street. 'The Leatherhead Savoyards,' he added, with a note of pride.

'Savoyards?'

'You must know Gilbert and Sullivan?'

Stavros groped. Intellectually he wasn't having a good evening at all. 'Weren't they contemporaries of Shakespeare?'

'That's Beaumont and Fletcher. Have you never heard *The Mikado*?' He started to sing, in a flat staccato voice: 'To sit in solemn silence in a deep dark dock, in a pestilential prison with a life-long lock, awaiting the sensation of a short sharp shock . . .'

Stavros interrupted desperately. 'I have to talk to you.' This killing was such a fragile enterprise: it was like trying to make love at the wrong time, in the wrong place, in the wrong mood. He marched Tight to the lift while the Gilbert and Sullivan was still in him, before the terror had returned . . .

'Where are you taking me?'

'Somewhere private.'

'My room's on the ninth floor. I don't want the basement.'

'You'll come where I tell you.' His voice should have had an iron quality, but he felt no stronger than Tight. 'You killed Kim,' he said as they got out of the lift. 'You killed Kim.' An executioner wasn't a machine: he had to keep his victim's crime before him at all times.

'Kim?'

'The girl at Pussy's.'

'Yes.'

'And you tried to kill me. During that black-out at the conference.'

'Yes. I'm sorry.'

'It's too late to be sorry.'

But suppose it wasn't too late? The candour of the answers unnerved him even further. He had expected denials, evasions, protestations of innocence. Tight accepted responsibility so *easily*, like a party-guest reaching for a canapé or a gin and tonic. What did it mean, this assured, open contrition? They moved in silence past a row of deserted shops – a hairdresser's, a chemist's, a tailor's – and found themselves by the side of the hotel swimming-pool. The water was a dark sheet, broken only by the moon's reflection; at the far end a couple kissed chastely under a palm-tree. Tight looked at the water and shivered. 'I have a child, you know.' The charge has been admitted, but there were still the pleas in mitigation.

Stavros winced.

'And I have an Irish wife who drives me up the wall. I have a mother who worries herself sick whenever I get in an aeroplane. We're all human and cared for, if you dig deep enough. But they don't matter – those other things. You killed

Kim.' It was like a primitive incantation. Would it stir him to action if he said it often enough? 'You killed Kim. You killed a woman you'd never met in your life because a crazy American paid you to. Try telling your child that. Or Kim's child. How do you know she didn't have one?'

Tight nodded sadly. Stavros didn't have to frighten him into guilt: it was there already, like a shabby, too-familiar piece of furniture in the corner of a room. 'I suppose . . .' He stared down into the water, like a poet looking for inspiration. 'I suppose I thought I was part of a larger struggle. Human rights and all that. It all seemed so important – when *he* talked. Poor defenceless people being tortured in lonely jail-cells.' And perhaps he was a bit of a poet: new facets were opening the whole time, like spring-buds.

'You're a fucking mercenary,' Stavros shouted. Perhaps if his language got violent, the rest would follow . . . 'You didn't kill for a cause. You killed for money. Ten thousand dollars of it.' The couple by the palm-tree looked up from their kiss. 'What are you going to spend it on, Tight?'

'There's no question of money.'

'Ledgerwood's paying you, isn't he?'

'I'm giving it to charity. I'm not keeping it. It wouldn't be – right.' And if he meant it, he had saved his life – for what terrible sea-change had brought him to this point, on the high plateau of decency, so far from the meanness and the haggling over twenty *baht*? He explained: 'It was hideous – that poor girl. I'll have nightmares all my life. The other man wasn't so bad: it was dark, it happened quickly, there was no mess or struggle. With the girl I only had a razor. She was young and she put up quite a struggle. Look, I'll show you.' He struck a macabre pose by the side of the pool.

Stavros shuddered.

'You fucking idiot. I don't want an action replay.'

'But I have to show you – how it was.'

'What's the point? She's dead, isn't she?'

The moon disappeared behind a cloud; the couple by the palm-tree resumed their kiss. Tight held his position, his right arm raised to slash an imaginary woman's throat with an imaginary razor. It was like a grotesque tableau from a production by the Leatherhead Savoyards.

'If only you'd been there, Stavros, you wouldn't be so brutal about it.'

'Me brutal?'

'You judge and condemn, but you haven't suffered like me. If you'd watched the whole thing, you'd feel sorry for both of us – me and the girl. Look.' He brought down his arm with a sudden slashing movement, then changed roles and imitated Kim's struggles. It was all done with such gusto that he lost his footing and fell backwards into the pool.

'You fucking comedian,' Stavros shouted. He wondered if his nerves would be strong enough to kill him as he got out of the water. When would it come, that pure, clean moment when anger would overwhelm pity? He waited tensely, rattled by the absurd pool-side pantomime. Tight didn't resurface: he went to investigate. A single foot was visible above the water: it had got caught and twisted behind the aluminium steps leading down into the water; the rest of the body must have been dragged inexorably below the surface. It was an apt memorial to the man – for who but Tight could have drowned in three feet of water?

The couple by the palm-tree interrupted their kiss.

Christine said: 'It's Stavros.'

Helmut the Lufthansa steward said: 'There has been an accident, I am thinking.'

SEVEN

I

'Dear colleagues, fellow parliamentarians, we can now resume the debate on human rights which was interrupted in such tragic circumstances yesterday. I propose that we defer the debate on refugees and migration until this afternoon's sitting and that the business *originally* scheduled for this afternoon – the debate on the Report of the General Sub-Committee on Parliament, Minorities and the Media – should be amalgamated with *tomorrow's* business, that is to say, the emergency debate on East–West relations in the light of the situation in the Gulf, which will take place under Rule 17(2) of the Rules of Procedure on a substantive motion in the name of the *Italian* delegation. Are those proposals agreeable to delegates? Have delegates understood those proposals? I shall repeat those proposals. The debate on refugees and *migration* . . .'

A Spanish vice-president was in the Chair, so Sophia was interpreting. Her precise, slightly breathless, diction, so grating in other circumstances, fell sweetly and soothingly on Stavros's ear. After all the excitement, that little prefab booth was like home – what home should have been. He looked at the earphones and the duty rotas and the half-written postcards and the carafes of water and the little scraps of paper with odd doodlings on, and he felt – not alive, but *safe*. In the Chamber the head of the French delegation was kissing the head of the Nigerian delegation on both cheeks: they swayed to and fro like trees bending in the wind . . .

'. . . agreeable to delegates? Does anyone wish to move an amendment under Rule 12? There is no opposition? Then the proposals are *agreed*.' There was a little flutter of applause.

He glanced across at Christine's booth and thought about forgiveness. The subject hadn't used to engage his interest: it had been way down the list of things to worry about, with nuclear fall-out shelters and flowers for Monica's birthday.

Yet if he could forgive Tight – and he nearly had – shouldn't he be able to forgive Christine? Just an innocent flirtation, she'd said; she'd been lonely, frightened, worried about him; it was reassuring to be held by a man, *any* man; Helmut was flying out the following morning; and no, of *course* they hadn't slept together. He remembered the 'of course' and, looking at her smooth, generous face – made absurdly girlish by the earphones, which resembled a child's plastic Walkman – wondered how far he could trust it. Then he remembered Tilda rubbing the back of his thighs, Kim kneading the muscles of his back with her tiny fingers – trust was a rare commodity in the City of Angels. If only they could talk properly . . . No sooner had they made it up over Helmut than she had shot off again, muttering dark, inexplicable nothings about the dangers of being seen together. It made no sense at all.

'Before we resume the debate, we have another melancholy duty to perform, dear colleagues. I must ask you all to stand in silence for one minute to commemorate the distinguished parliamentarian who lost his life in such tragic circumstances yesterday. One minute please, gentlemen.' The delegates rose to their feet.

Stavros hissed at Sophia: 'If it wasn't Arnoux, who was it?'

'Didn't you hear? It was Boff.'

'*WHAT?*'

'He and Arnoux took an early-morning swim and put on the wrong jackets afterwards. Their badges got mixed up.'

'But, but – this is insane. Boff wasn't a distinguished parliamentarian, he was a fucking bureaucrat.'

'We're all distinguished parliamentarians when we're dead – oh, shit.' The President was saying something. Sophia snatched the earphones and bent over the microphone.

'There seems, there seems to be an unfortunate disturbance in the interpreters' booth. In deference to Herr Boff, I propose that we start our minute's silence again. Is that agreed? It is agreed. Let us stand for one minute, gentlemen – starting *now*.'

Stavros banged his head on the ceiling and had to put his hand over his mouth; Sophia scribbled something down on a piece of paper. The minute seemed to go on for ever. Happy images of the dead man should have been flooding the vacuum – Boff's lighter moments, Boff's kindness, Boff dandling children on his knee, Boff trampling the Bavarian mountains with his *rührstock* humming the 'Ode to Joy' . . . But nothing came, nothing at all. He squinted at Sophia's note.

'BEFORE YOU LEAVE BANGKOK, I WANT A LIST OF ALL THE CONFERENCES YOU ARE DOING BEFORE 1993, SO I CAN AVOID THEM. I MEAN IT, STAVROS. ALL OF THEM.'

She had underlined the second 'all' three times and each line was a fresh wound: his own track-record belied it, but nothing hurts a Greek like losing friends. He forked out of his pocket the soggy bankroll he had retrieved from Tight's body and wrote: 'HERE. A FINE AND A PENANCE. LET'S STILL BE FRIENDS. I'LL DO GERMAN-INTO-ITALIAN NEXT TIME. MY STEPFATHER WAS ITALIAN.'

The President banged his gavel and there were shufflings and scrapings as delegates resumed their seats. Sir Rufus Barnacle waddled up to the rostrum and handed the President a note. Sophia stared at the money.

'Stavros, there are thousands of dollars here.'

'You deserve it, old pudding. I've let you down. I've been a complete joker.'

'Where did you get it?'

'Tell you later. There's quite a – history.' He stopped: the President was speaking. Sophia interpreted.

'Sir Rufus Barnacle of the United Kingdom delegation has just told me some distressing news. It seems, dear colleagues, that another distinguished parliamentarian has met his death in tragic circumstances. His body was found floating in the hotel swimming-pool this morning. He was secretary to the British delegation and his name was Kite.'

'Tight,' hissed Sir Rufus, in a loud stage-whisper.

'I'm sorry – White, Peter White. I regret that I must again ask delegates to rise for a period of respectful silence. Let us all spend thirty seconds remembering Peter Knight's contribution to parliamentary democracy. Thirty seconds please, gentlemen.'

Delegates rose to their feet again: the grumbles of the older ones were plainly audible. Sophia switched off the microphone.

'What *was* his name? The President didn't have a clue.'

'Tight. Knight has more dignity. You were right to stick with it.'

'Why did he only get thirty seconds? Arnoux got two minutes.'

'Arnoux was a delegate. Tight was only an official.'

'Even Boff got a minute.'

'The Germans gave a reception last night and the British didn't. Come on, Sophia, you know how this place works.'

2

Congressman Bill Ledgerwood stood at the side of the rostrum and waited to resume his speech on human rights. His arms hung easily by his sides; his shoulders were solid as a rock; a massive confidence surrounded him. He looked like a heavy-weight boxer about to remove his dressing-gown for a fight which could have only one outcome. Stavros's hatred suddenly faltered. Suppose he was what he said he was – a standard-bearer for human rights? And suppose lesser mortals had to be treated as pawns in that struggle – or the struggle would be lost? It didn't sound as convincing as the other explanation – that he was a dangerous maniac who should be put down like a dog. But then the sense of certainty had gone altogether from Stavros's neat, tidy universe. He could no longer plan or anticipate: he could only surrender to the emotion of the moment, whatever it was. He had been a Greek intellectual, now he was just a Greek – it wasn't an easy transition.

'. . . debate on human rights can now be resumed. There are ninety-two speakers left on the list and, since the debate on refugees and migration must start by two p.m. and some allowance must be made for lunch . . .' Sophia was interpreting in her usual flat style, so the import of the President's announcement was slow to register. '. . . limit of two minutes per speaker. Is that proposal agreed? It is agreed. The next speaker is Mr Ledgerwood of the United States, who had the floor when our proceedings were interrupted in such tragic circumstances last night. Mr Ledgerwood, please.'

The Congressman stepped forward to the rostrum, his shoulders slumped in disappointment. Two minutes to address his favourite theme, two minutes to stir his audience's emotions, two minutes to dress down the Thai delegation . . . It was the Gettysburg Address meets the Keystone Cops.

The President tapped the desk with his gavel.

'Mr Ledgerwood, I had forgotten that you had already used up some of your allotted time. You spoke for three minutes and thirty seconds last night when the time-limit for speeches was five minutes; therefore under Rule 47(4) (Procedure for interrupted speeches) your present time-limit must be reduced proportionately.' An official with a stop-watch was consulted. 'According to our calculations you have thirty-six seconds left, Mr Ledgerwood. Thirty-six seconds, please – starting *now*.' He banged the desk again.

The Congressman erupted. 'Of all the goddam horse's ass bullshit.' There was a shocked silence. The French interpreters went into a huddle round their dictionary. 'Mr President, will you please exercise a little common sense? You're making a monkey of this Assembly. Our proceedings have been interfered with enough already – I appeal to you to rescind your ruling.'

'I'm sorry, Mr Ledgerwood, Rule 47(4) is quite explicit. It applies equally to all Members of the Assembly. The only way in which the rule could be suspended . . .' Stavros started to laugh: he looked at Christine and, with a strange excitement, found she was doing the same '. . . would be for a motion under Rule 8(1) to be carried by a two-thirds majority. Do you wish to move such a motion?'

'Yes, I do, Mr President. Not in my own interests, but to protect the good name of this Assembly in the outside world. I beg to move.'

'Very well.' The President's voice dropped for a moment and Sophia had to press her headphones to her ear. 'I have a motion under Rule 8(1) to suspend Rule 47(4) and allow Mr Ledgerwood to speak for a full two minutes. Rule 8(1) requires me to permit one brief speech *against* the motion and then put the matter to the vote. Does anyone . . .' There was a shout of 'Get on with it, you oaf!'; the Dutch delegation banged their desks. 'I'm sorry, was that a point of order? It was not a point of order? Then I ask again: does anyone wish to speak *against* Mr Ledgerwood's motion? Yes, Mr Kalugin.'

A Russian delegate got up: Kristyan took over the interpreting from Sophia. 'Mr President, Mr Ledgerwood's motion is an outrage. It is a typical example of American arrogance and American greed. Why is it always the United States which has to have the biggest share of the cake? My advice to Mr Ledgerwood is this . . .'

Stavros leant towards Sophia and whispered: 'Did the President say Kalugin?'

'Do you know him?'

'I think a relative of his tried to kill me yesterday.' He looked from Kalugin to Ledgerwood and a scenario of dizzying complexity began to form in his head. Why wasn't his mother with him? She could tell whether to trust people just by looking at them – but she hadn't passed on the gift.

'. . . bourgeois petty-mindedness and insolence. The Russian delegation will oppose this motion.'

'Thank you, Mr Kalugin. I will now put Mr Ledgerwood's motion to the vote. Unless a roll-call vote is requested by three or more delegates, we shall vote by show of hands. The motion we are voting on is: That Rule 47(4) be *suspended* . . .'

A Turkish delegate stood up. 'Mr President, I request a roll-call vote.'

'Seconded,' shouted a Zambian.

'Seconded,' shouted someone else.

The President leant wearily forward. He wore a look Stavros had seen many times before: the look of a man who wished he'd never gone into politics in the first place. 'A roll-call vote has been requested. Members know the procedures. Voting will begin in three minutes. Three minutes, gentlemen.' He switched off his microphone and the delegations conferred about how they would vote; the Congressman stood marooned on the speaker's podium like a great sea-animal stranded by the tide. Stavros winked at Sophia. Roll-call votes were an interpreter's dream: they took up a lot of time and involved no speeches. He went out into the corridor to refill the carafe of water and found Christine doing the same.

'Stavvy. What are you doing?'

They looked nervously over their shoulders: the moment of privacy seemed unendurably fragile, like a kiss stolen in the corner of a room. The sense of dislocation, of their lives being dominated by events beyond their control, was overwhelming.

Impatient, he said: 'When can I talk to you?' She bowed her head and brushed her hand against his – so tenderly. He couldn't think what she saw in him sometimes – perhaps she just enjoyed the simple things in life.

'Soon, Stavvy. We shouldn't be seen together. I told you.'

'Why not? Who says?'

'I can't explain. Trust me, Stavvy.'

'I trusted you before.'

'I know. I'm sorry.' An old man passed sweeping the floor and there was a brief, strained silence. 'Helmut's gone back to Germany,' she added, with a wan smile. Bells rang to signal the start of the voting. She pulled a newspaper cutting out of her jacket-pocket and pressed it into his hand. 'This explains. We'll be all right, Stavvy – don't worry.' And before he could say anything, she had gone. Did she *really* expect him not to worry? The cliché ambushed him with an effect of pathos. It seemed such a very forlorn thing to say – the sort of forlornness you saw in mothers who loved without counting the cost . . .

'. . . voting will now take place in accordance with the practice of the Assembly. Mr Secretary-General, please.' The President nodded to the official sitting next to him, who dipped his hand into a box and pulled out a slip of paper. In the WLP roll-call votes were taken alphabetically, starting at a country chosen by lot – a device which exonerated Afghanistan and Algeria of the leadership of world opinion. 'Sweden!' the President announced flamboyantly, like a bingo-teller. There was scattered applause. The head of the Swedish delegation rose to his feet and those now relegated to the end of the queue – the Spanish and Sudanese – disappeared to the bar.

'There have voted for the Swedish delegation eleven Ayes, three Noes and two abstentions.'

'Thank you, Mr Wickbom. Switzerland?'

'Fourteen abstentions.'

'Thank you, M. Piquet. Syria?'

'Ten Noes.' The Noes overtook the Ayes on the electronic scoreboard and a few Danish delegates cheered. The President banged his gavel for order.

'Thank you, Mr Malik. And now – Thailand. Can I have your votes please, Thailand?'

The Thai delegates were still arguing among themselves: one

of them stood up and said something which was immediately contradicted by someone else.

The President raised his hands to his earphones.

'Was that six Ayes and eight Noes or eight Ayes and six Noes? It was ten Noes and four abstentions? There were only three abstentions? Does Mr Suthee wish to abstain? Mr Suthee wishes to be deemed absent? Thank you, Mr Suthee. That is ten Noes and three abstentions – three abstentions. Thank you, Thailand. Can I now have the votes of the delegation from *Togo*. Togo? Are you there, Togo?'

A black man hurried down the aisle zipping up his trousers; he shouted something in French which had to be interpreted into Spanish for the President and then back into English by Sophia.

'Togo one abstention, Togo one abstention.' The electronic scoreboard didn't record the vote; a Japanese delegate rose on a point of order; the Italian socialists started humming a chorus from *Il Trovatore*; Sir Rufus dipped into his briefcase for some angostura bitters . . . Stavros took his eyes off proceedings and studied the newspaper cutting Christine had given him. Even the best-rehearsed farce could pall after a while.

3

A printing mistake robbed the headline of its impact. US PRESIDENT-ERECT KNOCKS THAIS RIGHTS RECORD. It was on the front page of the *Bangkok Post*, between a story about an international drug-ring (POLICE SWOOP, QUIZ TWO, WIDEN PROBE – the house-style was American with a vengeance) and an advertisement for evaporated milk by the Thai Dairy Industry Co. Ltd. Above the article was an agency photo of Luciano Pavarotti and underneath: 'Controversial Sen. W. Ledgerwood speaking yesterday.' After that the journalism improved.

A power cut interrupted one of the more intriguing contributions at yesterday's seance of the 37th Conference of the World League of Parliaments in the Europa conference center.

US Senator Wm Ledgerwood was about to attack the host country's record on human rights when a problem in a fuss-box plunged the Assembly into darkness. A German official later died in circumstances sub judice and the debate adjourned till this morning.

White Mouse-hopeful Ledgerwood said afterwards: 'I haven't declared yet, but I guess there's a 50–50 chance I'll be running. It depends on getting the backing and improving my voter visibility. We have a great country and I want to unite it around the great tissues.'

In the margin, Christine had scribbled in tiny letters: 'This man's got to be stopped – he's absolutely bananas!' Stavros grinned. He caught her eye in the next booth and imitated a gorilla beating its chest – she shook her head. He imitated the same gorilla peeling and eating a banana – she looked at him as if he were completely unhinged. He scribbled a note (I AGREE – A REAL JUNGLE CASE) and slipped it under the door of her booth – she glanced at it and scrumpled it up in annoyance. Again that inexplicable feeling of rejection . . . He re-read what she had written in the margin. Perhaps 'bananas' wasn't 'bananas', but 'brains'? In that case what was the 'absolutely'? And why had she told him it would explain things when it explained nothing at all – except why nice boys didn't become politicians or journalists, which wasn't such a mystery anyway?

'. . . Belgium, please? Who will announce the votes of the Belgian delegation? Thank you, M. Gutman. Belgium, ten Ayes, one abstention. Bolivia?'

'Six Ayes, two Noes.'

'Thank you, Señor, Señor – thank you, Señor. Brazil? Can I have the Brazilian votes now, please? Could you repeat those figures? Again, please.' There was a hiatus while the bastardised Portuguese used by the leader of the Brazilian delegation was unscrambled by three different interpreters. 'Was that three Noes or four Noes? Do you *hear* me, Brazil?' The President was nearing the end of his fuse: it was on course to blow somewhere between France and Greece. 'Brazil, could you indicate three or four?' The Brazilian leader held up an outstretched hand. 'Is that three fingers or four? It is four fingers? It is four fingers. Brazil, ten Ayes, four Noes, two abstentions. Bulgaria now. Yes, Mr Popivanov?'

A stolid man with a face of corrugated iron had risen to his feet.

'The votes cast by the delegation of the National Assembly of the People's Republic of Bulgaria are as follows. For the motion: no votes. Against the motion: thirteen votes. Abstentions: one. Mr President, the delegate who abstained, Mr Belchev, wishes to make an explanation of his vote.'

The President banged his desk.

'Mr Popivanov, that request is out of order. Under Rule 82, explanations of vote take place after the voting has been completed. *After* the voting. We now turn to Burma. Is the Burmese delegate in the Chamber? He is not in the Chamber? Yes, Mr Popivanov?' The Bulgarian was still on his feet, with one hand raised above his head. 'Mr Popivanov, on a point of order. Briefly please, Mr Popivanov.'

'Mr President, my colleague cannot defer the explanation of his vote until the time proposed.'

'Why not?'

'He has an important lunch engagement.'

'Order. *Order!* That is not a sufficient reason for waiving the Rules of the Assembly. I am taking the vote of the Burmese delegate. Where is Burma? Yes, Mr Wang?'

A Taiwanese delegate explained that Mr Min, the Burmese delegate, had eaten something disagreeable in the grill room of the hotel and was indisposed; he had asked Mr Wang to exercise his voting rights in his absence. The President ruled that the arrangement was inadmissible: Rule 15(3) stated that proxy votes could only be exercised by members of the same national delegation as the absent Member. Mr Wang said that, with the greatest respect, Mr Min was the *only* Burmese delegate to the Assembly – wasn't the effect of the ruling the dismemberment of Mr Min? An Australian shouted: 'Disenfranchisement, you oaf!' Everyone looked hopefully at the interpreters. About a dozen delegates rose on points of order . . .

On the speaker's podium, the Congressman maintained a dignified aloofness. It was more than an hour since he'd insisted on his extra speaking time; but if he felt any embarrassment, he didn't show it. He was fighting for a principle, for the right to be heard, for the right to speak his mind, for the right to tell the world about Thailand and human rights and God knows what else ... If pig-headedness could be admirable, Greeks were quicker to admire it than most. Stavros watched that great brooding figure – noting how each delegation voted, seeing who was on his side and who wasn't – and wondered if it would be as hard to kill him as Tight. That he had to be killed wasn't in question. A girl was dead and Stavros had to avenge her because the girl had been good to him – the chain was inexorable, each link forged in ancient piety. The most lily-livered of his compatriots would have agreed with him where his duty lay. If only he could stop looking *up* to the man ...

The voting ground to its end. The Ayes had a clear lead, but there was some doubt whether they had the necessary two-thirds majority. The President consulted his officials; one or two delegates took out pocket-calculators and did their own sums. Apart from a steady chatter from the Czech delegation, who were engaged in a game of poker, the result was listened to in silence.

'Ayes three hundred and forty-one, Noes ninety-seven, Abstentions sixty-two. The votes cast for the Ayes exceed two-thirds of the total cast and I therefore declare Mr Ledgerwood's motion *carried*. You may address the Assembly for two minutes, Mr Ledgerwood – two minutes.' There was desultory applause and quite a lot of booing. The booers, mysteriously, seemed to outnumber the applauders by about two to one – either delegates had voted the wrong way by mistake or there were some bad losers around. The Congressman cleared his throat and bent over the microphone. The President tapped his desk.

'I'm sorry, Mr Ledgerwood, before you resume your speech, I have to give the floor to delegates wishing to give an explanation of their vote under Rule 82. Yes, Mr Marquez?'

A Mexican delegate explained that he had the highest regard for Mr Ledgerwood's qualities, but had voted against his motion in protest at American policies in Central America. A Swedish delegate said that he regarded Mr Ledgerwood as a dangerous ideologue and had supported the motion only to register his concern at the situation in the Gulf. The head of the Iraqi delegation announced that his colleague had voted the opposite way to the Iranians as a matter of principle: in other circumstances they would have abstained. A French-Canadian delegate expressed the view that the exercise of the right to vote was like the act of love – a distillation of the intensest personal feelings, *un cri de foie*. He had therefore . . . Another half-hour passed and the Congressman had to take a handkerchief to his brow. When he finally got to the rostrum, his voice was tired and strained, as if he'd already been speaking for an hour.

'I guess it's tough to speak your mind on something important in two minutes. But that's politics – you win some, you lose some. I'm going to say something to our Thai friends which may hurt them . . .' He cleared his throat and paused – long enough for Stavros, in a rare moment of incisiveness, to dart round into the Thai booth and hijack the microphone. Instead of interpreting what the Congressman was saying, he produced pure gibberish in Thai: 'My mother goes to the market every morning. Sometimes she takes her daughter, my sister. She looks for fruit first. A pineapple costs five *baht*. What beautiful weather. The sun is shining in the temple.' The Thai delegation looked baffled: Stavros grinned demonically. At *last* – he was getting his own back.

'Your prisons are a *disgrace*,' thundered the Congressman. 'My aunt is a small woman with white hair,' Stavros chirruped. 'I have first-hand evidence of serious mistreatment of prisoners.' ('She is eighty-one years old, but young in heart.') 'For God's sake, *get your act together* and regain the respect of the international community.' ('She likes to sing in the bath, *ti-tum, ti-tum, ti-tum*.')

A great wave of applause swept through the Assembly; some delegates were on their feet with excitement. The Thais, in some bewilderment, joined in; their leader stood up and waved at the Congressman with a big smile on his face. The Congressman nodded grimly. 'I see my message is getting home.' ('I send you fraternal greetings from the land of Mickey Mouse.') 'Let's hope, when the WLP meets again, there is progress to report.' ('Please give your children a kiss and a cuddle from me.') 'Thank you for your attention, gentlemen.' ('That's enough crap for now.')

The applause swelled to a crescendo and the Congressman strode back to his seat; a photographer darted in front of him to take his picture; the entire Thai delegation swarmed forward to shake him by the hand. Stavros switched off the microphone and turned to the Thai interpreters. 'I'm sorry, you probably thought that was rather silly.' Some of them nodded; others shook their heads; words failed them completely. As he left the booth, a man with a notebook accosted him.

'Prem Sapavasu, Reuters. Were you interpreting? What did he say just then?'

'Mainly how hospitable he found the Thai people.'

'Nothing on human rights?'

'Not a word.' Other reporters had gathered: it was like an off-the-record press briefing. He loved it. 'Mr Ledgerwood did make the point that, now he was no longer running for President, his observations would be inappropriate.'

'Did you say he wasn't running for President any more?'

'Is that official?'

'Are you sure about that?'

'Of course I'm sure. I'm a professional interpreter, aren't I?' Nobody dared take issue with the description: they scribbled down his every word as if he'd delivered the speech himself. He returned to his own booth: Sophia was interpreting an intervention by the President.

'. . . most stimulating contribution, Mr Ledgerwood. I'm sure your words will be taken to heart by Thai parliamentarians. The next speaker is Signor Meravalle of Italy. Before Signor Meravalle starts, I regret that I must make yet another contribution on the question of time-limits for speeches. Ninety speakers remain on the list but, because of the time taken on the roll-call vote and the explanations of vote, there is less than an hour's debating time left. I therefore must propose, in the interests of fairness, that speeches be limited to forty seconds – forty seconds, gentlemen. If delegates confine their comments to essentials and take their place quickly on the rostrum, we should still be able to hold a worthwhile debate in the best parliamentary traditions. That is my proposal, colleagues – forty-second speeches. Is that proposal agreeable to delegates? Is that proposal not agreeable? Would delegates to whom the proposal is agreeable please rise in their places?

Thank you, Mr Cacoyannis. Would delegates to whom the proposal is *not* agreeable please rise in their places? Thank you, gentlemen. The Assembly has voted decisively – the proposal is *not* adopted. I shall therefore make a *further* proposal, in accordance with Rule 21(6) . . .'

A tomato the size of a hand-grenade – for a moment it looked like a hand-grenade the colour of tomato – was lobbed from the public gallery on to the rostrum and made a mess of the Secretary-General's jacket. A second tomato skimmed the President's head; a third scored a direct hit on the official clock. Between a hundred and a hundred and fifty delegates leapt up on points of order – someone appealed for calm in Hungarian. A second volley was fired – eggs mainly, with the odd small pineapple. The throwers were finding their range: twice the President suffered a direct hit. Sir Rufus Barnacle's voice rose querulously above the hubbub.

'I spy strangers! I spy strangers!'

'What is your point of order, Sir Rufus?' Egg was streaming down the President's face, but he refused to be intimidated.

'I'm moving for strangers to withdraw, Mr President.'

'Strangers withdraw?'

'It's how we clear the gallery at Westminster.'

'This isn't Westminster, Sir Rufus. The Rules of Procedure –'

'It's a parliament, isn't it? We have to protect free speech. Chuck 'em out.'

A mango caught him on the back of the neck and he fell to his knees. Scuffling broke out in the gallery between the attendants and the demonstrators. An Iranian delegate shouted that it was all an Iraqi plot. Someone picked up an orange off the floor and announced that it had come from South Africa. The President crouched by the microphone with his arms protecting his head: Sophia interpreted faithfully till the last breath.

'I think, colleagues . . . that the debate on human rights may have to be resumed in Bucharest next year. Is that proposal agreeable to delegates? Does anyone wish to speak against the proposal? Are there any amendments to the proposal? Will delegates wishing to support the proposal please rise in their places? Do three or more delegates wish to request a roll-call vote? Will those who wish to abstain . . . ?"

EIGHT

I

'Shi-i-it!'

Only an American could have wrung three syllables out of the word; and only a very angry American could have spat between the first and second syllables and again between the second and third. The Congressman had just read the news-tape in the lobby of the hotel. His whole face was disfigured by an uncontrollable fury.

'What kind of two-cent reporter dreamt up this horse-shit? I'll kick his ass into 1992.'

'Is something wrong – Bill?' Stavros glided up behind him, his eyes puckering with concern. Greeks weren't naturally subtle actors, but he was getting the hang.

'I'm going to look like a dickhead. A duck-assed dickhead. Who wrote this dumb-dog crap?'

The leader of the Belgian delegation wandered over to listen. Interpretation was going to be difficult: the Congressman's vernacular wasn't as accessible as his pronouncements on human rights. Stavros looked at the offending item on the tape.

LEDGERWOOD QUITS – URGENT

US PRESIDENTIAL HOPEFUL BILL LEDGERWOOD OF DELAWARE PULLED OUT OF THE WHITE HOUSE TODAY WEDNESDAY STOP HE CHOSE THE WLP CONFERENCE IN BANGKOK TO MAKE THE ANNOUNCEMENT STOP STUNNED DELEGATES APPLAUDED SYMPATHETICALLY STOP TOMATOES WERE THROWN BY DEMONSTRATORS PROTESTING LEDGERWOOD'S VIEWS ON HUMAN RIGHTS STOP END REUTERS 1210

He shook his head mournfully: he hadn't enjoyed anything so much in years. 'Can't you just issue a denial?'

'From this shit-hole? The news will be all round DC before I can stop it. No, Stavros, I'm stuffed. The other guys will say I don't know if I'm coming or going.'

'You've got a telephone in your room. If you ring Washington now, you can limit the damage.'

'I guess so. Good thinking, Stavros.' He shook hands with him, as if to say: 'Good to have you back on the team.' There seemed to be no guilt in the man at all, no recollection of his conversation with Tight on Monday: his perception of people, his allegiances, shifted with terrifying ease.

Stavros said: 'Of course I'm just a faggot,' and that did disconcert him. Half-remembered conversations were circling round on his face as they got into the lift together.

'Which floor, Stavros?'

'Seventh.'

'I'd forgotten we were the same.'

'You forget a lot.'

'I'm a politician, Stavros.' He wasn't being ironic: he was making a statement of faith. 'You have to live in the here and now. Today's problems today: that's the way to do business. Leave guilt to the faggots.' It sounded like the title of a novel.

They went into the Executive Suite. 'Fix yourself a drink, Stavros.' He fixed himself a drink. 'Sit down.' He sat down. 'Hell, take your jacket off.' Hell, he took his jacket off. It was like a dog being obedience-trained. The Congressman struggled through a directory of international dialling codes and tapped out a number. It started to ring. He winked at Stavros. 'The head of Reuters is going to get his ass kicked from here to Louisiana.' There was an appalling sameness in his imagery. Stavros had a sudden picture of his election poster: THE AMERICAN DREAM – A PRESIDENT WHO CAN KICK ASS . . .

'Yes? Yes? Is that Brad? How you doing, Brad? Brad? Can you hear me, Brad?' He put his hand over the receiver. 'I don't think it's Brad.'

'Do you want me to try?'

'That's kind, Stavros.'

'Is that, uh, somebody called Brad?' A torrent of angry Italian engulfed him. '*Scusi, Signor, molti scusi.*' He replaced the receiver. 'What number did you dial?'

'My private office in Congress.'

'You got a bookshop in Verona.'

'Shi-it.' The Congressman snatched the directory of codes and tried again. As he dialled, his finger got stuck: he pulled it out and used a pencil instead. 'Goddam Asian contraption.' A jug of water overturned on the table and dripped on to his patent leather shoes. Stavros poured himself another drink. What serious vendetta was possible in the face of such engaging incompetence? He tried to remember Kim, tried to rekindle the rage he had felt the day before, but the fires were cold. He had wanted so badly to be an actor in the drama: it seemed he was doomed to permanent spectatorship. He wandered across to the window. Even the weather was on the side of inactivity. The midday sun had emptied the streets of all but the intrepid; a haze nestled over the skyscrapers. Perhaps the violent hour would come later, when the temperature had dropped.

'Brad? Jeez, am I glad to get hold of you. Have you seen the tapes? . . . Well, get off your ass and look at them. Reuters have said I'm quitting the race . . . Yeah, quitting. Horse's ass stuff. Get a statement out saying it's a load of bull and tell Don to ring Chuck . . . Chuck's on vacation? Well, Jody then . . . Yeah, that's it . . . Say, Brad, how'd the Redskins do last night? . . . They did? That's great.' A huge and authentic smile appeared on his face – and Stavros suddenly realised that he too was a victim. Politics had chosen him, he hadn't chosen politics: if he'd had his choice, he would have been watching the ball-game with a can of Budweiser in his hand. Brad was saying something: the Congressman loosened his collar and rested his huge hand on his hip. 'Brad, *I* don't know how it happened. Just one of those things, I guess. This place is fifty-language city – some goddam interpreter probably bitched it up . . .' His gaze settled on Stavros and it took him a second or two to draw the obvious inference: by the time he had, Stavros was nearly at the door.

'Of all the goddam . . .'

'I'll just go and take a shower.'

'Shower, my ass. You wait right here, Stavros. Stavros! What's that, Brad? Oh, some Greek gofer . . .'

He ran back to his own room and bolted the door. His shirt was sticking to his back and his hands were shaking. He was just a nice Greek boy with the gift of tongues: he didn't belong in this adult world of fear and suspicion and violence. There was a telephone message on the table beside the bed: he threw off his jacket and lay down to read it. YOUR WIFE CALLED. (Yes, that figured.) HER GUARD SICK WITH FLOO. SHE GO PARTY ALONE BUT WORRIED MISTER BIG-JOHN. The telephonist obviously spoke a little French, but hadn't heard Irish before. The message was meaningless – Monica's obsession had been to *avoid* Grandjean, so why . . .? He rang the desk.

'When did my wife call?'

'This morning, sir. Can I give her a message if she calls again?'

'No, don't bother. Is Miss Golding in her room?'

'No, sir.' And that figured too. He wandered into the bathroom, heavy with defeat. How nice it would be just to talk to her on the telephone – but what chance was there of miracles like that? His life had reduced to three brutal constants: a wife who wouldn't let go of him; a mistress he couldn't get hold of; an extraordinary number of people who wanted to see him dead. He looked in the mirror. Mr Achapong was standing behind him with a gun in his hand.

'Put your hands above your head and turn round.'

His heart didn't even miss a beat. Wearily he did as he was told, like a member of the chorus-line who had long stopped dreaming of a solo part. Achapong pulled a card out of the voluminous folds of his national costume and showed it to him. He nodded.

'What are the CIA doing in Bangkok?'

2

The man who had called himself Achapong said: 'If I wasn't a democrat, I'd shoot you.'

It was rather an impressive line. Stavros felt like saying

'Now tell me the good news', but his jokes hadn't translated too well lately. He said: 'Thank you very much.'

Achapong frisked him for weapons and found a fork in his hip-pocket.

'What are you doing with this?'

'I dropped it on the floor at breakfast.'

'Why didn't you put it back on the table?'

'The waitress was watching.'

'So?'

'I would have lost face. Thai women never marry men who drop things. It's a local superstition.'

'She's a friend of yours?'

'Never seen her before.'

'And you've had this thing sticking up your ass all day?'

'I forgot it was there.'

The man gave him a long hard look. 'You're crazy, aren't you? I thought you were just dumb, but you're crazy. One crazy Greek.' Beneath the scorn there was a tinge of admiration. 'Hold this – we don't have much time.' He handed him the gun.

Stavros pondered it.

'I thought I was a crazy Greek.'

'You're a crazy *gutless* Greek. You couldn't pull that trigger if my name was Adolf H. Hitler. Now sit down on the john and can it.'

He did as he was told. Achapong turned to face the mirror and slowly peeled off his moustache; then he removed his glasses, snapped them in two and threw the whole lot in the bin. A brisk application of flannel revealed a smooth, almost boyish, black face. Stavros glanced at his ID card again: '*BEV COULT, Central Intelligence Agency*'.

'I thought Bev was a woman's name.'

'Never heard of Bev Koestler?'

'No.'

'Bev Delany? Bev Brooks? Bev Vanderbilt Jr?'

'Not that I remember.'

'Then can it, smartass.'

'What's a CIA man doing with a card anyway? You're working undercover, aren't you? What if you were caught?'

'Would you believe a guy worked in the CIA if he had a

card saying CIA in his wallet? Have you seen the back?'

Stavros turned it over. There was a logo of a laughing dog, and below, in small letters: 'WANG NOVELTIES INC. Made in Taiwan'.

Coult grinned.

'Good cover, huh? They made the guy who thought it up head of section in Madrid. I'm only telling you straight because you're so crazy nobody would believe you. We could do with more guys like you in the Agency.'

'I'm not in the Agency.'

'We're making you a temporary grade five.'

'Does that pay well?'

'Not bad, not bad.'

'Thanks – Bev.' His head was throbbing with bewilderment; he went over to the basin and swallowed a couple of aspirin from a small green bottle.

Coult took a toothbrush out of the recesses of his clothes and spoke slowly into the bristles. 'I've apprehended the giraffe. The ostrich is angry. Proceeding as planned. Out.' He put away the brush and explained: 'The guys in Singapore thought it would be a bit obvious if we made Ledgerwood the giraffe, seeing as he's so tall. So we swopped you round. Neat thinking, huh?'

Stavros nodded. His mother had used to say: 'If you don't understand, ask – like Sophocles' (whom she confused with Socrates). But he couldn't think where to start. 'Where is Mr Achapong?' he tried.

'Resting.'

'Does that mean dead?'

'It means resting. We've put him up in Hong Kong for the week – his wife likes shopping. The Congolese don't go much for this parliament crap.'

'Does he know you're impersonating him?'

'Sure. He gave me a speech on arms control to read out on Monday. These countries get more Congressional aid if they make the right noises on that. Good speech, enjoyed doing it.'

'Wasn't that risky – getting up on the podium in front of everybody?'

'Only if anyone had listened. We created a diversion in the bar.'

'A diversion?'

'Someone said it was his birthday and bought everyone drinks. It's all on expenses, that's the nice thing about Agency work.'

'Those people throwing tomatoes today? Another diversion?'

'Sure. We figured that debate had kinda run out of ideas. Did you see the speech the guy from Warsaw was going to make? I guess not. Biggest load of bullshit I've ever read.' He peeled off his African robes: underneath were a pair of boxer shorts and a T-shirt saying IT'S NOT THE VOTING THAT'S DEMOCRACY, IT'S THE COUNTING. 'Funny, huh? Got a shirt, Alfonse?'

'Here. And it's Stavros.'

'Of course it is. What does Chris call you? "Stavvy"? That's neat – sounds like a flower.' He put on the shirt Stavros had handed him, then went over to the wardrobe and took out his spare suit: it was too small for him and he had a struggle to do up the trousers.

Stavros fingered the gun: perhaps if he shot him in the leg, it might slow down his conversation to manageable speed; he couldn't take this verbal bombardment much longer. 'Where is Christine now?' he asked with prim accuracy, as if she were the last person in the world he cared about.

'Chris? Should be having lunch in the Chinese restaurant in the basement.'

'Is she all right?'

'Do you want me to check?' He took out his toothbrush again. 'Please confirm squirrel's movements. Out.' He stuck the other end of the brush in his ear and grinned at Stavros. 'Get that. She's having sweet and sour pork. My sister makes the best sweet and sour in Washington.' The grin widened. 'Want to know why we call her squirrel?'

'Yes, please.'

'Because she likes eating nuts. Your nuts.' His shoulders shook with ribald, unrestrained laughter.

Stavros looked at him with utter loathing: a blind hatred of the man and everything he stood for welled to the surface. He pointed the gun straight at him. 'You bastard.' Then he shut his eyes and fired. Eight feet to the right of his target, a mirror shattered.

Coult wrestled the gun from him.

'You crazy Greek maniac. What did you do that for?'

'I didn't like what you said.'

'Jesus H. Christ, we're on the same side, aren't we?'

'Are we?'

'You've got one friend left in Bangkok and you pull a gun on him because he makes a joke about your broad.'

'She's not my broad. She's my – friend.'

'*Friend?* Mother of Liberty, I've got a head job on my hands. A real head job. Fourteen languages and brains in his testicles. If I wasn't a democrat . . .' Fire-alarms started ringing along the corridor and a woman's screams could be heard. Coult used an undemocratic expletive. 'You've done it now, Alfonse, you've really done it.' He seized the toothbrush. 'The giraffe is suffering from the heat. I have remedied the situation. Other animals restless. Please advise.' He noticed that the head of the brush had been shattered by the bullet and used another unparliamentary expression. 'You dumb Greek asshole, that was Government property. Let's move it.' He opened the door into the corridor, then shut it again. 'We can't go that way. He'll see us.' He crossed over to the window: someone knocked loudly and insistently on the door. 'We'll have to use the fire-escape.'

Stavros looked out and shook his head. 'I'm staying here.'

Coult prodded him in the ribs with the gun. 'You shift your ass or I'll shift it for you.'

With less than his normal enthusiasm, he shifted his ass.

3

Twenty-five feet from the ground, the fire-escape ran out: the rickety aluminium steps just stopped. Perhaps the builders had assumed people fleeing a fiery death would accept lesser risks stoically – but Stavros wasn't fleeing a fiery death and he wasn't a stoic. He pondered the drop in silence: there was a car-aerial right in the middle of the landing area.

'What do we do now?'

'We jump.'

'Are you mad?'

'Completely tonto. If you don't jump, I'll push you.'

He jumped. His legs juddered as he hit the tarmac and he fell forward on his knees; his back was on fire with pain as if half his ribs were broken. Coult landed beside him, stood up and brushed a speck of dust off the knees of his trousers. A Thai girl walked past unconcerned, as if this were the main exit from the hotel.

He gave a low moan.

'I think my leg's gone.'

'Your right leg?'

'Left.'

'Then you can drive a car. Shift it, Alfonse. This isn't a cocktail party.'

'I thought it was a cocktail party.'

'Is that a joke?'

'It was trying.'

'It can stop trying. Joke time's later. This is car time.' He hauled him to his feet and frogmarched him across the car-park towards a white Mercedes. A red and green flag fluttered over the bonnet.

'Don't tell me – the Congolese ambassador's?'

'Check. If you weren't so dumb, I'd say you were quite smart.'

'It's just practice.' He got gingerly into the driver's seat, relieved to find that both his legs were still functioning. The key was already in the ignition. 'Now I drive you to Pussy's?'

'Now you drive me to the police station.'

'Any reason you don't drive me?'

'I can't drive.'

'Are you kidding? Any idiot can drive.' He reversed out, scraping the next car. The car-park attendant shouted at him in Thai. He tried to indicate left and the windscreen-wipers came on. Coult muttered something under his breath.

'What was that?'

'I said, I failed the test.'

'Smart guy like you?'

'Seven times.'

'God Almighty.' He manoeuvred gingerly into the traffic on the highway: the slowest vehicle seemed to be going at seventy with its horn blaring. 'Is that why they give you the Mickey Mouse assignments like this one?'

'Check.'

'Anything else you can't do?'

'I can't whistle.'

'The girls must love that.'

'They do. Hey, Alfonse – will you do something about the wipers? They're bugging me.'

'Sure.' He tried a switch and a red light started flashing on the dashboard. He tried another switch and the car radio came on. A bus overtook them at speed on the inside, followed by a couple of *tuk-tuks*. The radio announcer wished a girl called Prang a happy birthday and played a Bruce Springsteen song. They came to rest at a traffic-light.

Coult strummed his fingers on his knee and looked anxiously to right and left.

'Know where you're going?'

'Not a clue.'

'I think it's right at the Hilton.'

'Isn't it left at the Sheraton?'

'Do you know the one-way streets?'

'First time I've driven here. Isn't there a map? Who usually drives you?'

'Hale. He's having lunch with Christine.'

'Couldn't we change to a taxi?'

'Against regulations. Know anything about security?'

'Not a lot.'

'You surprise me.' The lights changed and the traffic swarmed forward; a lorry behind them gave a friendly reminder on the horn. Stavros turned down a side-street and weaved through a crowd of people going into a temple. They passed a cinema, a canal, a couple of restaurants. Two Westerners in jeans were walking along the pavement to their left. Stavros glanced at their faces in the mirror and pulled over to the side of the road.

'Know those two? They spiked my drink in the hotel.'

Coult looked back over his shoulder. 'Rudi and Hanna Schrijnen. Small fry. Drive on, Alfonse.'

'I'd have been dead if they'd had anything to do with it.'

'They didn't and you're not. Shift it.'

'Can't we just shoot the bastards?'

'Not worth it. They're only tools.'

'And the guys who threw me in the river?'

'Also tools.'

'What about Ledgerwood?'

'He's his own tool.'

'That figures.' He started the car again. The Dutch couple were now level with them on the other side of the road. He pulled down the window, shouted something in Dutch and drove off at speed.

Coult stared at him.

'What did you do that for?'

'I'm a Greek. I have to speak my mind.'

'What did you say?'

'I told them to eat their own shit and fuck off back to Amsterdam.'

'You know that in Dutch?'

'It's a knack I have.'

'Useful, useful. You know we've got a languages section in the Agency – interesting work, pays well, you could settle down with Chris in Washington.'

A *tuk-tuk* roared up behind them. Coult looked in the mirror and swore.

'Step on it, Alfonse. I said *step* on it!'

'What's wrong?'

'They're after us. Mother of Liberty, why did they give me a big-mouth like you?'

Stavros stepped on it. He turned left on to a main road and tore down towards the river in the outside lane. The *tuk-tuk* lost ground, then regained it at a traffic-light. On amber the two vehicles shot forward together, leaving the other traffic behind. A bus barred their way. Stavros veered down a side-street, turned left and then right; the *tuk-tuk* turned right and then left and rammed into the side of him. He reversed, did a U-turn and drove the wrong way down a one-way street; the *tuk-tuk* followed. Coult maintained a stream of invectives: about Greeks, about big-mouths, about working for the Agency when he could have gone to law school . . .

Stavros took a bridge over a canal at ninety miles an hour. 'Why didn't you?'

'Why didn t I what?'

'Go to law school.'

'My father died.'

'Too bad.'

'He was forty-seven.'

A vegetable-truck was blocking the road ahead. Stavros went up on to the pavement and scraped the side of the car against a fire-hydrant. The wing-mirror snapped off and a red light flashed on the dashboard. He stabbed at the accelerator.

'This thing insured?'

'I guess so.'

'Premiums must be high.'

'The Agency doesn't count the cents.'

'Count the sense?'

'That neither.' Coult looked over his shoulder. 'They're still after us. I thought you said you could drive.'

'I can drive in Switzerland. It's different. People stick to the speed-limits.'

'Never mind Switzerland. Shift it.'

He shifted it. The speedometer passed a hundred at the intersection of Sukhumvit and Wit Thayu; two police cars joined the chase. He took a side-street, did three sides of a square and shot into a multi-storey car-park. The *tuk-tuk* missed the turning; so did the police cars. He switched off the engine and grinned like a schoolboy.

'Can I drive or can I drive?'

'You can drive, you can drive.' Coult grinned back: Stavros hadn't liked anyone so much in years. 'You're just not suited for undercover work, you Greek big-mouth.'

4

Ukrit greeted Stavros with weary familiarity, like a cat coming in out of the rain. 'I thought we'd seen the last of you, Mr Battista.' He showed him into a chair and conferred with Coult in the corner: their whispering was just audible above the hum of the air-conditioning.

'What did you bring the Greek for, Bev?'

'He's crazy. I can't leave him alone.'

'Has he screwed things up with Ledgerwood?'

'He's screwed everything up. You should see the guy – he tried to shoot me.'

'No shit?'

'He didn't like something I said. Dumb fucking asshole. We get on fine now, but he's a head job – you can't tell what he's going to do. If I wasn't a democrat . . .'

'You guys known each other a long time?' Stavros called out jocularly. Many more compliments and his ears were going to catch fire.

Coult scowled.

'Ever run out of questions, smartass? Superintendent Ukrit and I went to the same police college in LA. Satisfied?'

'Old boy network, huh?'

'Can it, Alfonse. This is work we're talking. If we have a language problem, we'll call you.'

He canned it. Coult and Ukrit carried on whispering in the corner. He picked up two or three expletives and something uncomplimentary about Greek sexual habits – nothing else. The clock above Ukrit's desk said five to three: outside a grey haze hung over the city and the skyscrapers had a leaden, monumental quality as if they had been there hundreds of years. He tried to picture Christine eating sweet and sour pork and wondered what Monica had worn at Mr Grandjean's party: simple, uncluttered thoughts, the only kind his brain could still cope with . . .

Coult's voice rose suddenly. 'Mother of Liberty, that gives us three hours.'

'Four,' said Ukrit. 'The plane was late refuelling.'

'You're sure he'll take it?'

'Pretty sure. Listen.' He crossed the room and switched on the tape-recorder.

The Congressman drawled above the static: '. . . and I want an aisle-seat if you've got one.'

'Smoking or non-smoking?' asked a Thai voice.

'Non-smoking. When does the plane get to Washington?'

'Five a.m. local time.'

'Five in the morning? What half-brained faggot thought that one up?'

'I'm sorry, sir?'

'Forget it. When do I have to check in?'

Stavros smiled and called out: 'Nice to know I'm not the only faggot in his life. Those sort of things give you a complex.'

Ukrit gestured to him to be quiet and rewound the tape.

Coult said: 'Can the complexes, Alfonse.'

The tape resumed.

'. . . have to check in?'

'Four-thirty this afternoon, sir.'

'Can I check my bags straight through to Washington?'

'Yes, sir.'

'OK. Thank you very much.' There was the click of a receiver being replaced.

Ukrit switched off the tape and said to Coult: 'That was an hour ago. He's moved fast.'

'Any idea why he's in such a hurry?'

'He's worried about the Washington end. There was some stupid story he'd quit running for President.'

'Joseph H. Stalin, who thought that one up?'

'Some idiot in Reuters.'

'Jesus, I could kill the bastard.'

'You can never trust the press.'

'I'd like to break his legs in twenty places.'

'Excuse me . . .' Stavros rose unsteadily to his feet: there was a churning sensation in the pit of his stomach and he had difficulty focusing. 'Do you guys mind if I take a walk outside?'

Coult had other ideas. 'Put your ass back on that chair.'

He did as he was told. Coult whispered something to Ukrit, who went into the next room and made a telephone call. Stavros stared out of the window at the skyscrapers: the haze had got darker, foreshadowing the evening storm; a wind was getting up from the river. A couple of minutes passed in silence. Ukrit returned smiling. 'All ready, Bev.'

'Quick work. How many did you get?'

'Four.'

'Will that be enough?'

'The judge won't be counting.' He nodded in the direction of Stavros. 'Will he do his bit?'

'I'll break his ass if he doesn't.'

'He can have as many goes as he likes.'

'Up to five?'

'Up to five.' They laughed. 'Up to *five*!' Coult repeated, wiping the tears from his eyes. 'He'd have to be some dumb Greek to get it wrong.'

Ukrit giggled. 'Wait till you see the other four, Bev – you'll love them!'

Coult had to lean against a chair to steady himself. Stavros folded his arms and looked at the ceiling – his mother had said to ignore people who laughed at you. A mosquito buzzed past his head and he made a vain attempt to swat it.

'Come on, Alfonse,' said Coult, the laughter still echoing in his voice. 'We're running out of time.'

'Where are we going?'

'Memory Lane. Then the airport.'

'No time for dinner?'

'No time for dinner.'

'Too bad – I could have killed some beansprouts.'

Ukrit led them along a corridor, down three storeys in a lift and along another corridor. Stavros followed uneasily. They seemed to be in the same part of the building where he'd identified Kim's body the night before. He wondered if she was still lying there or how they had disposed of the body – it was a melancholy speculation. Ukrit ushered them into a small, darkened room and gestured to them to be quiet. As the light cleared, Stavros saw that one of the walls was a one-way mirror: on the other side five men had been drawn up in a straggly line. His brain switched on again.

'Identity parade?'

'Clever boy,' Coult whispered appreciatively. 'You Greeks aren't all shit.'

Ukrit addressed him more formally. 'Mr Battista, I want you to look at those men and tell me if you recognise any of them.'

He went up to the glass and peered through. The man standing second from the left was wearing a suit and had a scar on his right cheek: it was the ring-leader of the gang who'd beaten him up and thrown him in the river. To make his task easier, the other four wore police uniform: they were younger and at least six inches taller; their faces were unmarked. He pointed firmly at one of the policemen. He was a proud, free-thinking Greek: he wasn't going to be pushed around by anyone.

'That one.'

'Which one?'

'That one at the end with the moustache. I know that guy, I just *know* him. Now where . . .' In the darkness he could sense Coult's angry breathing, but what the hell – a man had to enjoy himself sometimes. 'I've got it, I've got it. Monday night I went downtown. I did some shopping, took a taxi to the Oriental, had a beer, then took a taxi back to the hotel. That man was driving the first taxi – I'm sure it was him.'

Ukrit bit his lip. 'Anyone else?'

'Hang on, hang on, don't rush me. Christ, this is so *hard*, I just wish I had my proper glasses. You Thais all look the same sometimes. I guess Greeks are no different – it depends on what you're used to. Wait, wait, I've got it.' He picked out another policeman at random. 'That man's wife is an interpreter. I met him at a party on Sunday. Not much English, but a lovely smile. He's an insurance salesman. Lives out of town, drives a –'

'Can the jokes, Alfonse.' Coult kneed him hard in the kidneys: he gasped in pain.

'Just joking, Bev. The man with the scar – he beat me up on Monday night.'

'Where was this?' Ukrit asked sharply.

'I don't know. I'd been kidnapped.'

'Anyone else with him?'

'Three men. Younger. That man was the ring-leader. They asked me some questions, then they tied me up and threw me in the river.'

'What were the questions about?'

'A packet I'd given Ledgerwood.' Ukrit and Coult exchanged glances. 'A secret packet.'

'Forget the packet, Mr Battista. Tell me about the man. Did he hit you?'

'Several times.'

'Hard?'

'Very hard. On the face.'

'Do you still have the marks?'

'I'm not sure.' He ran his hands over his cheeks. 'I don't think so.'

'A pity. The judge likes marks. But you're willing to testify, Mr Battista?'

'Certainly.'

'Good. I'll take your statement now.' He opened the door and took him into an adjoining room; Coult followed. A man was sitting waiting at a typewriter: Ukrit dictated something to him and the click-clack of the keys reverberated round the tiny room. Outside in the corridor a man laughed, then a woman. Stavros asked Coult if he ever watched the Washington Redskins: no answer.

'Sign,' said Ukrit.

Stavros looked blankly at the sheet of paper.

'It's in Thai.'

'I thought you were an interpreter.'

'I speak Thai, I don't read Thai. I did two weeks in a language laboratory. What does it say?'

'It says: "I testify that the man I have identified subjected me to grievous bodily harm."'

'Isn't "grievous" a bit strong?'

'The judge will like "grievous". "I was later tied up and thrown in the river on his orders. I am willing to so testify in a Bangkok court of law." That's it.'

'Just like that? No small print? I don't have to buy the *Encyclopaedia Britannica*?'

'No, Mr Battista.'

'Or make life insurance payments?'

'*No*, Mr Battista.' Ukrit scowled. His patience had lasted longer than Coult's, but it wasn't limitless: the lines of a life spent doing serious things were scored on his face.

Stavros borrowed a Biro from the typist and signed. As an afterthought he put 'Profession: polyglot faggot' – if he sounded like a joker, he might get out of the court appearance. Ukrit didn't notice the embellishment: he took the paper, folded it in four and put it in his pocket. They left the room together and marched down the corridor to the lift. As the doors opened, Ukrit said: 'You're a very brave man, Mr Battista.'

'Brave?'

'I can't get anyone else to testify.' The lift rose slowly and jerkily to the second floor. Stavros stared at him.

'What are you saying? Who was that man? Why won't anyone else testify?'

'Other witnesses have disappeared.'

'Disappeared?'

'In the river mainly. You were one of the lucky ones.' The lift-door opened and he stepped out: Stavros spun him round and gripped his lapels.

'Talk straight, Ukrit. Who was that man?'

'The worst man in Bangkok,' Ukrit muttered, with sudden intensity. 'I've been trying to nail him for ten years. You've been a great help. Bev will tell you – I'm short of time.' He eased himself free and bustled off down the corridor. Coult pressed the button for the ground floor.

'No!' Stavros shouted. 'No! I can't take any more of this. I demand to know what's happening.' He put his foot in the doors and stopped them closing: Coult tried to pull him into the lift, but he resisted. 'You must tell me what's happening,' he repeated. For once his indignation was impressive rather than ludicrous: it had a determined quality born of desperation.

Coult looked at him thoughtfully, almost sympathetically.

'Cool it, Stavvy, just cool it. You'll be all right if you do as you're told.'

'And *don't* Stavvy me. Christine Stavvys me, you don't Stavvy me.' A middle-aged man wandered past with a cup of coffee in his hand. 'I'm not Stavvy and I'm not Alfonse. I'm Stavros. Got it?'

'Got it.'

'Now tell me who that man was.'

'Mr Thuang?'

'Is that his name?'

'One of his names. He has several.'

'Who is he?'

'An international businessman.'

'Why does he have it in for me? Why's he so interested in human rights? Whose side is he on? Is Ledgerwood with him or on his own? What's happening in this hell-hole of a city?

I'm not going anywhere till you tell me.' He stopped for breath: Coult put a friendly hand on his shoulder.

'Want to see Christine?'

'Of course I want to see Christine.'

'Then you'd better come – we're running short of time.' He pressed the button for the ground floor again: Stavros stepped reluctantly back into the lift and the doors closed.

'Where are we going?'

'I told you. The airport.'

'To catch a plane?'

'Catch anything else at airports?'

'Who's going to do my interpreting at the conference?'

'We've arranged a substitute.'

'What sort of substitute?'

'He's a driver at the embassy.'

'Does he speak French?'

'He can use a dictionary.'

'Oh that's great, that's just great. What about Christine? Is she coming on the same plane? Who's doing *her* interpreting? The gardener?'

'The ambassador's daughter.'

'With a dictionary?'

'She's got a phrase-book.'

'How old is she?'

'Fifteen, maybe sixteen.'

'God almighty, Coult, who do you guys think you are? We'll never get work for the WLP again. These are serious professional people you're buggering about.'

The lift-doors opened: Coult turned and smiled. 'Serious? No way. Professional? No way. People? Maybe, maybe not. We're the professionals, Alfonse.'

'Who says?'

'We say.' A police officer came up to him and handed him an envelope: he glanced at the front and put it in his pocket. Another policeman escorted them to the exit. They passed a man walking an Alsatian, two drunks collapsed on a bench and a queue of people filing through a door marked VISITORS.

'Who are they visiting?' Stavros asked the policeman, in Thai.

'Prisoners who've just been charged. We detain them here overnight.'

'Can they have as many visitors as they want?'

'Of course.'

'No restrictions? That's great.' He nudged Coult. 'Did you get that? Unrestricted visiting.'

'Are you surprised? This is a very civilised country.'

'Is it?'

'Of course it is.' They waited while their escort went into an office adjoining the corridor. Coult smiled and put a fraternal arm round Stavros's shoulder. 'Want to know something, Alfonse? Help you sort your ideas out a bit?'

'Sure.'

'Everything that man Ledgerwood has told you about human rights in Thailand is bullshit. Every last thing. He wanted someone dumb to believe him, so he found you.'

'But why?'

'It's simple. If you want someone dumb, you look for a Greek.'

'No, why did he tell me all the bullshit? What was in the packet?'

'I'll tell you.' The policeman emerged from the office with another envelope which Coult pocketed. 'Later. It's confidential.'

'I realised that.'

'Use your brain – if you've got one.'

Stavros stamped his foot on the floor. 'Cut this brains crap, would you, Coult? You think Greeks are dumb? You're too dumb to know dumb. Most of the greatest minds in human history are Greek. Ever heard of Plato? Aristotle? Thucydides?'

'They're dead.'

'They're still Greek.'

'Seems like Greeks are either dumb or dead. Which are you, Alfonse?'

'You black fucking bastard.' He lifted an arm to hit him, but the policeman restrained him.

'Can it,' Coult said. 'There's no time.'

At the far end of the corridor a red-haired woman started screaming abuse at another policeman. Stavros listened, puzzled.

'She's speaking Russian. Who is that woman?'

Coult glanced down the corridor. 'Funny you should ask. That's the Soviet ambassador's wife. Mrs Kalugin. Do you know her?'

'Not personally. She tried to kill me.'

'With a gun?'

'In a car. She swerved right up on to the pavement.'

'Nasty.'

'It wasn't a plot?'

'Of course not. She just drinks too much. Well-known local dipso.'

'Can't anything be done?'

'Want to start a world war? She's got diplomatic immunity.'

'Suppose I'd been killed?'

'If you'd been *killed*?' The very possibility sent Coult's body into fresh spasms of pleasure. 'If you'd been killed, they'd have given her the Order of Lenin. Now shift it, Alfonse – we've got a plane to catch.'

NINE

I

They shifted it. A police car rushed them to the airport at fantastic speed: the driver was a pale-faced woman in her early twenties who treated the accelerator like an insect she was trampling to death.

'She's good,' Coult whispered to Stavros on the back seat. 'If you'd been driving, we'd have missed the flight.'

'If you'd been driving, we'd have needed L-plates.'

'I suppose that's funny?' The car roared into the airport forecourt and screeched to a halt: a phalanx of porters rushed forward to open the doors. Coult looked at his watch and swore.

'What's wrong?'

'We're early.'

'Does it matter?'

'We don't want to hang around – it will look suspicious. Ask her to drive round the block for twenty minutes.'

'And that won't look suspicious?'

'Not if we shift it.'

Stavros spoke to the woman in Thai. She smiled at him in the mirror and said something back; he laughed. The car glided off again and back on to the highway. Coult pulled the collar of his jacket up around his face and wriggled down in the back seat.

'Nice work, Alfonse. What did she say?'

'She said you Agency people never know what time of day it is.'

'And what did you say?'

'I said you might be dumb but you meant well.'

'Robert H. Redford, whose side are you on? Here.' He took an envelope out of his pocket and produced a passport.

Stavros opened it.

'This isn't mine. It's Spanish.'

'The documents section figured you looked more like a Hispanic than a Greek. Good likeness, huh?'

Stavros turned the page and a rather severe version of his face stared up at him from in front of a puce curtain.

'Where did you get this?'

'They took the usual mug-shot in the hotel lobby and tarted it up. Speak Spanish?'

'Sure.'

'Well, speak it – Mr Sanchez.'

'Sanchez?' He looked at the facing page: *Señor Alfonso Sanchez. Country of origin: Mexico. Profession: Engineer.* 'Oh, that's smart, that's really smart. The amount I know about engineering, you'd better hope nobody asks me any questions. Who are you going as? Achapong?'

'Too risky. Carlton May, research scientist.'

'Know anything about science?'

'Not a bean.'

'What do I call you? Carlton or May?'

'Neither. You don't know me.'

'How come we're arriving in the same car?'

'Coincidence.'

'We've driven out from the town centre without introducing ourselves?'

'We're the strong silent types. Correction, *I'm* the strong silent type.'

'And why the police car?'

'There wasn't a taxi.'

'In central Bangkok?'

'Good point. Let's say we've just been let out of prison.'

'What were we in for?'

'You for drunk and disorderly, me for currency offences.'

'Couldn't we make it the other way round?'

'Not credible.'

'None of it's credible.'

'That's why we don't want to have to tell it. Use your head, Alfonse – it doesn't hurt when you get used to it. Now get out and walk. This is where we split.' The car had come to a halt in a traffic jam about half a mile from the airport.

Stavros looked doubtfully out of the window at the muddy verge.

'Any reason you don't walk?'

'I'm a scientist. I'm too important.'

'Check. One last thing – why don't I have any luggage?'

'You left it at the hotel.'

'All of it?'

'You're a head job, you forget things.'

'Why don't I have an epilepsy at check-in? It would fit the character.'

'Alfonse, *nothing* fits your character. Now shift it.'

The car drove on towards the airport and he trudged after it on foot: his shoes stuck in the mud and he had to skirt the big brown rain-puddles which lined the road. The first spots of the evening storm began to fall: he quickened his step. A girl in the back of a Mercedes made a silly face at him and a driver sounded a gleeful, mocking horn. From the direction of the city, lightning zig-zagged down above the skyscrapers; thunder followed. Twice he lost his footing and found himself ankle-deep in mud; then the clouds opened and he had to do the last hundred yards at a sprint. Was this what they meant by foreign travel broadening the mind? He'd be better off playing tiddlywinks in Geneva.

The Washington flight was checking in at the far end of the concourse. He joined one of the economy-class queues and tried to scuff the mud off his trousers with the side of his shoe. 'You've been out in the rain,' an American man noted. 'It's the rainy season,' he added helpfully. Stavros winced. 'Stormsville, Asia, I call it.' He changed queues. Three ahead of him was Coult, looking cool, dry and unconcerned. Coult's passport was cleared without comment and he was handed a boarding-card; looking more like a football-player than a scientist, he padded off to the departure lounge. The queue inched forward. The woman checking in next was a vegetarian: she made querulous inquiries about the meals to be served on the flight and an official in red uniform had to be sent for. Stavros looked around for Christine: there was no sign of her. To his right, in the first-class queue, a stentorian voice broke in.

'I don't want a goddam window seat, I want somewhere I can stretch myself. Smoking, non-smoking, I don't mind. Jesus Christ, isn't there a guy here who speaks English?' The Congressman looked over his shoulder like a hunted animal.

Any cosmopolitan veneer had long gone: the day he'd left Delaware he'd moved way out of his depth. His eye fell on Stavros just as Stavros had reached the front of the queue and the check-in clerk was looking at his passport. 'That guy,' he rasped, pointing crudely. 'The Greek. He's a professional interpreter.'

'You an engineer, Mr Sanchez?' the clerk asked. 'My brother engineer. Very honourable profession. Where you from?'

'Mexico,' Stavros mumbled.

'He's a Greek,' boomed the Congressman. 'Just ask him to step over here for a minute.'

The second clerk crossed the floor and touched Stavros's shoulder. 'Are you the Greek interpreter?' The Mexican engineer nodded unhappily. 'Can you help, please? The American gentleman is being difficult.'

'The American gentleman is always difficult. Tell him to get stuffed.'

'I can't, sir. He's a VIP.'

'Viciously inclined politician?'

'Sir?'

'Never mind. OK, I'm coming.'

The desk-clerk handed him his passport and boarding-card. 'Enjoy your trip to Mexico, Mr Sanchez.'

The other clerk looked bemused.

'Is Mexico in Greece?'

'It's one of the smaller islands.'

'I never knew that.'

'They do a lot of engineering there.'

'Is that so? One day I would like to travel in Europe. More exciting than Bangkok.'

'Stay clear of Geneva.'

'Is that another Greek island?'

'Sort of.'

They had pushed their way through the crowd to the Congressman. The clerk introduced him with a flourish. 'Here is your Mr Sanchez, Senator.'

The American shot him a look of the deepest suspicion.

'I thought you were called something else.'

'Thais get European names confused,' he said firmly.

Back in economy, Christine was just checking in. 'Miss Millicent Parks,' he heard her say, in her most English voice. 'I'm an Australian diplomat.'

2

The Jumbo 747 paused at the end of the runway, then accelerated into the storm. Mechanics scurried for cover across the tarmac; raindrops bounced a foot in the air off the huge white wings. The plane lifted off, seemed to think better of it, then climbed on and up into the night like a golfer marching down a fairway into the teeth of a gale. The woman sitting next to Stavros made a discreet sign of the cross: the man on his other side asked the steward for a brandy and ginger. He undid his seat-belt. Air hostesses demonstrated how to use the life-jackets, incomprehensible nothings flooded the public address system, a child was sick into a bag. He felt strangely at home. He pulled a *Time* magazine out of the compartment in front of him and read about a new drug which could cure insomnia. The woman next to him asked him something in Spanish. He ignored her. She asked him again. He remembered.

'*Sí, sí. Alfonso Sanchez.*'

'*Maria-Luisa Pueblo.*'

'*Buenos días, Maria.*'

'*Buenos días, Alfonso.*' They shook hands: he remembered that Hispanics were particularly keen hand-shakers. Across the aisle Coult watched his every move. '*¿Es Español, Alfonso?*'

'*Mexicano.*'

'*¿Mexicano?*' She explained excitedly that her brother had been to Mexico: he was a freelance journalist and travelled the world looking for material. She also had a cousin living in Mexico City whom she had never met: her mother had had eight sisters, so the family was extensive. In 1968 –

Stavros made an idle calculation: if the woman talked two hundred words to the minute and the plane travelled at five hundred miles an hour, how much of her life story would she get through before Washington? He waited till she paused for breath, then excused himself and made his way up the aisle towards the toilets. A stewardess rammed him with a drinks-trolley and he toppled on to somebody's lap. Apologies were exchanged in four different languages . . .

The toilets were engaged. He wandered forward into club-class and caught a glimpse of the first-class cabin through a half-drawn curtain. The Congressman's long legs were stretched out into the aisle; a steward in a white jacket served him champagne. Across the aisle a small girl was clutching an enormous teddy bear: her hair was tied up in a pink ribbon and she chattered little nothings to nobody in particular. He retreated. The toilets were still engaged and there were now two other men in front of him in the queue. He wished them good evening in Spanish and hummed a snatch of Puccini. The light on one of the toilet-doors changed to VACANT and Christine stepped out. They looked at each other hesitantly.

'It's Millicent Parks, isn't it?'

'Ye-es. I don't remember –'

'Sanchez. Alfonso Sanchez. We met at a party . . . somewhere . . . some time.'

'Of course we did. You're, uh, Spanish – in trade?'

'No, I'm an engineer. From Mexico.'

'Of course you are. How silly of me to forget. I'm still in the Australian diplomatic corps, would you believe?' Her attempt at an accent was risible: she sounded as if she'd never left the Home Counties. The corridor between the toilets was getting congested: three more people had now joined the queue. They pressed happily against each other and smiled.

He said: 'I'd like to talk to you about the Australian position some time.'

She giggled. 'You Mexicans are fast movers.'

A voice behind them growled: 'Move along there. This isn't a debating society.' It was Coult.

Stavros turned and did an exaggerated double-take.

'It's Carlton, isn't it? Carlton May, the research scientist?' Coult froze, his whole face rigid with hatred. 'Say, Carlton, how's the research going? Were the Bangkok laboratories up to speed? Did you find the pherodoxin formula yet?'

Coult smiled politely and kneed him in the groin. 'The research is going just fine, Mr Sanchez.'

He doubled up in pain. One of the toilets became vacant and Coult shepherded him into it: he sat down and took deep gulps of breath. In the mirror, his face was suddenly that of a man twice his age: lined, careworn, flecked with stubble. He reached for a bar of soap, but the plane lurched without warning and deposited him on the floor; the seat-belt sign came on. He crawled out and scrambled back to his seat. Coult watched with detachment; Christine was hidden behind a magazine. The plane did another lurch and the cabin-lights dimmed; a beer-can fell on the floor and rolled back down the aisle. The captain spoke in English over the intercom.

'We have a small technical problem. Is there an engineer among the passengers?'

At the same time a stewardess with a placard saying MIS-TER SANCHEZ PLEASE arrived at his side.

3

With Coult's eyes boring into the back of his neck, he stumbled forward to the flight-deck. An Englishwoman murmured to her companion: 'I hope he's not going to be flying us.' Two Italians clapped. He passed through club-class, then tripped over the Congressman's outstretched legs in first. ·

'Taking a stroll, Stavros?' came that dry, contemptuous voice.

'I have to interpret. They've found an engineer who only speaks Polish.'

'Well, don't louse this one up, whatever you do.'

'I won't.'

He carried on up the aisle. The girl with the teddy bear buried her head in her mother's lap. 'Mummy, I scared.' The plane did another lurch. He took a deep breath and opened the door to the flight-deck. Three absurdly young-looking men, wearing clean white shirts with various insignia on the shoulders, were seated at the controls having an animated discussion. They turned and welcomed him with huge, terrifyingly huge, smiles: his arrival had Messianic overtones he didn't like one little bit.

'Mr Sanchez, are we ever glad to see you. I'm Captain Dersu. This is Second Officer Prem and Flight Engineer Cha. Mr Cha has a problem.'

Stavros stepped forward in an advanced state of nervousness. Yes, Mr Cha did have a problem. A blue light was flashing on the control-panel; a second light flashed when the plane lurched, which it proceeded to do three times in quick succession. He nodded thoughtfully. The first light was labelled *Kgh/1000*, the second *Em Par St*. Beyond a sinking feeling that *Em* stood for *Emergency*, he was no wiser. He opened his mouth to explain that his engineering skills didn't extend to aeroplanes and that he'd spent most of his working life in Mexican cobalt-mines, when the captain broke in.

'We spoke to air traffic control in Tokyo and they said their computer showed we had a Mr Sanchez on the passenger-list who was an expert in aerodynamics. Do those Tokyo boys ever know their stuff.'

The plane lurched again, more violently than before. Mr Prem fell off his chair; Stavros was thrown against the left-hand wall. When he regained his balance, he saw that he had accidently pressed a button marked IFM which now glowed a deep scarlet colour.

The captain reassured him.

'Don't worry about that, Mr Sanchez. You've just started the in-flight movie. Good thinking – it will relax the passengers.'

'What's the film?'

'*Three Men and a Baby*.'

'Well, I'm the baby here,' he said quickly, with what was meant to be a disarming smile. 'You gentlemen have been flying for years. I'm sure I can leave everything in your capable hands.'

'Mr Sanchez, please – this is no time for modesty. We would welcome your advice.'

The plane lurched again. Stavros clung miserably to the back of the captain's chair.

'How old is the plane?' he asked in a small voice. He sounded like an inexperienced second-hand car dealer.

'Eighteen months.'

'No trouble before?'

'Nothing.'

'And there are – two engines?'

'Four. It's a standard 747, Mr Sanchez. Please, time is short. What is your theory about the flashing lights?'

'I think . . .' He peered at the controls. The plane shuddered, as if it were passing through heavy turbulence, but outside there was just the moon and the stars and a vast empty heaven. A button marked CORRECT caught his eye and his finger hovered over it. 'Have you tried . . .?' He held his breath and took his life, everyone's life, in his hands. The plane seemed to stall, then plummeted. The crew were flung forward from their chairs; the control-panel lit up like a fruit-machine disgorging its contents. The captain took corrective action and the plane righted itself. Prem and Cha looked at Stavros in horror. With hollow nonchalance, he straightened his tie.

'How far are we from Tokyo, Captain?'

'Three hundred miles.'

'I suggest you land and get the problem looked at by a professional.'

He turned and left the cabin. The plane did a final lurch, then wheeled through ninety degrees and started its descent. In first-class, the girl with the teddy bear was crying; the Congressman was slumped back in his seat as if he had seen a ghost.

'You cack-handed Greek mother-fucker.'

Being naturally an optimist, Stavros always hoped that one day the insults would stop and people would be nice to him. But it was a long shot.

4

The stop in Tokyo took ten minutes exactly: mechanics in white overalls swarmed aboard and found a dead bird in the starboard engine. The plane lifted off again and dinner was served. Señora Pueblo told Stavros eight more instalments of her life's story and he drank eight whisky miniatures: when Coult scowled at him, he retaliated by shouting, 'Hi, Carlton, how you doing, you old asshole?' – which did the trick. The lights were then dimmed for the in-flight movie and he nodded off to sleep. When he came to, everyone else had done the same and the cabin was in darkness. He peered at the luminous figures on his watch: 11-37, Bangkok time. They had been flying seven hours and the whisky, by an old familiar process, had descended from his oesophagus to his bladder. He clambered over the man next to him and zig-zagged forward, waking a couple of people on either side. Someone swore at him in Chinese. Coult watched him through half-opened eyes.

One of the toilets was engaged and energetic puffing noises could be heard from inside: a woman let out a moan of protest and a man made a joke in German involving the Teutonic equivalent of the five-mile-high club. Stavros felt slightly ill. He turned towards the other toilet and tripped over someone in the dark: it was the little girl from first-class, curled up on the floor with her teddy bear. She was wide awake and watching him.

'Mister peepee,' she announced. She was at the pre-syntax stage: it was unclear if it was a question, a description or an order.

'Yes,' Stavros stammered.

'Daddy peepee,' she went on.

'No,' he said firmly. 'Not Daddy. Stav-ros.'

She tried to say the name without success.

'I'm Greek,' he added.

'Geek!' she said delightedly.

He stooped to pat her on the head. 'That's it, darling.'

A stewardess appeared round the corner. The little girl pointed at him and said shrilly: 'Geek peepee, Geek peepee!'

He blushed: the stewardess beat a retreat. In the toilet, the couple copulating reached a new pitch of ecstasy. He banged the door. 'Cool it, you two. There's a child listening.' There was a brief, confused silence. He squatted on the floor and picked up the bear: it weighed a ton and had a face disconcertingly like Boff's. He looked at the girl.

'Is this yours?'

'Ess.'

'It's big, isn't it?'

'Ess.'

'Did Daddy give it to you?'

'Ess.' The toilet-door opened and a red-faced woman emerged hitching up her knickers under her skirt. 'Mummy peepee!' shrieked the little girl. A bearded man followed after a short interval. 'Daddy peepee!' Her notions of parenthood

178

and urinating were charmingly unformed. Stavros put a big clumsy arm round her and she clung to him happily.

'What's the matter, darling? Can't you sleep?'

'O.'

'Is your Mummy asleep?'

'Ess.'

'Do you like flying?'

'O.'

'Does your teddy like flying?'

'Ess.'

Coult's rasping voice broke in. 'Tried asking her if she wants to be an interpreter when she grows up?' He was standing behind them with his arms folded and a strained, uncertain look on his face: the CIA training manuals hadn't taught him about children or, for that matter, Greeks.

'Daddy,' the girl cooed. 'Daddy back.'

Coult shuffled his feet and attempted a smile. 'I'm not your Daddy, sugar, and I haven't been away.'

'Daddy back,' she repeated.

'I think,' said Stavros, 'it's your pigmentation she's talking about.'

Coult growled. The girl's face broke into a huge toothy smile. They suddenly seemed a long way away from the *tuk-tuks* and the interpretation booths and the woman's body laid out cold on a slab.

'How long are you going to be fooling around here?' Coult snapped.

'As long as I feel like it. Is there a problem?'

'You're supposed to be undercover, you Greek big-mouth. You've been clowning non-stop since we left Bangkok. One stupid stunt after another. I could break your ass.'

'He means bottom,' Stavros explained to the girl.

'Botty,' she said cheerfully. 'Daddy botty!'

'And get that kid away from here. She's a security risk.'

'KGB, you reckon?'

'You can't trust children to keep their mouths shut.'

'Should we confiscate the bear? It could be bugged.'

'Alfonse, I'm warning you.' Coult took a belligerent step forward: a stewardess appeared with a polite smile.

'Can I help you, sir?'

'You can take this child back to her seat. She's blocking the passage.'

'Certainly, sir.'

The girl was led away clutching her bear in one hand and waving at them with the other. 'Bye bye Daddy. Bye bye Daddy back.'

Stavros said: 'Ever worry about mislaying your sense of humour, Coult?'

'All the time.'

'What do you do about it?'

'Kill a Greek.'

The Congressman's voice suddenly boomed out from around the corner. 'Where's the john in this goddam contraption?'

Coult hustled Stavros into the toilet and squeezed in after him: they held their breath as the American's heavy step approached and he tried to open the door. Stavros's face was pressed against the mirror and his legs were bent double; Coult's elbow gouged into his armpit. Had two fully grown adults made love in *this*? The Congressman tried the door again. Coult's mouth pressed against his ear and told him to can it or he'd eaten his last moussaka. He canned it: he was fond of moussaka. They could hear Ledgerwood breathing heavily on the other side of the door: in-out, in-out, as if he'd been running. A second passenger joined him. 'Is it taken?' he asked: another American by the voice.

'I'm afraid so.'

'Too bad. Free when you don't need it, taken when you do – that's flying. Say . . .' there was a short pause, time for Stavros to get an itch in the back of his neck and elbow Coult in the eye '. . . aren't you Bill Ledgerwood?'

'I am.'

'Well, get that. Congressman, this is an honour, a real honour. I'm a Delaware man myself. Pete Palukis.'

'How are you doing, Pete? Palukis – is that a Greek name? I've got a great affection for your countrymen.'

'Now, that is handsome of you – Bill.' There was a fleshy smack of outstretched hand meeting outstretched hand.

Stavros made an involuntary movement of his knee and flushed the toilet. 'Not long now,' the Congressman announced. In the mirror, Coult's tense, contorted face reached new heights of fury.

'Do you mind if I ask you something, Bill?'

'Go right ahead, Pete.' Water was streaming down Stavros's trousers: outside, the conversation was urbane and relaxed.

'Are you running next year or not? There've been so many different stories.'

'I guess I'm running, Pete.'

'Well, you can have my vote right now. Anyone who brings a decent face to politics in Delaware gets Pete Palukis's support. Remember the name – Palukis.'

'Hey, Pete, am I voting for you or are you voting for me?'

'I'm a salesman, Bill, always have been. It's the way God made me – I'm a Greek.'

'Wonderful people. Warm, spontaneous –'

'The best, the best.' In the toilet Stavros whispered: 'You see? Not everyone thinks we're schmucks.' Coult hissed: 'He's a schmuck himself, isn't he?' The Congressman rattled the door. 'Say, is there anyone in there?' Stavros and Coult looked at each other in the mirror. 'You answer,' Coult mouthed. 'Why me?' 'You're the talker. Say you're constipated.' 'Why can't you be constipated?' The door rattled again. 'Whoever you are, hurry up. We've been waiting ten goddam minutes out here.' Stavros called out something in Spanish. Palukis said: 'I think he's French.' The Congressman said: 'Jesus Christ, we'll be here all night.' A stewardess's voice broke in: 'Is there a problem?' The Congressman barked: 'Some goddam Frenchman with bowel trouble is monopolising the facilities. I want him out of there.' 'There are other toilets,' she said. 'Back down the plane.' There was a confused silence, then the sound of receding footsteps. Stavros breathed out, misting up the mirror: his legs were shaking uncontrollably.

'That was close. Our cover could have been blown.'

'Can the cover,' said Coult. 'And shift it. I have to shit.'

'Can't I go first? I'm desperate.'

Coult said something quite unprintable.

An earnest, clean-shaven official looked at the picture in Stavros's passport and tried to reconcile it with the bleary-eyed wreck standing in front of him. Something made him suspicious and he fired off a volley of questions: Stavros played dumb, Mexican dumb.

'What is the purpose of your visit, Mr Sanchez?'

'Vacation.'

'Ever been to Washington before?'

'*Si.*'

'Where are you staying?'

'A hotel.'

'Which hotel?'

'I haven't decided.'

'What sort of engineering do you do, Mr Sanchez?'

'Aerodynamics.'

'Interesting work?'

'*Si*, it pays well.'

'Do any engineering in Bangkok?'

'No, that was a vacation.'

'That's two vacations.'

'I'm between contracts.'

The official's eyes narrowed. 'Are you married, Mr Sanchez?'

'*Si*, but we're just good friends.'

'Humorist, huh?' The joke was a mistake, a serious mistake. Jokes weren't expected of passengers arriving at Washington airport at five in the morning; they bucked the system. The man pressed a button under the desk and another man sauntered across with a walky-talky. Stavros looked round for Coult and saw him standing on the far side of passport control reading a newspaper. The man with the walky-talky was about six-foot-eight and had a face without finer feelings of any sort.

'This gentleman giving trouble, Ben?'

'Yes, sir.'

'What sort of trouble?'

'Verbals, sir.'

'Can I see his passport?' He leafed through it, spending a long time studying the photograph, and put it back on the desk.

'Did you imbibe any alcohol on your flight, Mr Sanchez?'

'Is that an offence?'

'It is if you verbalise my boys when you get off the plane. Don't do it again – this isn't Gringoland.' He waved him through.

Coult put down his newspaper and walked beside him towards the customs-hall.

'What kept you? Put your foot in your mouth?'

'They didn't take to me.'

'Warm, spontaneous Greek like you?'

'I tried making a joke.'

'Ronald H. Reagan, will you never learn?' They had reached the customs-hall. The other passengers were waiting round a carousel for their luggage. The Congressman stood slightly apart, leaning on a trolley; the little girl sat on the floor feeding her bear a biscuit. Coult gestured to Stavros to follow and they slipped through a side-door and up a flight of stairs. A short man in glasses greeted them at the top.

'Have a good flight, Bev?'

'Terrible. This is the Greek comedian I told you about.'

'How you doing, Stavvy? I'm Don. Let's move it, shall we?'

'Don't you mean shift it?' Stavros murmured.

Don chose not to hear. He opened a door marked OPs IV into a small, cramped room with no windows. A group of men in uniform were sitting in front of a bank of closed-circuit TV screens watching the passengers in the customs-hall. One of them pressed a button and a camera closed in on a woman in tight-fitting jeans. 'Get a look at that ass!' There was the crackle of dry masculine laughter.

One of the men turned and saw Coult.

'Nice work, Bev. How many bags has he got?'

'Two. Plus the briefcase he's carrying.'

'Anyone travelling with him?'

'I don't think so.'

'Well, we're about to find out.' Luggage started to arrive on the carousel and the passengers reached for their bags. The Congressman pulled out two matching grey cases and put them on his trolley. One of the watching cameras homed in. The cases were made of soft-grain leather, with combination locks: the initials W.L. were printed on one of the corners. The Congressman glanced at his watch and wheeled the trolley towards the exit marked NOTHING TO DECLARE. As he passed the girl with the bear, he absentmindedly bent down and patted her head.

'Get that,' said Coult. 'Five in the morning and he's playing to the gallery. That's politicians for you.'

'Perhaps he just likes kids,' said someone else.

'That asshole – forget it.'

The others laughed nervously. By now there was a definite tension in the room. Someone pressed a switch and a fresh bank of TV screens came on. A camera panned over the Congressman's head as he pushed his trolley slowly through the customs-hall. 'Now,' Coult whispered.

'Get the bastard,' said someone else.

As if on cue, an official at the side of the hall held out his arm; the Congressman looked up in surprise and wheeled his trolley across to a waiting table; a camera homed in on his face, another on his bags. Everyone watched intently. The bags were snapped open and their contents lifted out on to the table: boxer shorts, paperback books, disposable razors, an interminable supply of neatly folded white shirts . . . Stavros said: 'I like a man who dresses simply.' Coult told him to can it. Bottles of shampoo and after-shave were added to the growing pile. The Congressman looked patient and unconcerned; once he made a joke, at which the official laughed without conviction. The cases were now completely empty. The official ran his hand round the lining and made a meticulous search of the stitching on the leather panels: there was nothing untoward. In the control-room six frustrated faces were glued to the screen.

'I think,' Stavros began.

There were ritual shouts of 'Can it!', but he was too excited to hear.

'No, wait, you guys, I think I've worked it out. Human rights was just a cover. Ledgerwood doesn't give a damn what goes on in Bangkok prisons. He's just a crook, a drug-smuggler. That's what was in the packet I picked up at Pussy's and that's what the other guys were after, the guys who threw me in the river. Ledgerwood wanted to use me as a courier to

Washington, but I wouldn't play along so he's had to try something else. Is that it?'

'Check,' said Coult. 'Clever boy.'

The Congressman's belongings were being packed back into his case: the watchers in the shadows were heavy with disappointment. Stavros looked up at the screens and saw all the other passengers streaming through the customs-hall: the small girl dragging her bear along the floor; two men in sunglasses laughing at a joke; a woman in a white cotton dress stopping to put on a cardigan. Everyone looked tired but happy: it was hard to believe that something criminal was taking place under their very noses.

He said: 'Has anyone checked out the bear?'

6

The bear's stomach was slit open and disgorged its contents on to the table: tiny plastic pouches, hundreds of them, filled with a white powdery substance. A customs official ran an expert eye over the haul. 'Heroin,' he said. 'The best. Street value in millions. You could run for President on that.'

Coult patted Stavros on the back. 'Neat thinking, Alfonse. When you use that brain, it's good.'

A dozen happy, smiling faces surrounded him. In the corner the girl was sobbing. A tall man in glasses loured over her. 'Who gave you the bear, darling?' The question drove her to fresh paroxysms and Stavros swept her up in his arms without thinking: her head buried itself in his shoulder and she clung to him like a small animal.

'Where's her mother?' he asked. 'I saw her on the plane. She must be in on this.'

'She shifted it,' said Coult with a shrug. 'Jumped into a taxi before we could reach her. We won't see her again.'

'But this is her child.'

'Maybe, maybe not. Drug-dealers aren't philanthropists, Alfonse.'

'And what about Ledgerwood? Aren't you going to arrest him?'

'No evidence. The kid's too young to testify.'

'So he's got away with it?'

'He's got away with nothing. The drugs are right here.'

'And Kim? The woman he had killed in Bangkok?'

'That's five thousand miles away.'

'You nauseate me, Coult.'

'The feeling,' said Coult, 'is mutual.'

The girl sobbed a little harder and Stavros had to walk up and down to comfort her. The sobbing stopped. A brisk-faced woman in a black dress appeared at the door and said to Coult: 'Is this the child? We can take her now.'

Stavros handed her over reluctantly.

'What will you do with her?'

'Unless the mother shows, we'll have to give her to an adoption agency.'

'She'll hate it.'

'She'll be in experienced hands.'

The girl started to cry again and the woman patted her ineffectually on the head. Stavros looked exasperated. 'Here, let me.' He took her in his arms and walked her up and down: again the sobbing stopped instantly, as if a tap had been switched off.

Coult shook his head appreciatively. 'You know, Alfonse, I figured there had to be *something* you could do properly. Maybe you should turn pro – childminding isn't megabucks, but you'd be dealing with your own age group.'

'Can it,' said Stavros.

Coult grinned. 'Now you're picking up the language too. Agencyspeak is tricky, but you're a clever boy – underneath.'

Stavros grinned back. 'Can the underneaths, Coult.'

The girl shrieked and pointed at the remnants of her bear, which were being bundled into a garbage bag. 'Bear gone, Daddy! Bear all gone.'

He held her tight and turned to one of the airport officials. 'Is there a toy-shop around here?'

'On the ground floor, sir.'

'Thank you. Come along, darling.' He carried her out of the room and down the escalator. Nobody said anything or tried to follow: he had the feeling they wouldn't mind if they never saw either of them again. He bought the biggest bear in the shop and they sat down together on the floor and discussed

186

what to call it: 'Bobo' seemed to be the girl's first choice and he couldn't get her interested in 'Boff'. In the distance he could see the Congressman surrounded by reporters, towering above them all like some strange prehistoric pachyderm; and a few tantalising fragments were just audible.

'. . . very disappointed indeed to be pulling out of the race, but if the people with the money won't back you . . .'

'. . . a sudden decision? No, gentlemen, I've thought long and hard about this one . . .'

'. . . nobody's put pressure on me to quit, no, sir . . .'

'. . . I shall, of course, continue to fight for human rights as best I can. Bill Ledgerwood's a lot of things, but he's not a quitter . . .'

Repelled and nauseated, Stavros also felt it was symptomatic of returning health that the bear's name meant more to him than what the Congressman told the papers and whether anyone believed him.

TEN

I

The view from the hotel window was like a parody of what he had looked out on all his working life: skyscrapers bunched together under a leaden sky, cars crawling bumper to bumper along straight narrow streets. The leaves on the tree in the hotel forecourt were beginning to turn and he could just see the top of Capitol Hill in the distance: he assumed this meant he was in Washington in the fall, but it might just as well have been Seoul in winter or Paris in the spring. The once fixed parameters of his life had changed. There was still a message to ring Monica on his bedside table, he was still waiting for Christine to ring him – but now there was a third claimant on his time.

He looked at the child sleeping on the spare bed in the corner of the room and felt a great weight of panic. He realised with dismay that he didn't even know her name. Her bear was called Mac because that was what she said when she clutched it or tried to tickle its tiny black nose; but who she was and where she came from was unknown, perhaps unknowable. She looked quite plump, quite contented, quite ready, if it came to it, to accept him as a father. But how long would the honeymoon last?

There was a knock on the door and, with a sudden flurry, Christine was in his arms.

'Oh, Stavvy.'

'Oh, Christine.' The words had the simple fervour of a religious chant: there was no need for original composition. She kissed him hard on the neck, then stopped abruptly when she saw the child.

'Stavvy. What's that?'

Shy, he took refuge in sarcasm. 'What does it look like? A goldfish?'

'Whose is it?'

'Nobody's. I'm looking after her.'

'For how long?'

'I'm not sure.' He explained what had happened. Christine's face softened and she bent to look at the girl, who was curled up under a blanket making light snoring noises.

'You can't keep her, you know, Stavvy.'

'Why not?'

'You're the original incompetent male. You'd never look after her properly.'

'Says who? She likes me. She laughs at my jokes.'

'She's only known you two hours.'

'We've never had a cross word. Really.' He tried one of his appealing looks, but she shook her head.

'Stavvy, you're dreaming. Where's she going to live? Who's going to look after her when you're working? She can't stay in hotel rooms all her life. She needs a stable home, schoolfriends, a mother . . . What does your wife think about all this?'

'That,' said Stavros, 'is a very good question.' In a daze of disappointment, he looked at the message beside the bed, PLEASE RING Mrs de BATTISTA – URGENT, and from the message to Christine and from Christine to the child. He suddenly felt like a poker player who had gambled everything on a poor hand and now had to show his cards. He picked up the telephone and dialled; Christine disappeared into the bathroom. A great anger flared in him: he'd been patient with Monica for too long; if she needled him, he was going to shout at her.

His mother answered the phone and spoke in Greek. 'Is that you, Stavros?'

'Yes, Mama. What is it?'

'Stavros, something terrible has happened.'

The child shifted on the bed and gave a gurgle of the deepest contentment.

2

Christine came slowly out of the bathroom: she wore the pain of a mistress on her face like a childhood scar. 'Well?' she asked in a flat voice, as if nothing that went on in Geneva could ever be any business of hers.

'Something wonderful has happened,' said Stavros. His eyes sparkled with an excitement he hadn't felt in years. 'You remember Grandjean?'

'The chiropodist who touched up your wife?'

'She's run off with him.'

'No.'

'Yes. She went to his party and never came back. They've gone to a hotel in Lausanne together. She left a note saying she was very sorry, but she had to find herself. To find herself! It's incredible.' He lay back on the bed and started to laugh. 'That's Catholics for you. She probably had a consuming passion for him all along. Mama was very upset. She said a woman who could behave like that wasn't worth crying over. I agreed with her on that.'

Christine lay down beside him and held him chastely by the hand. Their new freedom made them superstitious: it seemed profane to reach too hungrily for the nirvana which beckoned. When, after a long silence, they talked, they didn't dare discuss the future.

'What made you think the drugs were in the bear?' she asked, running her hands gently and proprietorially through his hair: he smiled at the new intimacy.

'Greek intuition.'

'That sounds like a language school.'

'You should meet my mother — now, she's *really* got intuition.'

'What happened to the intuition earlier? You acted as if you didn't have a clue what was happening.'

'I didn't.'

'I gave you a newspaper cutting. It was all there.'

'Are you sure?' He reached for his wallet, took out the cutting and unfolded it. On one side of the page was the story he'd read, US PRESIDENT-ERECT KNOCKS THAIS RIGHTS RECORD; on the other the one he hadn't, POLICE SWOOP, QUIZ TWO, WIDEN PROBE. He started to read.

'American undercover agents have joined local police in a bid to halt a major drug-smuggling racket. In a raid last night on Pussy's massage parlour in the Patpong district . . .'

'Ah,' he said. 'That explains.' He smiled sheepishly; it wasn't easy for a Greek with intuition to admit he had a brain the size of an olive-stone. He looked at what she had scribbled in the margin. 'This man's got to be stopped – he's an American bigshot.' That seemed to explain something too, although he couldn't for the life of him remember . . .

'Let's forget about Bangkok,' he said firmly. 'It was interesting and it made a change and the food was terrific, but it's over. We've got a conference here next week.'

'God, Stavvy, I'd forgotten. What's it about?'

'Third World trade, I think.'

'Are you sure it's not arms control?'

'It might be the position in Central America.'

'No, that was last year.'

'Talking of positions . . .' He took her strongly and confidently in his arms and they started to slither out of their clothes. A delirious merriment lit up his face. Greeks learnt caution in their mothers' wombs; they knew that what the gods gave with one hand they took back with the other; they didn't believe in miracles. It seemed like a disorder in nature that there should be such happiness in one room – but he didn't care. He felt simply, simply –

On the spare bed the child woke up and started to cry.

AS THE ACTRESS SAID TO THE BISHOP

DEREK NIMMO

Derek Nimmo has an actor's eye and ear for the odd incident and the bizarre story. He has played many roles and done many things – some of them strange in the extreme.

Showbusiness is an overflowing world of unlikely characters, farcical scenes and comic happenings. Here are stories of the big names, the bit players and the whole improbable off-stage cast: the eccentric landladies, over-sensitive writers, manic agents, erratic promptors, uncontrollable props and mad stage managers.

Together they add up to an hilarious collection of anecdotes from stage and screen, all told in the inimitable Nimmo style.

HODDER AND STOUGHTON PAPERBACKS